Birthmark

Kimberly Cruz

PAGE PUBLISHING, INC.
New York, NY

First originally published by Page Publishing, Inc. 2019

ISBN 978-1-64462-835-5 (Paperback)
ISBN 978-1-64544-113-7 (Hardcover)
ISBN 978-1-64462-836-2 (Digital)

Printed in the United States of America

Prologue

"*D*O YOU WANNA PLAY A game?"

"No, Lydia, I'm seriously not in the mood."

"C'mon, please, at least until something good is on TV."

"Lydia, I said no, I'm not in the mood."

Lydia gave me some sort of a sigh, but a sassy one, kind of like the ones kids half her age give adults when they're told they can't have cookies. I hated putting her on the receiving end of my bad moods, but honestly, that little girl just didn't understand. She never did. And when I was pissed like I was that day, I had no choice but to put her on the receiving end. Either that or I'd break down. It was an ultimatum, but I was always selfish. I'd yell at her for no reason at all sometimes, just because I knew I could.

"What're you doing now?" I refused to speak. "Mel, I said what're you doing?"

"Homework!" I shouted. "My gosh, Lydia. Can't you learn to just shut up every once in a while?"

Tears started to form in her eyes. I was too angry to say I was sorry. It always broke my heart to see her cry, but I was too stubborn to take back my words.

"Mom!" Lydia screamed.

"What're you doing to your sister?"

"Why don't you ask what this little brat is doing to me?" I asked.

"Mel, you're always treating your sister like crap, that's why I don't ask."

"Maybe if she could—"

"I don't wanna hear it! You're the one who needs to shut your damn mouth every once in a while, not her!"

3

Our so-called mother took Lydia's side over mine every time. As crappy as she was as a mom, at least she knew how to defend one of her kids, in some way. Right?

"I told her when I got home I wasn't in the mood, and because she's bothersome enough to ask five minutes later, I told her I'm busy doing my freakin' homework!"

"Mel, does it look like I care? Lydia isn't the one putting you in such a crappy mood!"

"I know, you are," I muffled under my breath, but still loud enough for my mom to hear.

Glaring at me, she said, "I don't even know why you're doing that damn homework. You're such a dumb-ass it's not like you're gonna finish school anyway. As far as school goes, you're pretty screwed."

"Says the whore who had a two-year-old kid by the time she was my age and didn't even know the father." I always meant every single word that left my mouth when I spoke to her; almost always did it result in a fat lip or me getting slapped. What one might call occasionally is when I'd get my hair pulled and thrown down the stairs.

Lydia never meant for things to escalate so quickly or to that degree. I knew that, but it was crazy to me how, after eight years of those sorts of reactions and violence, she didn't already get it. At that point, she still hadn't understood. That was something I never understood.

I rubbed some of the blood off my lip and then stared at Lydia. Every time I think about it, the intensity grows greater and greater, the length of the glare longer and longer. Too long.

I communicated something to her. I enforced in her this belief that anything that went wrong was completely and utterly her fault, no matter what. Before I went upstairs, I told her I wasn't going to talk to her for the rest of my life. Later that night, she came to knock nervously at my door.

"Mel, are you okay?" I didn't answer. "Are you still mad? You're really never going to talk to me again?" I heard her whisper, "I need you." I could hear the pain, the cry in her voice. I still didn't answer. I couldn't.

Shockingly enough, I meant it when I said I wasn't talking to her for the rest of my life. I left that night, without hesitation. I almost felt bad, but I couldn't go back.

*****

I remember that night like it was yesterday. But it's far from being just yesterday. It was lifetimes ago, literally. It was my first lifetime.

Now I know what you're thinking, and yes, I can remember my past lives.

I don't have superpowers or anything like that. It pains me to admit that I'm never born knowing how to speak, walk, or do calculus. Nope. All I do is remember. Some lives are more vivid than others, but all of them are a part of my memories and a part of who I am.

I could go on and on about other lives I've lived, but I'm going to take time out of this one to tell you about my most recent life, my favorite life.

Chapter 1

$\mathcal{H}$IGH SCHOOL IS TYPICALLY WHEN things actually begin to get interesting in life, and in this lifetime, it was no different. With that being said, I'll start at the very beginning of freshman year.

I was always a pretty quiet kid. I was never on anyone's bad side because no one really even knew of my existence. In the mornings, I hung out near the library, and honestly, no "regular" kid wanted to be anywhere near any library! At lunch, I hung out at a bench near the office. C'mon, that's even worse.

All my teachers found group work to be downright idiotic. The way they saw it, group work was just a way for the "stupid" or lazy kids to mooch off the overachievers or for friends to have the thumbs-up to make noise and get zero work done. To be fair, that's basically what it was. Everyone gossips and speaks nonsense until the bell rings then says, "I'll do it at home."

At the same time, group work was a way for students to have unfair advantages. One is stuck in one of three situations: the overachievers (if you're lucky, you're the odd one out and get to do virtually nothing), the screwed overs (because you all either are lazy or have no idea what's going on), or the screwed overs plus one (the screwed overs but with that smart kid who will do pretty much everything because they want their good grade, even if that grade is to be shared [if you're unfortunate, you're the plus one]).

Anyway, that's how I remained solitary in class.

And it's not like I was socially awkward. I actually had great social skills. I was just...antisocial. Admit it, at one time or another, we've all come to find ourselves declaring "I hate people." Some of us even have that as our go-to catchphrase. People are annoying, and when they're not, they're tolerable, I suppose.

Nobody in that school was worth knowing in particular (that included me), but some of them were known and acknowledged by everyone (that did not include me).

There was Julian. He was the guy everyone—and I mean everyone—went to for snacks. He had an entire backpack apart from his real one just to lug around snacks (and money). And his locker, full of books? Screw that! More snacks. Kids were dropping out and moving schools constantly, so he even got security to hook him up with a second locker. Located in the coldest hall in the school, that's where drinks and, yes, even ice cream went. Every year kids were sure to learn his schedule so just in case they missed lunch or if lunch wasn't enough, they knew where to find him.

Then there was Carol. She was Julian's best friend and the flashlight you needed in a dark tunnel. She knew everyone. How could she not? I mean she was best friends with the guy that everyone in the school needed. By the way, that included faculty. Because she knew everyone, she had dirt on everyone. Carol was on everyone's good side, but not everyone was on hers. Take my word for it; you wanted to be on her good side, because she could do you dirty real quick! She could up your class dues, charge you for lunches you didn't buy and books you never checked out, so when the time for graduation came, you were in more than enough debt. She could hack computers and change your attendance records. That town wasn't too bad, but it wasn't unheard of for parents to go ape shit on their kids for skipping school or cutting class, being under the safe assumption that they were up to no good. Bad attendance equaled trouble. She could also change your grades, so that A you were hoping for on that one test, it was kissed goodbye the moment you made Carol's "hit list." You were stuck with all the other average students with a B-. You might've earned it, but Carol didn't think you deserved it. Believe it or not, that was Carol being civil, because if you really pissed her off, you were done for. Yup, within seconds, you could turn into one of the blacklisted. Julian wouldn't sell to you anymore. It wasn't that easy to escape either because that meant that everyone you associated yourself with was put on watch—definitely no sharing. And everyone had someone just waiting to rat them out and get them blacklisted.

And finally, there were "the Fans," five girls who were "the biggest fans" of everything popular, and according to them, they were always the first ones to discover it all. There was Cynthia, Kathleen, Rachel, and Carter. The four of them weren't that bad. They were just as tolerable as anyone else, but there was one poison that made them all less than tolerable, very much so. Her name was Cara Montoya. "Not Cara as in Delevigne, Cara is in ——mel." I heard that enough times for the rest of my lives.

It's not like Cara terrorized the school, but when she did, she was disrespectful to anyone who didn't have some sort of status. She always got the good lunches. That meant the biggest slice of pie on our Thanksgiving meal day—with the good whipped cream, the softest cookies, and the cheesiest pizzas. She was captain of the volleyball and cheerleading team and top of our class.

Cara wasn't the best player on our volleyball team and probably not the best cheerleader, but she was smart, very smart. I'll give her that much.

Cara was by far the fakest girl—person—I ever came across in any of my lifetimes. She used to display her test scores up on the whiteboard just to make everybody else feel small. And when she felt like it, she put up everybody else's grades too. That included Cynthia, Kathleen, Rachel, and Carter, especially when their grades were way less than perfect. Cara never helped them with the things they didn't understand because she wanted to be as superior as possible.

I flew pretty low on everyone's radar, if I was on their radar at all. I was a dismissible kid; on top of being dismissible, I was quite smart. You can probably imagine how easily subjects came to me after living several lives and remembering them all. I might not have been born knowing calculus, but I sure as heck could learn it better and faster than everybody else. This was the situation in all my classes, especially history. Since I wasn't as gregarious as Cara, I had a lot less distractions. In class, the only things that captured my attention other than my assignments were my own thoughts.

Two weeks into freshman year, transcripts came out. All of us freshmen received the entire, big, and important lecture on how we needed to try our very best in school. After that speech, Cara and her little applaud squad—as I liked to call them—started handing out transcripts. It was pretty dumbfounding—and hilarious—when Carter announced to everyone that MC was number one in our class. Cara's face slowly but surely turned from a mocking "I'm better than all of you" face into a questioning "What the hell are you talking about?" face, because her initials weren't MC; they were CM. So who could've taken her rightful spot as number one? The only student with her reversed initials: Melenium Champion.

Of course, she had no idea who I was until I went up to get my transcript from Carter. I never had a single class with Cara, so she had no clue I was giving her competition, serious competition, a lot of serious competition.

It wasn't like I was behind her as a close second. No, no. I was first; that meant we were dead on tied. Anyone and everyone could've split as many hairs as they wanted, as humanly possible, but there was no way on Earth—or any other planet—that Cara had me beat. She wasn't superior.

I'm sure she went home throwing a huge fit, the worst tantrum any five-year-old ever threw. She just had to come to terms with the fact that there was a new sheriff in town…just kidding. I was the one who had to come to terms. I had to come to terms with the fact that I had just secretly, silently, and unknowingly declared war upon Cara Montoya and the Fans.

Yup. Five against one.

Chapter 2

*T*HAT WEEKEND WENT BY JUST as normal as any other weekend. I did schoolwork, listened to music, watched TV, and avoided my mom all day both days. The only thing slightly out of the ordinary was the fact that the house was actually quiet all weekend instead of filled with my mother's obnoxious hollering. But then, that's not so out of the ordinary when I come to mention that it was because she was passed out drunk the whole time.

However, come Monday morning, things started to go awry, if you will. Actually, things started to go more than just awry; they started to go wrong, very wrong.

I got a call from the school that morning saying that the buses were running late—well, my bus was running late. It had rained mildly as compared to other times when my bus still drove its regular route, sometimes at what seemed like record time. My bus always got us to school early, so finding out that it was running "late" for once was really no big deal. I could live with getting to school on time. I went to my living-room window, where I had a good view of the two stops before my own, sat down, and turned on my music.

I wasn't exactly anxious to get to school that morning; to be honest, I never was. But after so many songs had played, I decided it was taking a little too long for my bus to arrive, so I checked the time on my phone. It was seven thirty; the first bell rang at 7:35 a.m., and class officially began at seven forty. I got up to call the school and check my bus's status when I noticed there was a message. I must have missed the call listening to my music. The message informed me that my bus was incapable of getting me to school and that a route would not be ran until further notice.

Great, just great. I was positive this had nothing to do with the rain.

After taking some time to consider how screwed I was going to be for quite some time, if not the next four years, I got my backpack, threw on my hood, and started walking.

The bus ride to and from school always gave me a fair amount of time to think about things plentifully. But the walk to school gave me plenty of time to think about everything plentifully.

There were only fifteen kids who rode my bus, all of which came from about nine stops—eight excluding my own. Fourteen of those kids had parents or guardians who actually cared about them. I—a.k.a. the fifteenth kid—didn't, so I took a long and tedious walk to my high school. By the time I got there, I had already missed first and second period and enough of third period that I just decided to make my way to my fourth period: lodging management.

Everybody from my bus was excused, so maybe I should've gone to my third period, but it was Spanish class. I didn't figure it was all that important because I knew we had a substitute for the week. Plus everybody was excused from being late to first period or missing it entirely, but no one was going to understand why I didn't make it till third.

I got to fourth seconds after the bell had rung to release us all from third. I spoke my polite "Good morning" to Mr. Lewis and complimented him on his always "stunning" necktie. Our little student-teacher banter was something I always had seemed to look forward to those days. I guess little glimmers of positivity like that were basically what got me through my days till bigger things came along.

With my hood still on, I went to my seat and put my head down. I got pretty lucky freshman year. All my classes seemed to be small enough. None of them ever exceeded eighteen students. There were four tables in my lodging class; three of them filled two-thirds of the way with four people each. I sat alone at my table—of course, it was the table closest to the teacher, the table no one wanted, so even though the time to change schedules was up, Cara got her schedule to match mine. And of course, she couldn't be left alone, so Carter,

Kathleen, Rachel, and Cynthia all entered into that class and all the rest of my classes as well.

Solely for their amusement, the Fans decided to surround me at what I felt was completely my own table. I couldn't exactly demand that they leave me alone, leave the table, and much less the class, so I sat there with my head down and said "Here" when I heard Mr. Lewis call my name. I fought the urge to roll my eyes when I heard Cara's name called—I couldn't roll them every day; I'd probably get headaches after so long.

Of course, hearing all five of the Fans gave me headaches often enough. All they ever talked about was clothes, makeup—you know, just superficial things.

PE with them was strenuous in every form of the word. Geometry with them was horrible! Spanish with them was irritating beyond comprehension. Lodging management could've been worse. Thankfully, it was mainly a class where people did actual work even if it was supereasy. Those were my mornings at school in a nutshell. My afternoons, well, those almost killed me. I (I mean *we*) had health, science, and English. These were classes in which everybody actually spoke, and literally being required to hear the Fans talk was pretty unbearable. And of course, going home wasn't all that much fun either; it never really was, but at that point, it was also because I was stuck with an arduous walk home. Being home sucked. On the bright side, since I wasn't taking the bus home anymore, my mom had no signal of my arriving. Even so, I rarely went through the front door. Back door? Nope, not that either. I took my bedroom window.

It wasn't as if my mom cared a whole lot about when I got home, but I cared about not pointlessly getting screamed at. Especially with the Fans in all my classes, I cared very much so.

After so long, Cara decided that keeping an eye on me, observing me, just wasn't enough. She knew having my classes didn't make her excel in any way, shape, or form. That's when she decided that this whole top-of-our-class thing was going to become like somewhat of a paintball game. Since I was competition, I was also a target.

One day, I'm pretty positive it was just some random yet totally ordinary Wednesday—I was walking my then-regular way to school.

I was about halfway there when a huge car sped its way through what one might consider a puddle and what another might consider a lake; either way, you probably have already predicted, I got splashed bad.

Soaking wet and freezing, I made the decision to head back home and change my clothes. I also packed an extra outfit because, in all honesty, I couldn't be sure this wasn't going to happen again.

Once I finally made my way to school, it was about time to finish up with second period, but I went anyway. I had been refusing to wake up much earlier than I had when I was still riding the bus, so I had been missing a bunch of class time. That had to change, I guessed. It appeared as if I'd have to be waking up no later than five in the morning. Anyhow, I got to class, picked up my work, and made my way to Spanish, where I came to find the owner of the vehicle that left me drenched.

"Well, well, well. Looks like someone got herself all dried up."

"Yes, Cara. It's not that hard to change clothes," I snapped.

"I'm just saying, if it's not that hard, why weren't you in first period this morning, and barely second?" Cara mockingly asked.

"I'm sure you know damn well the answer to that frivolous question of yours." I was pretty taken aback by myself. I never really gave anyone back talk, given that no one ever really spoke to me.

Cara turned around after blatantly rolling her eyes at me. Then, she went and sat at her desk right next to Kathleen. I'm more than positive she would've said more had she taken the time to actually learn my name. She had a thing for turning people's names into something to be made fun of, even if it was seemingly the most ridiculous thing in the world, even if it clearly made no sense. She probably would've called me something like Meleni-dumb. I came up with that, so I'll admit that it's rather clever. She knew I wasn't dumb, but like I said, these nicknames of hers didn't even have to come close to making sense. I remember when they were first becoming friends, she used to call Kathleen "Caffeine" because she has ADHD and could almost never sit still.

Come Thursday (that's right the very next day), Kathleen was stuck doing some of Cara's dirty work because Cara needed, absolutely needed, a car wash. So that mini lake that always stuck around near my house after rainstorms was still present, and Kathleen splashed me like it was her job! Left drenched, I decided this probably wasn't going to end anytime soon, so I took that rather lengthy walk back to my house and grabbed two more outfits for backup. And I obviously changed the clothes I already had on.

I kept two backup outfits in my locker. I also kept another backup outfit in, guess whose locker, Carol's. Carol and I were on pretty good terms especially since that day that she found out that I was giving Cara a run for her money when it came to being top of the class. Basically, I knew if the Fans wanted to mess with my locker and get my extra clothes, they could. But there was no way on earth anybody was going to mess with Carol's locker.

I could go on about how that Thursday went on to be one crappy Thursday, but I'll spare you the details.

Friday was another day of receiving my own personal rain shower, but I at least didn't have to walk back home to change clothes. I only went to class a few minutes late because I had to go to my locker, get my clothes (that was no problem), then I had to wait for a stall to open up in the girls' bathroom. Yes, stalls stayed occupied basically all of class. I suppose I could have just dressed in front of everybody, but honestly, do you think that trusting Cara with the sight of my bare body would be all that smart? Okay, my seminaked body, but either way, it wasn't wrong of me to believe I could be wronged even if it would be weeks from that day. I've always been the sort of girl who couldn't care less about what other people thought and/or said. But I still did prefer that people left my name out of most conversations, especially the negative or problematic ones. Just to mention I find it pretty hard to be fully confident in high school in most of my lives, if not all. That was another reason I preferred having little to no attention.

It was maybe five weeks into freshman year; at least by the time the sixth week started, the so-called puddle evaporated enough so that Rachel and Cynthia didn't get their turn to use their cars as supersoakers. I'm sure either they felt some sort of relief, because, as I mentioned, they weren't bad people, or they felt like they were missing out on some fun.

I was lucky enough to have made a routine of changing clothes then washing and drying my original outfit of choice in the home ec. class. I did indeed become acquainted enough with the home ec. teacher to be one of her favorite students. (Yes, I'm a bit cheeky about it.)

All the classes in the school got called together at the end of the day for a class meeting. We mainly talked about things like class budget and our contributions to our pep rally for homecoming. The class council was to help make things happen like encouraging all of the class to participate during spirit week and help build the infamous freshman float, which was supposed to be built by council and all the homecoming candidates, but a ton of students always got talked into helping. Anyway, by the time we—Cara (*cough, cough*)—got finished with talking about that, the topic of grades got brought up by a certain someone.

To Cara's complete shock, and rightfully my own, she and I were still tied for valedictorian. I wasn't very interested in school, especially not more than your average bear. But I did my work and had a decent-enough reputation among teachers by having no reputation at all. Those were the things that made the staff figure I had reason to miss class time, so work assigned and done was technically an A. If there was such thing as extra credit when it came to our class rank, Cara would have been in first place. She was always in class on time; I obviously wasn't. She frequently stayed after school; I was already getting home late because I had to walk; why would I stay after seventh period? Plus I rarely was presented with concepts I didn't tackle; if I came across one, I would learn it myself within the week. Cara was so much more dedicated than I was, and in a way, I guess it means that she deserved valedictorian more than I ever did. In my opinion, the outcome came out fair and very much so as it should have.

Who ever really heard of getting extra credit for things like that? Right? Well, that school had a way of figuring out, more so choosing, who deserved what.

On top of being the first one to arrive and last to leave class, and maybe even school, Cara did sports: volleyball, basketball, and track.

No one got extra credit for being in sports, but teachers were a lot more lenient toward the kids who were in them.

Take note of all this; just acknowledge and notice all the assistance Cara got in school. I'm definitely not trying to discredit her in any way; I'm just saying, imagine all the incredible things I could've been if I actually gave a damn about school! Yeah, well, I supposed that was just something to remain in our imaginations, never actually something that I'd figure out because I didn't really want to give a damn about school. It was school; all I had to do was pass. Nothing was hard for me, so I gave the least I could possibly give without becoming a problem. I was good enough, average, absolutely nothing more. And for some unknown reason, I was completely fine with that.

I suppose we'll talk more about that later; let's go back to the fact that Cara's plans were being soiled. She had to crank up the effort.

I was a smart kid with good behavior and got my work done. If making me late to class wasn't enough to make Cara win, then she had to sneak her way into my grades. How? You might ask. Simple, Cara had her way with words, and well, the principal was her auntie.

Attendance and whether or not we got to class on time became a weekly grade. In certain classes, we also started having Socratic seminars, which were more of participation grades than anything else. How could I participate if I wasn't around? Exactly. These were small grades, ten to twenty points, but Cara and I weren't stupid. We both knew they would add up.

In gym, the Fans would mess with my locker, so I could rarely get to second period on time because of troubles I dealt with in first. I didn't want to risk them stealing my things, hiding them, or even throwing it all in the showers, so dealing with it all being stuck in my locker was really my best option. Collecting what I missed in second made me late for third, and my workbook went missing in fourth. That meant that I had to copy the workbook pages onto a piece of notebook paper then start the work. It really wasn't that big of a deal, but it did take away the time that I used in that class to finish other work. That led to me having more work at home and less sleep. Still not a huge deal, but it did make a difference.

The Fans didn't really do anything to my afternoons, but I had no doubt they would figure something out. In the meantime, they still came to splash me on the mornings that it had rained—and our town never really went through a drought. Come winter, it all would freeze, and then the Fans wouldn't be able to torment me. Cara didn't want top of our class so bad that she would risk sliding and hitting me, at least I hoped not.

The first snowfall of the winter had proved to be the school's first cancelation—our first snow day! I didn't exactly have to sit there and ponder what I should do, because I had something I should've been doing: homework. I did, however, stay pondering the decision of whether or not I felt like doing the work. I decided against it. I didn't feel like doing anything at all, but I also decided that I had discipline, and discipline was doing what I knew needed to be done, even if I didn't want to do it. So I spent my morning finishing up my workbook for lodging and finally began my geometry assignment, which was a more lengthy assignment than usual, therefore taking me to waste more time than usual. By the time I finished with my geometry homework, it was just before two o'clock. I figured while I was at it, I would get the last of my work done. It'll probably come as a shock to you, but the homework I had left was actually for...PE! I know, I know. What sort of madness even is that? Well, apparently, it was our school's sort of madness.

All I had to do was run, jog, or speed-walk a mile and record my time, tell that time to Coach Jo, and try to beat it on at least one of our mile runs for the month. It's pretty obvious that not many kids did it. I don't think anyone even believed I did it. Everybody basically just came up with a number and claimed it to be their time, but almost always, when the day came to compare our times for the month, the numbers were so far off it was unbelievable. Coach Jo never told us our actual times, so no one really knew if they were in a ballpark range or not. Mainly everybody failed when it came to the honesty part of our grade, but heck, what did Coach Jo care? It was our grade.

I value honesty a lot, and I feel like having goals is a wonderful and important thing. It helps in making you better as a person. So I got some money, set foot out the door, and went to the market. I figured the market was about a mile away, at least, and if not, it gave me some wiggle room for the next time we got timed on our mile in class. I jogged most of my way there, then when the market was in sight and in fair-enough distance, I would run, straight-up book it like my lives depended on it, all of them. After catching my breath, I'd walk into the market and buy mostly snacks—that's what I lived off. But from time to time, I'd buy real-deal things like chicken, never without barbecue sauce though.

On that particular run, I had run my mile in twelve minutes and forty-one seconds. It wasn't horrible, but I wanted to cut down my time more than anything. I wanted a time of nine minutes flat; like I said, it's a wonderful thing to have goals. I knew that even in my first lifetime. I had sped up from my last run of twelve minutes and fifty-two seconds, so I decided I could go all out with my snacks.

As I was walking home, bag full of snacks in hand, it started to snow again. By the time I got home, it was still snowing, harder now, and it was sticking. Something told me that I didn't even have to do all my work that day. And guess what? I was right! Wednesday was canceled and Thursday as well. By Friday, it was still snowing; however, it wasn't snowing as harshly as the other days in the week. School probably would've been canceled that day, but being that Monday was the only other day we went to school that week, we settled for an in-between—a two-hour delay. That was pretty insane, because typically, either there was school or there wasn't; never was there an in-between. Our principal hated the idiotic schedule we had to follow when school was delayed, but the idea of cutting into our summer break sounded worse to her so…

The day went by fairly quickly considering every day felt sluggish while waiting for Thanksgiving break and Christmas break. I was never able to help myself from the anticipation of not having to be around my school for lengths at a time.

That weekend, I came to the realization that I actually always had work. I was never overwhelmed, but I was occupied at all times.

I didn't have time to just do nothing anymore. Yeah, that was not good. Cara had to have known about that. She also was still gunning for me; I just knew it. As soon as she figured out how to affect my afternoons, I was going to be screwed. I'd start drowning in work, my grades would crash, and Cara would no doubt start "winning." All this trouble because of something that ultimately meant nothing to me.

This kept up. I was struggling to keep up in school, but I was surviving. If I was lucky, I'd get to school with just my pants drenched because of walking in the snow. Other times I'd get to school drenched because of reasons you're now already well aware of. And other times, what I'd call often enough, I'd get to school covered in mud.

Frustrated with having to stay after school to gather my laundry, which got lost with the home ec. class, I took some time to raid the counselor's office for snacks before walking home, which I'm glad I did. All that frustration and tension completely faded away when I noticed the school's newest student the day before Christmas break. Weird, right?

Well, this wasn't just any student. This was Lydia Legend, my sister.

Five against two!

Chapter 3

I RAN UP TO THIS GIRL at least at the speed of a nine minute mile, that's for sure. And I jumped on her, tackled her almost.

You must think that that's weird, and you must think she thought I was insane, right? Wrong! Well, the first part is right, but Lydia most certainly did not think I was insane. I did this almost every lifetime, because I found out in my second lifetime that Lydia remembers everything just as I do. So she stumbled a bit, and we both ended up falling. Laughing and feeling tons of relief, we were both amazed that we found each other for this lifetime, finally. Her mom, of course, was puzzled, so Lydia told her that I was an old friend from a school she went to before, which wasn't entirely untrue.

That Christmas break turned out to be one of the best Christmas breaks I've ever had, and I've certainly had many. I actually would call that my favorite break, but we'll talk about that later, I guess.

Lydia and I spent at least 90 percent of that Christmas break together. Strangely enough, Lydia and I got along so much better when we weren't sisters; maybe it was because I came to find out what life was like without her, and she came to find out what life was like without me. We both learned that neither of us were all too fond of life without the other around to bother—oh, I mean talk to and bother. So after our first lives, we couldn't really stand to be apart and adored every second we had together. Don't get me wrong now, Lydia and I would bicker still, but it was more so sarcasm and smart-mouthed remarks than arguments. I never really took things that seriously. Lydia rarely took things seriously, and even if we did, we would always remain in the same room. Because we would rather be together arguing than apart moping and feeling angry. We need each other, always.

The few days that we weren't together, I was in my room watching movies, reading, and eating buffalo-style boneless chicken. I might've spent the whole break with Lydia, but although Lydia had known me for lifetimes, her family had just become aware of my existence. I could be understanding enough to let them have a nice Christmas with just family as well as a few days for the same nice family time. Lydia told me I could've stayed the entire break, that I'd be more than welcomed, but I knew I wouldn't have preferred to impose. In due time, her family would get used to me, so I was fine with my alone time.

By the time we went back to school, I started to feel better. I can't legitimately tell you that things were all good, but some things were better. Lydia didn't make Cara go away or leave me alone. She gave me someone to vent to and someone who actually listened to me when I felt the need to rant. It's always better to be alone than badly accompanied, but sadly, I could not and cannot escape the company of my own poor thoughts. But thanks to Lydia, I had less poor thoughts and wonderful actual company.

Lydia switched her schedule to match mine. I couldn't change my schedule sadly, so now we both had to deal with Cara. I wasn't in first period our first day back, so I made sure to find Lydia right after class.

"So you weren't lying about the whole 'basically having another wardrobe at school' thing, were you?"

"Nope. Almost every day I come to school soaked."

We both gave a small laugh. Lydia more so gave a half laugh, thinking to herself, *That just kinda, sorta sucks.* I noticed that look that she would give me every so often. She felt apologetic, guilty even, for everything that had happened before. Obviously, nothing was even close to being her fault, but I guess when you care about somebody, you're always going to wish that you'd gotten there earlier or been there to keep something from happening, maybe even to just be there as a shoulder to lean on when things were getting rough, to make things easier. I know that I'll always wish that I hadn't left Lydia that night.

Yup. First-lifetime problems.

Anyway, back to the first day back at school.

"Well, I'm sorry I didn't bring this up during break, but maybe I could bring you clothes? Just so you can have one less thing to worry about," Lydia suggested.

"That would be amazing. Thank you!" I said, practically in awe of my sister for taking some weight off my shoulders.

"And just to save you even more trouble, I'll just bring you some of my clothes," she said, laughing a little as she spoke because of the enthusiasm she'd heard in my voice.

"Are you sure? I mean, they're in huge danger of getting dirty, beyond dirty," I explained.

"Yeah, I'm sure. That's what sisters and best friends do, right? We share clothes, but for every outfit I give you, you'll give me."

So that was it, my little smart-ass of a sister had herself a deal. Being sisters and sharing clothes, as sisters—and best friends—do. I could've sworn that I had better taste in clothes than my sister, but come this lifetime, I supposed she learned a thing or two from yours truly. Then again, she'd use the clothes I left behind my first lifetime, so maybe she was milking it for my own sake.

Lydia's mom was a bit iffy about this whole deal going down. What if I didn't give her the clothes back? What if I got things torn or stained? And just because I gave her some of my clothes didn't mean it was fair. That last one basically meant "Your clothes are more expensive, more than likely." I guess I wasn't as pleasant to her mom as I had hoped. I would think to myself, *Sorry, Mrs. Legend, that my way of making a first impression on you was me tackling your daughter.* But Lydia trusted me, and after so long, she got her mom to trust me just enough, or at least pity me enough—either one was fine, I guess. And when it all came down to it, clothes were just clothes.

Day after day, Lydia and I would get to school early, and depending on whether or not my "lake" was around, we'd swap clothes and finish getting ready. In most cases, I would just start to get ready all over again. Surprisingly enough, there were days when Cara decided to spare me or just forget about little insignificant ol' me. If neither was the case, I suppose I just wasn't worth her time or any of the Fans' for that matter. It just took too much time and effort to torture me, I guess. Oh well, that was in my favor.

One thing not in my favor, Rachel had a creative little idea of her own so they didn't have to settle for just rainy days and melted snow. Can you say *water balloons*?

I knew it was Rachel because one morning she was getting to class late with me—like me—and carrying them, a huge, prideful smile plastered on her face. When we walked in, she instantly told Cara of the wonderful thought she had the night before. So at that point, it was every morning Lydia and I were swapping clothes. She might deny it, but I at least lost track of which clothes belonged to whom.

Obviously, the spring semester has more breaks, so it at least helped a little. It gave me more time to catch up on work, because yes, at that point, not only was I swapping clothes every morning with Lydia; I was also legitimately falling behind! It was a big help when school got canceled too.

Spring break came along, and I spent a good 60–70 percent of those two weeks doing work. Some of the work was late, some of it would be on time, and I was going at it trying to get ahead so I could fall back into being on time. Lydia didn't really mind; she'd work too, but not if she felt like being lazy. She could afford that. It's not like I didn't take breaks. I was and have always been way too easily distracted to not take breaks, but for the most part, we'd talk while I was writing summaries for plays like *Romeo and Juliet*.

I had two months left in freshman year, then I'd be home free. What could possibly go wrong within that amount of time that I wasn't used to at least? I figured, if anything, perhaps something would go right. I could actually get back into my old scheduling of school; I could keep up maybe? What if my bus would start running its route again? Maybe Cara would notice I had started to seriously fall behind and she'd let it all go and leave me alone and she'd just go back to forgetting I existed?

Yeah, none of that happened. Obviously, I survived because, well, even though none of that happened, something very right did happen, but after summer vacation, but we'll get to that. We're close.

Every so often, Lydia would bring us lunch randomly, or I would. Sometimes we ended up doing it on the same day and just added to the surprise. We would, more so I, would just work through lunch. I'm pretty damn blessed that Lydia loves me enough to have stuck around. After April, there wasn't too much for me to fall behind on, so we were basically golden once May came around.

We had three weeks of school to attend in May, which most people didn't attend any more than maybe eight days. We were given our first three finals the first week, the next two finals our second week, and obviously, our last two finals the third week.

I don't know if I mentioned this, but I don't exactly study, like ever. But Lydia always has. I have no idea why. Because finals were close and Lydia's studying habits were strict, I spent an entire weekend studying with Lydia and I ended up spending the other two weeks the same way. In the same way, I'm lucky that Lydia loves me; she's lucky I love her. There's nobody else I would've studied for or with at the time. I'm not going to lie though; there are plenty of places I would've rather been and plenty of things I would've rather been doing.

"I don't think I'll ever understand why you study so often," I said.

"Because some of us actually care about the grades we get in school. Actually..." Lydia trailed off and put her head back down, shaking it.

"What?"

"Well, I was almost thinking the same thing."

"Why you study so hard?"

"No, why you don't ever study at all," she said with a slight edge.

"Because I just don't. I mean, it's not like I really have to," I argued.

Lydia shook her head again, put her pencil down and her books aside. It looked like it was time for another small break. Great. Finally. But hey, guess what. It wasn't break time; it was talk time, which sometimes felt more like lecture time.

"Well, no, you don't. It's not like you have to do anything." Lydia put extra emphasis on *have* because she knew I would've been smart about what she said one way or another had she not put the emphasis "But don't you think that maybe it'd be nice if you did?"

"Not really, no," I quickly replied; almost instinctively I went against what she said. It wasn't because I wanted to argue but because I saw no reason in being better if I was good enough. "Plus, if I start studying now, do you realize what that'd mean?" I asked.

"Not really, no," she mocked.

I rolled my eyes and responded, "It would mean that Cara and the Fans would terrorize me even more than they already do. I mean, probably."

"And that's another thing," Lydia started. "Cara and her little entourage—"

"Applaud squad," I interrupted.

"Applaud squad," she continued, "do all this crap to you because you give her a run for her money, a good one at that. So if you don't care at all and don't want to try or study, why don't you just stop altogether? You'll lose top spot, second spot, stop being competition, and she'll leave you alone. And she'll tell her 'applaud squad' to do the same."

I looked at her with no response at all. She had some pretty valid points. Man, I sometimes despise my sister being so smart.

I shook my head and told her, "Listen, I just don't wanna really talk about it right now, okay? So can we just not?"

She tilted her head and gave me that look that said "I just want to understand so I can help" and respectfully went back to her books, picked up her pencil, and continued to study. I figured that meant break over.

I felt sort of bad because even though we didn't fight, I shut her out, and when someone does that, it never feels good, especially when it's someone you care about. As a consolation, I let her have all my Pringles and walked her home as we listened to a playlist of her own creation.

Walking back, I was basically mindless. I didn't want to think about absolutely anything until I reached the comfort—well, security—of my own bed. As if I were a supervillain, I did my fair share of monologuing. To this lifetime, I hope no one heard me, because I probably sounded insane! Just imagine hearing a fifteen-year-old girl trying to decipher the pros and cons of the Louisiana purchase and how mind-blowing the number zero is. Yeah, exactly, when have you ever been relaxing on a Saturday night hearing "I mean zero is the exact opposite of a prime number because every damn number in the freakin' world is a multiple of zero! Wow, that's mind-blowing! And the answer to zero divided by zero is what? Zero? One? Undefined? Who even knows?" Exactly, never, 'cause it's insane. Even harder to imagine being that girl, so only try if you can.

When I finally got home, I lay down and proceeded to stare at the ceiling and think about everything, actually just everything Lydia had said only hours before.

I didn't have answers to any of her questions. This sort of thing had never come up before, and I spent some time wondering why that was. I didn't know why I tried in school even if, to me, I wasn't trying all that hard. Why did I turn in work? Why did I finish work? Why did I start the work in the first place? I know that I didn't want to be the kind of kid who caused a ton of problems, that was too much work, but why did I care to be an actual good kid? I could've been the kid who was somewhere in the middle, turned in work most of the time but not always, listened to music in class, and got Bs and Cs along with the occasional A. It was a true mystery to me why I did indeed care, maybe not like Lydia did, but I did. I knew that if I were to have laid off and gave Cara the top spot in our class, I wouldn't have been in the situation I was in, so why didn't I just let her have it? Eventually, I came to the conclusion that I really didn't have an answer. Yeah, just wonderful; I lost an entire night's sleep to reach no answer. I should've listened to this one quote that I heard: "Never sleep on anything because then you won't sleep at all." Something along those lines. In that case, it proved to be truth.

"Hey, Mel."

"Hi, Lydia. Thanks for taking away my sleep last night," I said half jokingly.

"What do you mean?" she asked, confused.

"Well, you're basically the whole reason I didn't get sleep last night."

"Did something happen on your way home? I'm sorry, I didn't think to ask if you wanted to stay the night."

"You don't have to be sorry, it's just…"

"What's wrong?" She looked concerned.

"Nothing really. It's just I realized that I don't have the slightest idea how to answer those questions you asked me yesterday while we were studying."

"We?"

"Ha ha, very funny. Okay, while you were studying," I said. "I stayed up all night trying to make sense of it all, but nothing."

"Wow. It's not that big of a deal though. Sometimes we just do things because."

"Just because?"

"Just because," she assured me.

I took a deep breath feeling mostly better. "If you say so."

So Lydia smiled, proud of herself for curing me for the time being, then we got to work. Of course, after our second break, I decided I was all done, maybe for the school year. That sounded about right. Helping Lydia study was enough studying for me.

In gym, I aced that. I didn't get my nine minutes flat, but I got a time of ten minutes and sixteen seconds. Guess who tied; that's right, my partner in crime. She bumped up her time from a twelve-minute-and-two-second mile.

Geometry was pretty easy. What else would you expect from a girl who, in her spare time, discusses how amazing the number zero is, discusses with herself nonetheless? I got a well-earned 98 percent. Two words: *damn, negatives.* Lydia got a ninety-six; that's what studying gets you.

Last for that week and possibly least, Spanish. It was a simple test, multiple choice. I got a solid ninety. Lydia beat me there with a ninety-seven.

Two more weeks. The studying continued. Lodging was easy; we just had to answer some questions from our textbooks, not our workbooks, thankfully. That got me and Lydia solid hundreds. Fifth-period history got me a one hundred five and Lydia a one hundred two. Hooray for extra credit. Lastly, I ended my freshman year with a ninety-eight in physical science and in English; Lydia, a ninety-one and a ninety-three.

That was it; freshman year was over and done with. Lydia and I had our first summer vacation of this lifetime at our fingertips. But of course, something just had to go wrong. Lydia's grandparents got robbed. They didn't live very far away, but Lydia's family felt it best that they stayed with them for a few days. Thankfully, her grandma and grandpa had been out for maybe three or four days going to other graduations. So they weren't home. If they had been, who knows what would've happened?

Once her grandparents got set up with a bed and some other furniture, Lydia and her parents came back; at that point, the summer was ours to take over! I guess we didn't really do anything all that extravagant, but together, everything felt pretty badass! We went out for ice cream and tried every flavor there was to try, I'm almost positive. We went to watch movies and, to save money, sneaked into the ones we weren't sure deserved our money. If the movie was to our liking, we'd go back to watch it again and would pay. We took walks in the parks or just all around the town. We took some time to goof off in stores or look like idiots—compared to others—in gyms. That summer was good; its ending, not so much. Why? Well, because it ended.

Signing up for classes and registering for school was always… awkward, I guess. I'd tell my mom we were super late so we could go just late enough for some of the faculty to be there, enough to get me in. They would feel bad we made the trip for nothing, so they would sign me up. But it was always a day prior to when sign-ups started; this way, I could go with Lydia and tell her the classes we should get and when, and nobody would see my mom. It's not like she was around me any other day of the year. Sometimes kids from other grades would pull the sort of stunt I would and come the wrong day, but on accident for real. Let's just say that as Lydia and I were walking out all done, I saw someone worth tackling.

Yup, five against three.

Chapter 4

"*Y*OU SAW HIM?" LYDIA YELLED.

"Yes!" I yelled in return.

"You're positive? Like, you're one hundred percent sure?" she asked to basically clarify everything, even though it was needless.

"Yes, stupid, I'm one hundred percent positive."

"I'm not stupid, just in shock because this is insane!"

"I know it is! And you know I've never mistaken him. How could you doubt me? I, for one, am offended."

Lydia smiled knowing that I definitely wasn't offended. I was too excited.

"Who on earth are you two screaming about?" Lydia's mom, Francine, asked.

I looked at Lydia; Lydia looked at me.

"Mel's lover, of course, Mom." She pushed my shoulder and gave a teasing smile.

Francine rolled her eyes, smiled, and shook her head as we left the parking lot. It was amusing to her that we were such "crazy kids" obsessing over things like boys.

Lydia and I began to playfully hit each other. "I'm serious, Mom. She's been in love with Tyler pretty much since the beginning of time!" Lydia said that, looked at me, and knew I couldn't deny any of it. "In love with Tyler," "beginning of time"—yeah, that was about right. "See, Mom, she can't even go against me."

"Shut up, Liv!" I said and smacked Lydia.

"Liv?" Francine asked.

"Yeah. Since she's Lydia, instead of Lyd, I call her Liv. It just appealed to me." I shrugged.

Francine nodded and admitted that she liked it as well. She found it to be cute. Lydia glared at me in a mischievous way, realizing I wanted to change the subject and not talk about Tyler quite then. For the rest of the ride from school, we all mainly stayed quiet unless we were asking about or commenting on a song that played on the radio. I usually danced and sang along with the music, even if I didn't like the song that much, but it always felt strange to me in front of any parent.

Lydia and Francine asked me if I wanted to stay with them so Lydia could have someone to go to school with on the very first day of sophomore year. I said yes because I knew that Lydia was always very nervous on her first day of anything. It's not like I had to pick up anything because I was still sharing clothes with Lydia. I'm pretty sure Francine noticed that I didn't have any new clothes for the new school year, because she didn't ask me anything about having new things. Lydia told me that Francine always asked a lot of questions, and since she didn't ask me any on the car ride to their house, I sort of just inferred. As far as shoes went, I didn't really share with Lydia, not because either of us minded, just because we were really pleased with our own. We shared on occasion though. Francine was okay with that. I think at that point, she took a liking to me.

When we got to the house, the first thing Lydia did was drag me to her room. She sat me down and told me to wait there as she went to her kitchen to make us nachos. There was no way she was going to be without food as I told her all the details of this basically nonexistent gossip.

"Okay, so tell me everything. Don't leave out a single detail," Lydia demanded.

"I have no idea what you mean." I basically responded with a question.

"Yes, you do, it's Tyler we're talking about. There's always something to tell!"

"I get that, Liv, but there's not really anything to tell."

"Whatever, just tell me everything you got then. You like to talk too much anyway."

I rolled my eyes then tried to tell Lydia "everything," but her being the one who likes to talk too much also, she had to interrupt.

"So, did he see you? Did you two see each other? Did he wave? Did you wave? Did you both wave? How about smiles? Did you guys smile at each other? Actually, did you two even make eye contact?"

I think as she was rambling, Lydia noticed the situation was a whole bunch of nothing other than her own hype.

"Well, Ms. You Talk Too Much, if you'd let me talk, I could tell you all that." I paused for a moment, fully expecting for Lydia to make some sort of remark. When she stayed quiet for more than three seconds, I started, "I'm not exactly sure if he saw me, but he did turn back. I think he thought he dropped something. That being said, we obviously didn't wave to each other. Eye contact? No, it didn't happen. But yeah, of course, I smiled at him. Whether or not he noticed is beyond me," I answered.

Lydia nodded and, surprisingly enough, kind of just dropped it. We snacked on the nachos for the rest of the afternoon, then Francine called us to have dinner. I should've known that Lydia would bring up Tyler at the table at least once; she actually brought him up three times, but only once did she succeed. So I told Francine a little bit about Tyler. I told her we were friends for a long time—of course, I didn't mention how long—and basically that he was very nice and friendly. Francine thought that perhaps after getting reacquainted, Lydia and I would like to have him over. I found that sudden, you might say. It was just that every time I met Tyler, I felt like it was the first time we were meeting. Cute and cheesy and romantic and all that other stuff, right? Well, I guess kind of, but it was mainly because in a way, it was always our first time meeting. Tyler didn't remember anything.

Now before I go into starting the next chapter, I'll tell you a little bit more about Tyler because he's a pretty important person in my lifetimes—all of them.

Lydia told you a little; Tyler is the love of my life—lives—and that is for lack of a better phrase. He's my soul mate. That's pretty incredible, right? To think that every life we live and lived that our souls are meant to come and complete the other. Anyway, one important thing to know is that, like Lydia and I, Tyler and I don't always find each other at the same time. I could find him at thirty five, or I could grow up with him. But nonetheless, we always find each other.

Umm…another thing is that meeting him isn't always the easiest thing in the world for me to do. I was always just meeting the same old Tyler, but he didn't know that we were destined to fall in love and be together forever. He didn't know that he was basically already obsessed with me. And I couldn't just treat him like we knew each other as long as time, even though we kind of did. I mean, sometimes I couldn't help myself and did anyway, but it wasn't always the best idea.

Tyler is tall and kind of pale—well, not so much pale but white. I apologize for my poor descriptions. His hair is perfect. Sometimes it's short; other times, it's long. It's not ever extremely long but what one might consider long for a boy. Either way, his hair is always beautiful, very soft indeed. I love his nails. I actually just really love his hands. I'm going to be cheesy again and mention that it always has felt like my hand fits perfectly in his. I mean, I truly love everything about him. I adore his mouth, laugh, smile, nose, and especially his ears. I really liked to play with his ears for whatever strange and unknown reason.

Aside from all these physicalities, I love the way he sees things, thinks about things, and the natural curiosity he has—we share that. He's hilarious and joyfully weird in a very pleasant way. And somehow, him being as carefree as he is, he treated things so preciously. People, sentimental belongings, music—Tyler kept it extremely close to his heart because it mattered.

I'll tell a story; it's one of my favorites. Maybe that will help some colors shine through. This story is in one of the lifetimes that I found Tyler before I found Lydia. To be completely honest, I always liked it better when I found Lydia first; sometimes Lydia would find Tyler, then they'd both find me. Those lifetimes are cool too though.

I had just had a completely horrendous day, and I basically wanted nothing more than to just forget the world and not exist for a while—a long while. I was a junior in high school, technically because I had just finished up with my sophomore year. I had met

Tyler not even a month prior to that day. You could kind of say that we were actually friends, not just acquaintances, but nonetheless, he came to my rescue by surprise.

I was a random pissed-off girl in a park at eight forty-five at night. We weren't even dating yet. and for whatever reason, he decided it would be only proper for him to approach me and find out what had been wrong. I wouldn't call that being nosy, but you'd have to admit that's a not-so-common form of common courtesy. Right?

"Hey, Melenium," he said.

"Huh?" I asked, somewhat confused.

"That's your name, right? Melenium?"

"Oh, yeah, that's my name. I guess it's just different because we're out of school," I explained.

"Really? I just thought that since we see each other everyday…"

"No, no, it's fine. I agree that it isn't weird at all, Tyler, but I'm feeling pretty out of it tonight."

"Is there anything wrong? Anything I can help with?"

I can remember looking at him with what felt like very distressed yet also innocent eyes. I can also remember Tyler looking at me like he got it; he understood it all without me speaking a single word. I looked down again, and he faced straight forward. After about only two minutes, Tyler shook my leg, stood up, and reached his hand out for me to do the same. I hesitated before I made any sort of move.

"C'mon, we're going somewhere," he said.

"Where could we be going? A lot of places are closing right now, and other places will be closed by the time we get there."

Tyler smirked and said, "Don't worry about it, just trust me."

"Well, where are we going?" I practically protested.

"A place worth going." He stayed smiling. "I promise."

So I took his hand, and he helped me up. I gestured for him to lead the way; he laughed and gestured for me to follow. We arrived at his car. I got in, and I buckled myself. He got in, buckled himself, started the car, then we were off.

"So what kind of music do you feel like listening to?"

I panicked. I didn't want to give the typical, lame answer of "It doesn't matter. I listen to everything."

"Anything, I kinda listen to everything."

Yup, I screwed up anyway. I still sounded stupid despite my best efforts. If you couldn't tell, I'm somewhat of an idiot. I just face-palmed in my mind really quick. Tyler picked a radio station that "seemed pretty legit" because it was playing Green Day.

"Is this cool?" he asked.

"Totally, love Green Day." I gave a pathetic excuse of a smile because of how nervous I felt.

We came to an easy halt at a Stop sign, and he looked at me and nodded his head to the glove compartment.

"Will you get the black jacket that's folded up in there?"

I was so relieved hearing that he didn't want a cigarette. My asthma has always been supersensitive, and I've always thought that smoking is just plain gross!

"You can go ahead and put that on, it's getting pretty cold. It's not a heavy jacket, but it's something."

"Thanks, it is kinda cold." I put it on and cuddled myself in it.

I was pretty surprised that Tyler had noticed I was cold. I don't think I made it all that obvious, then again, he could have just made a lucky guess.

"So you wanna let me know what 'everything' is?" Tyler asked.

"What do you mean?"

"The music you like, you said you kinda listen to everything."

"Oh yeah. Well, I listen to punk rock, like Green Day. And I like alternative. Pop music is pretty dominant, I think, but I'm pretty into rap too, which I can't say strays extremely far away from trap music, so I like that too. Country is legit. Some country music is my jam. Christian music is cool. Back to rock music, I just feel this is important, the rhythm section is so underrated. I mean, guitar is awesome, like 'Sweet Child o' Mine,' and the solo in 'Dead' by My Chemical Romance totally prove that, but bass and drums can create miracles. Blink-182 in 'Here's Your Letter' is insane on both bass and drums. I could listen to that instrumental all day. But yeah, like

I said, kinda everything." I probably looked like I was mad, insane while saying all that, but whatever.

Tyler looked at me as if to say "Wow!" and "What!"

"Who on earth, who in the universe listens to trap music and country?"

I laughed pretty hard. "I have no idea. I'm insane." I shook my head. I'm pretty sure I was blushing massively hard. "Shut up and don't say anything. Like I said, I'm insane."

"No, no. It's cool, that's just hard to believe."

"Yeah, well…" I looked at him and asked, "What about you?"

"What about me?"

"Don't play dumb, what's your music like?"

"I'm sorry to say it's not as interesting as yours."

"If you wanna call mine interesting, okay. Just tell me." I encouraged his answer, me being all too curious.

"Mainly punk and rap, not much else. It's not really genre that even matters, just that it sounds good, you know, feels good, and has purpose. But outside those two genres, nothing has really captured me."

"I knew someone who listened to nothing but ballads basically, and I thought that maybe that'd get, not necessarily boring, but like I'd want to throw some fun in there. So I guess everyone has their own ears. It's no worries. We'll hang out more though. I'll show you a whole new world in music. I'm absolutely positive you won't hate all of it…more than likely, maybe, hopefully."

We both laughed and let the radio play. Tyler nodded in agreement, and we kept driving farther away from town. We both got quiet, but in a good way. It's like, I've always appreciated relationships where both people can just be secure in silence, comfortable without sound. Tyler and I have always had a relationship where conversation is natural, not forced and just flows. But whenever silence crept in, it was not at all awkward. We didn't feel the need to entertain each other just because.

When it started to get a little bit lukewarm, I unzipped the jacket I had on and rolled down the window. I let the wind blow my hair. In that moment, I felt so good, seeing all the signs, reading that we were leaving town and running away. But we weren't running away. We weren't afraid, scared, or angry. It was more like we were running free, because we were. We were free, and we were taking that freedom to our advantage, and we were escaping. We were escaping from the town, the people in it, the emotions, and the problems that we knew would be there waiting when we went back, but it was all right because, more than anything, we were escaping our realities. By running free that night, we gained the ability to just not exist and forget all that did. We just decided that we were going to not exist together. It was like being alive in a world where nothing was real unless you really wanted it to be. It was the most calming feeling I had ever felt; at the same time, it was the most exhilarating!

Tyler and I left our town behind easily; that wasn't too much of a shocker. Then we passed a second and even a third. By the time we reached the fourth town, I was sure I knew where we were going.

"Really?"

"What?" Tyler asked, smiling.

"You're taking me there?" I asked, rather confident in my answer.

"You think you know where we're headed?"

"I know, I know where we're headed."

"I'll bet you don't."

"I'll bet you, I do."

"Okay, but I doubt it 'cause not too many people know this place."

"Are you sure? 'Cause I think a lot of people do. You know everyone loves to go to the lake."

"Oh. Yup. You're wrong," Tyler said somewhat triumphantly. "I told you, but you just didn't wanna listen. Ha ha, I won."

"Okay, okay. You don't have to boast in your 'victory,' weirdo."

"Yeah, I do."

"And why is that?" I asked.

"Because I'm pretty sure you're the only one who'll let me."

So for a little while, I let him pick and tease. That only was a short while, of course, because I regained my curiosity of our destination. So I asked Tyler, very straightforwardly, where he was taking us.

"Well, you know where we're not going."

"Don't be a smart-ass, just tell me!" I whined. "At least I took a guess."

"That doesn't mean anything!"

"It should!" I crossed my arms and playfully pouted my lip. "I think it does," I mumbled.

"I sort of told you. I said it was a place worth going, which, now that I think about it, really kicks out the lake. Why did you think we were going to the lake?"

"You know, a lot of people would argue with you on that. The lake's pretty freakin' popular for a reason. Plus, it's close to here."

"I'll give you that much, but c'mon, I didn't want to drive you to some place that's ordinary. No, you're too special for that. That's too inside the box. You gotta think outside the box!" Tyler looked at me, probably hoping he had gotten through to me in some way, which he did, so I didn't ask any more questions. I just nodded. "It's a good surprise, okay? I promise. And I always keep promises."

"I always keep promises" makes my top-three list of "favorite things to hear" (especially from Tyler). Yes, I am that lame to have a list.

Anyway, the rest of the ride we spent quiet. We just listened to the radio and went way too fast. And of course, I'm going to tell you where we ended up. Yeah, we ended up in the middle of nowhere, with a flat tire, on the side of the road.

I'm just kidding. We were quiet for the rest of the ride with the radio playing, and we went way too fast because we were indeed in the middle of nowhere. No cops were around to care, so we both kind of figured, Why not? But we didn't end up with a flat tire on the side of the road. No, we ended up on the top of a mountain that has the most beautiful view I've ever seen.

"Wow. No one ever comes here?" I asked in astonishment.

"Nope. You can't really see it from the main roads. You have to either be really lost, which I was the first time, or actually trying to get here to get here," Tyler explained.

I stared out in awe. We both stared up at the stars too. Again, it was like the world was ours, because from up there, it seemed like, in the best way, we just didn't exist. The only thing you could see while looking out on the horizon was opportunity, the opportunity to create anything because the world looked like a blank canvas, rather than the horribly complex and abstract world we realize is already painted once we step back into reality.

"Tyler?"

"Yeah?"

"Thank you, for all of tonight, I mean."

"No problem. And you know what the best part is?" he asked with a smile.

"What's the best part?"

"That it's not over."

"What do you mean?"

"This was only a pit stop, my friend. I still have a particular place I really want to show you."

I looked at him with a suspicious smile then agreed with a simple "Okay."

"You're not gonna argue or ask millions of times where we're going?"

"No. I trust you. And I decided something."

"What's that?"

"I like surprises," I said. It seemed to have taken Tyler aback.

We got in the car and buckled ourselves. We kept the radio on but also had one of those conversations that are basically meaningless but are also very pleasant, because I think everyone likes to talk about nothing every now and then.

I told Tyler how it really irritated my life that I had the terrible habit of going to the refrigerator constantly even though I knew nothing good was in it. And Tyler told me that he couldn't stand it when people would put sugar in their bowls of Raisin Bran, because in all honesty, it just didn't make sense to him.

I think that on that mountaintop, we both decided that nothing heavy owned us, that we owned ourselves, and that we were always going to be better because of it. And I think that sitting back in the car and having those conversations about nothing was our way of promising each other that we truly meant it.

You see, everyone says that you own your own happiness and only you can decide if you're happy. In a lot of ways, that's true, but no one ever mentions that you kind of need some help. You need tools, you need people, and you need reasons. Tyler and I decided that we were going to be that for each other. We decided that if everything started to go wrong and everyone started to walk out on us and seemingly our whole world was falling apart right before our very eyes, we would still have each other; that if one of us fell into a funk, the other would be right there. We would always have a reason. We would always have a person. We would always have a tool— hope. We would always have each other, so the world would never be allowed or even capable of owning us; we would always be our own.

When we finally pulled up to what appeared to be an old barbershop, I wasn't disappointed or underwhelmed, just very, very confused and curious.

"'Kay, are you ready?" Tyler asked.

"Umm, I guess."

"You have no idea where we are, do you?"

"No," I said blatantly.

"Good."

Good? What the heck was that supposed to mean? With my heart racing at a thousand miles a second and my mind even faster, I tried to theorize what on earth was going on. I did not succeed. Honestly, if you stopped reading right here, could you guess what was going on? I think not. Still not knowing anything, I opened my door and got out of the car. The lights were off. I still didn't ask any questions, all because I really wanted my surprise.

"C'mon. I got a key if it's locked," Tyler said, urging me to follow him.

"I'm coming, just trying not to fall," I explained.

"That's all right. I'll get the light for you."

Tyler turned on both the inside and outside light. He waited for me at the door as I sped up my steps. I looked inside to what revealed itself to be, not a barbershop at all, but a tattoo parlor! There were tons of colors and creations on the walls and artworks in binders on the countertops. I wasn't positive if there was more than one artist that worked there. The room wasn't too big, relatively small actually. But all the creativity was amazing!

"Come here. These are all my favorites."

"And you did all of these?" I asked, very impressed.

"Oh, no. I wish. Actually, uhh…" Tyler looked at his phone. "It was my friend Larry. Yeah, he's on his way now."

"How come?"

"How come what? You mean, like, why is he on his way here?"

"Yeah. I mean, don't you think it's pretty late?"

"No, not really. It's pretty freakin' early, I think, personally."

I rolled my eyes at him and laughed a bit. I guess sarcasm never really takes a break.

"Anyway, no, he said he doesn't mind at all. Plus, he lives close by."

I looked around the room, observing all the tattoos a little more. Tyler explained to me how almost every tattoo Larry did was original. He said that there probably were times that people wanted something specific, something they'd seen done before, but for the most part, Larry gave his customers tattoos they could only get from him, 100 percent unique and one of a kind. Apparently, Larry even practiced calligraphy, so he had incredible fonts as well. The tattoos he displayed in his binders illustrated that fact very well, but there was nothing like seeing it in person. I guess it's sort of like with music. You can listen to albums, even live albums, and see videos, but the artist in person is just so much more.

"Oh, hey, I think I heard him pull up," Tyler said and got up to open the door.

"Hey, man, it's been a while!" Larry exclaimed and hugged Tyler.

"I know, I know. Just school, I guess."

"You better be keeping up those grades. Remember, man, you gotta give it your all."

"We talk about this all the time. I know!"

"Because it's not worth doing if it's not worth doing right."

"Larry…"

"Nope. Let me hear you say it."

"If you're gonna do it, you might as well do it right," said Tyler.

"That's not exactly it, but I'll take it."

Tyler rolled his eyes a bit then introduced Larry and me.

"This is Melenium."

"Hi. It's nice to meet you," I said. "I really like the work you do."

Larry nodded and thanked me causally. I was extremely impressed because Larry only seemed about twenty-two (so not that much older than I was) and his craft was tremendous! He wasn't even an apprentice. He was a legitimate tattoo artist, a damn good one too. As you might imagine with all that I've seen, I'm not exactly easily impressed, far from it actually.

"So what exactly were you two looking to get?" Larry asked.

"Oh, no. I'm not actually getting anything done," I spoke out shyly.

Larry looked at me somewhat puzzled. And Tyler looked at me too as if to ask what I was talking about.

"Yeah, you are," Tyler said, almost bossing me.

"And what would make you think that I even wanted a tattoo?"

"Well, doesn't everybody?"

"No, far from everybody, my friend." I laughed.

"So, you seriously don't want one?"

"I do, really."

"What's the problem then?"

"I don't have any money to pay for one. I mean, look at these tattoos!" I began to speak more to Larry. "These are amazing. I couldn't afford anything like these!"

"Well—" Tyler started.

"No way. I'm not charging you guys," Larry interrupted.

"You're not?" I asked, not believing him.

"Of course not. Tyler is like a brother to me, and well, if you're cool with him, you're cool with me too."

I smiled. I was pretty touched that in one night, I seemed to have gained two friends that seemed a whole lot better than any friends I had that lifetime. It turned out that it stayed that way too. I'll always encourage people to acknowledge the people who are really present in their lives—in a good way. Consistency helps make us feel a bit safer.

"Do you know what you wanna get? I already know what I'm getting," Tyler said.

"Uhh…well, I have a few things in mind."

"Just remember, it can't be too big. We're trying not to take eight hours."

"Damn, I guess I can forget about that colored octopus back piece I wanted for now," I joked.

Tyler and Larry laughed. I was glad that they didn't take me seriously because it wasn't one of those jokes that's even funnier when it's explained. I did have a few ideas of tattoos I wanted to get done. At that point, I knew I really only wanted Larry to do them, but it would have to wait. I did know I could get my smallest tattoo though.

"Yeah, I think I got something in mind."

"Sweet. I guess we'll just get started?" Tyler asked.

"For sure. Umm…who wants to go first?" Larry questioned.

"This is gonna be my first tattoo, so that means I don't have to get the first tattoo of the night."

I was relieved because both Tyler and Larry figured that, that made enough sense. Tyler shrugged then went to go sit in the chair. Larry went to get his sketch pad. Not sure what to do, I just followed behind Tyler.

"What are you getting?" I asked.

"It's just something really simple."

I nodded, still with complete wonder in my eyes. Yes, yes, I know I was way too curious. I always have been. So I just sat there in curiosity; Larry came in and did his thing. I saw him sketch something for Tyler and put his calligraphy to work. Since I decided that I loved surprises, I didn't sneak a peek at the sketch or the outline when Larry laid it on Tyler's wrist.

"All right, you're all done," I heard Larry say.

"Nice," Tyler said. "So, you wanna see it?"

"Yes!" I said, excited to see the final product.

Tyler pulled me over to his side and revealed his wrist; plainly— and beautifully—ran the word *alive*. It was right where you get your pulse checked, and for whatever reason, that hit me with a lot of meaning. I never asked him if he meant it to behold that much of a message, but I think he did because he's poetic like that.

If you're wondering what I mean by "a lot of meaning," I'll explain, of course. You see, it's the word *alive*, and the word *alive* means to be obtaining life. Obviously, I've obtained life many times, which is part of the reason that the tattoo meant so much, but life is so much more than breathing. Well, the word *alive* was across his pulse and doctors check your pulse to determine that you are indeed alive, but to me, Tyler got "ALIVE" on his wrist to sort of indicate that breathing or not, he would always be alive. Sadly, not everybody lives or becomes alive. You hear all the time how life is great and wonderful, right? And a lot of the time, we think *No, it's not* or *Mine isn't*. But really, that's because we're not alive! *Life* means "breathing"; *alive* means "being lively and happy." *Alive* means "being in knowing that you have something to live for and believing that you are deserving of life and all its possibilities." The truth is that despite the fact that some circumstances are more fortunate than others, no life is more capable than the other. Tyler's tattoo represented all that to me and also that when it all came down to it, Tyler was alive, forever and for always.

"I love it!" I said with a bright smile. I turned to Larry and repeated myself. "I love it. I think you did an amazing job. I'm obsessed with the lettering!"

"So what do you have in mind?" Tyler asked.

"My tattoo, well, uhh…I kinda wanted to make it a surprise for you, like you did with yours."

"Okay. That's fair enough."

"C'mon over!" Larry called.

I walked my way over and explained to him what I wanted. With words that gave not the best description, Larry managed to draw up exactly what I had imagined, if not better. I gave the thumbs-up on his design, and Larry began tattooing.

All the hype about tattoos and how much they hurt, in my opinion, is completely false! I personally don't think they're all that bad, a discomfort maybe, but once you stop paying attention, the feeling is barely there. The first time I got a tattoo, I prepared myself for teeth-clenching, fist-biting, breath-holding pain, but it wasn't even close to that. I suppose it depends on the placement.

Anyhow, when Larry finished up my tattoo, I made my way to his mirror, and a smile longer than the Nile River found itself growing on my face. I instantly became obsessed with it.

I don't find Larry every lifetime, but when I do, he's the only—and I mean only—person allowed to tattoo me. Let's just say there are those who imitate art and those who create true art.

Tyler came up behind me "Wow! That's sick."

"Thanks. Larry did amazing," I said.

"He sure did."

"Hey, thanks, guys. That's always nice to hear, but I think I'm starting to feel how tired I actually am, so I'm headed back home. You guys wanna close shop?"

"Nah. I think we're headed back too, Larry, but thanks so much for hooking it up."

"No problem," Larry said, then he turned to me. "And remember, if you ever want anything else, I'm available, okay?"

"Okay, I'll remember. Thank you," I replied.

We walked out of the parlor and exchanged some more good-byes and "see you laters," then Larry got in his car, and Tyler and I got in our car, and we all left. Tyler and I drove for about half an hour before Tyler started our conversation.

"So, why a lighthouse?"

"It's somewhat of a long story," I said shyly.

"It's not like we don't have time."

"I'll make it long story short, okay?"

"Okay. That's cool too."

"Okay, long story short, it's pretty symbolic, which you might've guessed. The lighthouse takes care of those out in the ocean. It provides light, in turn guidance. People, a lot of the time, overlook it's importance, but it's always there simply because it's still needed even if some don't notice it. The lighthouse is sort of a safe place, but it also cautions people to avoid it, because, well, if they don't avoid it, they'll wreck into it, and they, as well as the lighthouse, will break and become damaged, sometimes beyond repair. It's like deer don't run towards headlights and you don't 'run into the light' because in essence that means death, metaphorically, of course. So, the lighthouse kind of shows you that it's not calling out to you, it's guiding you on the path that you're choosing on your own. The only people that really get to see the lighthouse are those who want, and dare, to see inside. Those who care enough." I picked my head up from staring at the car floor and awaited Tyler's commentary.

"Wow. I mean…wow. Not so short, but I'm glad 'cause that means a lot. It's badass. I never would've guessed. I'm just so glad I asked…wow!" He laughed a bit, in probable astonishment.

"Thanks. I didn't think anybody would care, really." I put my hand behind my neck.

"Well, no, that's awesome. It just sucks because they don't know."

Being the loser I am, I blushed and tried too hard to hide it. Tyler pretended not to notice, but I knew he did.

"So, why on the hip? Was the placement significant?" he asked.

"Well, yeah, but I said long story short, remember?"

"Yeah, but I thought you could break the rules a little."

"Some rules are meant to be broken," I admitted, "and some aren't. This one isn't."

Tyler and I exchanged looks and then stayed quiet again for a while.

"Random question," Tyler said. "It's a good one, I promise."

"Okay. Shoot."

"I know that this is only your first tattoo, but now that you have it, do you feel a little bit more, I don't know, more complete, I guess? Like the tattoo was always a part of you but you had to find it first or something?"

"Yeah! Actually, extremely! You basically took the words right from my mouth, mind, and heart," I exclaimed.

"That's awesome. I'm not crazy! I used to think that tattoos were kinda like pieces of us, things that made us more ourselves, and now I describe them more as like our personal birthmarks."

"That's a cool way to look at it," I agreed.

"We just got birthmarked."

"This is true." I looked at my tattoo and finished, "And I like it."

We continued to drive back to the city mainly in silence, but not awkward silence, calm silence. We definitely were more talkative and awake on the way up, but at that point, we could feel the sleep deprivation.

I told Tyler that despite the fact that he made me feel a million times better, I still wasn't all that ready to go back to my so-called home. So instead he took me back to the park and we just sat in the car. We probably would have sat on the hood of the car—like we were cool—but it grew colder that night despite the fact it was summer.

"So, I'm guessing you have somewhat of a curfew," I said.

"Mmm, not really. Before anyone realizes I'm gone."

"Well, it's pretty early, so maybe you should head home. I wouldn't want you to get in any sort of trouble, you know."

"No, it's really not a big deal. But it is getting pretty early."

"Yeah, it's cool if you wanna go home. I can just stay here."

"I'll get going now, but I, umm..."

"What is it?"

"I just thought that maybe that you'd wanna come with me. Only if you want to, of course," he said.

I can remember him asking me that. He was really nervous, for obvious reasons, I guess. And I'm sure that I didn't take forever to answer, but it felt like it. I just needed time to process the fact that someone actually wanted me around and wasn't trying to get rid of me as soon as possible. It felt weird to know that someone cared where I was and if I was all right.

"Umm...yeah. That'd be nice, but uhh, would that be okay?"

"I think so. Yeah. It's really only important that I'm home."

And we left. The entire ride there, I was really just trying not to fall asleep, staying awake while I am tired; driving in a car has always been pretty difficult for me. Tyler and I talked through the short ride there, but I was still rubbing my eyes every five seconds to ensure I didn't pass out.

"So we're gonna have to go through my window because the back door leads to the laundry room, and that's where we keep the dogs. I don't want them freaking out and waking everybody up, and I don't have the key to my front door."

"Okay. I've done my fair share of sneaking in through my window, so I think I'll be fine."

Tyler took my hand and led me around the side of his house. Once we got to his window, he turned on the flashlight on his phone, and he gave me a small boost so I could get inside.

As soon as he stepped inside, Tyler started to get comfortable, extremely ready to lie down and go to sleep. He took his socks and shoes off, then his jeans to reveal the shorts he had been wearing underneath, finally his jacket and T-shirt. As long as he was getting comfortable, I figured I'd do the same. Of course, the only thing I did was take off my jacket and bra.

"Are you hungry at all?" he asked.

I looked at his bloodshot eyes with my bloodshot eyes and gave a slight nod. He went into his kitchen and got two slices of cheese pizza and a pack of Pop-Tarts. Despite how sleepy we felt, we both couldn't ignore the emptiness we felt in our stomachs, so we each ate our slice of pizza and s'more Pop-Tart. After, Tyler got up to get mouthwash from his bathroom. We both rinsed our mouths then went back into his room.

"So how do you wanna do this?" he asked.

"It doesn't really matter, I guess."

"You don't need to sleep on a specific side of the bed or anything like that?"

"No, I am fine, either side works," I responded.

Tyler took the side he had been standing closest to, and I lay opposite him. I stared out the window for a while, still feeling tired, just not tired enough to shut my eyes. I turned over to stare at the ceiling and listened to the silence. Tyler started scrambling to find comfort as well.

"Hey, Melenium."

"Yeah?"

"Is it okay if I...hold you?"

"Is it okay if I...let you?"

Our bodies met in the middle of the bed, and Tyler held my hand; after only seconds, we both turned to our sides. I pulled Tyler's arm over me; shifting only slightly, he lifted my shirt and unveiled my freshly tattooed lighthouse that lay on my hip. He kissed my shoulder, laid his head back on his pillow, and whispered a quiet good night. I listened to his heartbeats and whispered a quiet good night in reply then fell asleep to the sound of his breaths.

Come morning, Tyler and I were still asleep. We woke up more around eleven thirty, maybe twelve o'clock! We were that tired. When we finally got up, Tyler found a note on his door that read, "Glad to see you made it home okay. I might work late, but I'll try to call"; at the bottom of the note, there was a small heart. I always thought small notes like that were the absolute best!

I realized how late in the day it was and remembered how much my dog hated being left alone for long amounts of time, so I told Tyler that I thought I should be on my way. He took my hand and pulled me in to kiss my forehead then walked me to the door.

"Do you maybe want something to snack on, on your way home?"

"No thanks. I'll be good."

"And you're sure you don't want me to give you a ride?"

"Yeah, I am sure. I like walks."

I was on my way when I stopped after a few steps to turn around.

"Tyler, does this mean that..."

"I hope so." He smiled.

So I went up to him and kissed him as though it was my best response, which, in retrospect, it kind of was, and just told him that I would see him later.

"Not today. I just wanna sleep and cuddle my dog," I said.

"Good deal. I just might do the same."

"So we're on for tomorrow then?"

"Totally. I'll meet you at the park."

Smiling like an idiot, I headed home already anticipating the next day.

Yup, well, that's my story. Hopefully, you have more of an idea of who and how Tyler is. And yeah, Lydia's right. I talk too much!

Chapter 5

"*W*AKE UP, LYDIA!"

"Ugh! Mel, why are you waking me up?"

"Because we have to go to school."

"I know! You realize how early it is, right?"

"Yeah, but I also realize how long it takes for you to get ready."

"Give me five more minutes—no, ten more minutes, or you're walking to school."

I rolled my eyes at Lydia and continued to get ready. I was freaking out a little, maybe a lot, because it was not only the first day of school but also the day that I was first going to talk to Tyler. I made sure my hair was particularly straight. I ironed my clothes completely flat. I brushed my teeth for at least six minutes and wore my best perfume and best lotion.

Somewhere between me finding socks that wouldn't slip and making dumb faces in the mirror, Lydia actually woke up! Trust me, her getting up on her own is far beyond rare. She took her time in the shower, probably calming herself down, because as I mentioned, she always has nerves the first day of anything. When she was done with her thirty-minute shower, she stepped out and realized she hadn't picked out what she was going to wear, so she came out in a towel and we chose her clothes together. She didn't want to seem like she was trying too hard, but let's face it, everyone always tries too hard on the first day of school. We ended up pretty much synchronizing our outfits, both of us wearing short shorts and tank tops, but she wore boots and I chose to stick with sneakers. As she went to take forever on her hair, I went to fix both of us breakfast. I only made breakfast burritos and coffee but took long enough because I only had one pan to use. After I had finished, I went to wake up Francine. She didn't really need to get ready because all she was doing was dropping Lydia and me off at school. I remember she didn't work that day, so I felt bad not letting her sleep.

"Is Lydia ready?" Francine asked.

"Yeah. I only had to wake her up once this morning."

She raised her eyebrows, making a facial expression suggesting that it indeed was something that didn't happen all too often.

"Here, I brewed enough coffee for you to have some if you want."

"That's all right, I'll probably wait till after I drop you two off."

"Oh, okay. Yeah, I just wanted to let you know it was there."

"Thank you. That was very thoughtful."

"Uh-oh, Mel, you're gonna make my mom hate me," Lydia said coming in.

"That's the goal, Liv," I replied.

"I don't mind," Francine added.

Lydia and I laughed. I think part of what made what Francine said funny was that it didn't seem too far-fetched, the idea of us childishly competing to be someone's favorite. And the fact that it was her mom was the icing on top. Obviously, Lydia is her "favorite," and despite the fact that she was joking, I think Francine did enjoy us bickering to have her favoritism.

Despite all of us being ready to go, we all decided to take some time to simply sit down and relax. Lydia and I thought about getting to school nice and early, but that day, it just felt better to go only on time. We had every other day in the year to go early.

When we got to school, the first thing Lydia and I did was go to the cafeteria. Our school was cool enough to give free breakfast every morning to all the students, because they cared enough to make sure we had the opportunity to eat, and from what I saw, all the students took advantage of that, especially the ones that needed it. Not everybody got free or even discounted lunch; as you can imagine, our school didn't have that much money, but sometimes the school store decided to be generous. I will always applaud the school for having the main school fund be the free meals because, well, I think all schools need and could really use and appreciate a fund like that as opposed to getting a new track, football field, soccer field, and basketball court every year or every other year. After eating the breakfast I had made, we took advantage of the free breakfast from the school just in case. The first bell rang, and boom, that was it. I took a long, deep breath in, and Lydia took a long, deep breath out; with no way to avoid it any longer, the both of us got up and made our way to class: first-period biology.

Even though we both had nerves going through the roof, Lydia and I made it to class early—well, what students considered early, because that's just what felt the most comfortable; that was the only way the teachers let you choose your own seat. But the popular kids were fine with almost anywhere they sat, and majority of the time, they were popular among staff as well, so they were all good just arriving late to class. It's no shocker, but guess who came in just before the last bell rang. Yup, the Fans. Lucky for us, Cara, Rachel, Cynthia, Kathleen, and Carter didn't have enough room to sit near us. That meant that they couldn't mess with us during biology.

The teacher seemed nice, but on the first day, don't most, if not all, teachers seem nice? And the class seemed simple enough. Science was never my best subject, but it always was the subject that cut me slack if I ever needed it and even when I didn't. Like every year, all we did was pick up a list of supplies we'd need for the school year and go over the basic class rules, which were almost the exact same in every class every year!

Once the bell rang to go to our nutrition break, Lydia and I stayed behind to snack on the breakfast we frivolously picked up from the cafeteria and looked at our supply list to decipher the supplies we would actually need. We had it finished after about ten minutes had passed, then we picked our things up and headed for the door, when Lydia took hold of my arm and pulled me to and out the other door.

"Okay, it's go time," she said in a hollering whisper.

"What the heck are you talking about?"

"What the heck could I possibly be talking about except—"

"Oh my gosh, you just saw Tyler," I said with my jaw dropping.

"No. I'm just messing with you."

"I hate you!" I yelled, smacking her shoulder.

"Okay, okay, now I'm actually kidding with you. He's in the room. He must have this class for second period."

I poked my head in barely to get a slight glance, because I didn't fully believe Lydia the second time. When I caught sight of him from the corner of my eye, Liv pushed me back into the class. I was surprisingly able to catch myself and saw Tyler turn his head just a tad, probably because he heard Lydia being a jerk and laughing at me. I had no other choice than to continue to walk in, but instead of being awesome and brave, I punked out and went up to the teacher to ask her for a second copy of the supply list despite the fact that I had a perfectly legible one right in my backpack.

I thanked her and walked out acting as calm as I could. Once I got into the hallway, I went up to Lydia and pushed her into the lockers, not as hard as I felt I should have, so don't worry.

"Yeah, now I hate you!"

"What are you talking about? I should hate you, you totally punked out in there!"

"No freakin' duh! How'd you figure that one out, Sherlock?" My voice grew in volume the farther we got away from the science room. "I didn't want to talk to him right away, at least not until we figured out if we have a class with him!"

"So you're telling me you would rather wait to talk to Tyler in a class we have with him, which we might not have, so possibly tomorrow, than talk to him between classes for a shorter time with nobody else around?"

"Well yeah." I paused. "I'll admit you have some good points too, but my plan was already settled in my head...yours is too sporadic right now."

"Nope! C'mon, we're going to talk to him," Lydia said, grabbing hold of my arm again. I'll admit that I didn't exactly put up a fight to keep her from dragging me along with her. But then, the bell rang.

Slightly disappointed, I still pointed my finger in Lydia's face and expressionlessly said to her, "Ha ha." We turned right back around and started our walk to class. It sort of seemed and even felt like we were the only kids actually making their way to class; I had a notion that it was going to stay like that for a long while, so I made a note to myself to get used to it. Perhaps it was because everybody else had friends to see and tell things to, and Lydia and I had only each other, and being that we were together almost always, we didn't have to die waiting to tell each other something that happened. I guess, depending on how you look at it, we were a pretty boring scene.

Our second period was Spanish II, which was pretty cool because we had the same teacher from the year before. The sophomore Spanish teacher quit; we were indeed notorious for making teachers quit, Spanish teachers in particular. I know it's bad, but I was always kind of proud of that. I thought it was cool to be known for something, even if it was that. Another thing that was cool was that a lot of kids didn't like that Spanish teacher, but Lydia and I did, and in return, she took a liking to us as well. And we didn't even have to fight for that favoritism.

Since we got to class before everyone else, we got to choose our seats again, and being the lame kids we are, allegedly, we sat in the desks that were basically right in front of the teacher's desk. They were just off to the side. The Fans came in not too long after us, and since they didn't want to be in front of the class or next to Ms. J, again they kept a decent distance from our seats. At least at the rate it was going at, Cara and her applaud squad couldn't torment Lydia and me the entire day. The last bell to get to class went off, but we waited a few more minutes before getting started. We all came to notice that the class size was quite small. Other than the seven of us, there were only three other students and then Ms. J, and even though that school wasn't that spectacular and huge, it was still awry to have a class that small—only ten people in that class. It probably would've been smaller if the Fans didn't all have to be together and also if those other kids had passed Spanish II the first time.

We again did a whole bunch of nothing, which, spoiler alert, is basically what we continued to do all year. So the bell rang, and Ms. J said bye to us, and we said bye to her, and by "we," I mean me and Lydia. Next we had humanities. Just in case you don't know, humanities is a mixture of English and history, world history to be exact. And that class was far from small! Everybody wanted that class because some kids got in, then those kids told their friends to get into the class, then yeah. You get the idea. There were about forty, maybe forty-two students in that class, but I loved it.

The teacher was Mrs. Rose, and even though she wasn't the most laid-back teacher, pretty much everyone loved her. She really knew how to teach well and made it just about as fun as anyone could. Mrs. Rose only taught humanities and these other electives— genocide and mock trial—because she hated basically everything else! This school would've been nothing without her, so the principal didn't even try to make her teach anything else. Humanities counted as two classes because, like I said, it was a mixture of English and world history, so after the bell for third, Lydia and I just stayed in the classroom. No one actually got to choose their seat in that class, but luckily, Lydia and I got sat together!

When fourth period ended, all I wanted to do was stay in class at the risk of seeing Tyler and Liv making me actually make contact with him.

"Hey, what are you doing? It's time to go to lunch," Lydia said.

"I know, I know, but I don't really have lunch money anyway."

"Really? I thought I saw you get money this morning. Well, I guess it doesn't matter. I brought some extra money, so I'll buy us something we can share."

"You know, I'm not all that hungry. And we have art class right across the hall, so maybe for today we won't go to our bench, we'll just chill here?" I suggested.

"Mel, you're being chicken."

"I know that, and you know that, let's not let anyone else know that."

"Seriously? C'mon, you have to meet him eventually."

"Gee, Liv, you're just wonderful at pointing out the obvious today."

She rolled her eyes and started pulling me, insisting we had to go to the lunchroom at least for the sake of her. Before we got out into the open area, I was pulling myself back and onto the floor, because there was no way she could pull all of me, right? And even if she could, she would not be willing to cause that much chaos, right? Wrong and wrong!

I was always a sucker for the old "If you love me…," so I caved in and the two of us made our way to the cafeteria. I don't know about Lydia, but I was not at all looking for Tyler. I wasn't trying to find him, nor was I looking to find him so I could avoid him. It was just too much pressure. So all I did was walk behind Lydia with my head to the ground. I'm lucky I even got away with that. I'm also lucky that Lydia didn't walk me into anything.

"Are we at least going to go back to our bench and not stay in here?" I asked.

"Yes. Don't worry, the only time I'll force you to be in here is when we're waiting in line, but there'll probably be exceptions," Lydia said with her infamous grin.

"Oh, I know there will be!"

Waiting in line didn't necessarily calm me down, but it made my nerves a bit more stable. I got a grip on the fact that Tyler could've gotten in line right behind me or could've asked to cut in front of Liv and me. At that point, I was keeping an eye out for him; luckily, he didn't find me. Even more lucky, Lydia didn't find him. I saw him in the opposite line farther behind than us. I said nothing, but I did know what I was looking for by or right after seventh period: black skinny jeans, a band shirt, a snapback, and maybe a red backpack. I wasn't sure if I saw it right or if it was his friend's backpack.

"You saw him and didn't notify me?"

"Of course, Liv. And you don't have to say 'notify,' I'm not Twitter."

"I'm just expanding my vocabulary. Mrs. Rose said that's important."

"This is true. Anyway, I did notify you, just not right away."

"Still. What good is it that you told me now? You know I'm too lazy to walk back to the cafeteria! Not only were we just there, but it's also way too far away from our bench!"

"Exactly!" I mimicked her infamous diabolical grin.

As Lydia glared at me, I grabbed for one of her chocolate chip cookies. She pulled away her tray; she still let me have one but only the one with not so many chocolate chips baked inside it.

"How's he dressed like?" Lydia asked.

"You didn't notice this morning?"

"Not really. All I saw was his hat and red backpack."

"Okay, so it was his," I said to myself.

"So are you gonna tell me?"

"All right, all right. Calm your ass." I laughed.

"Hey, you're the one who made best friends with this nosy girl."

"That's true. I forget that sometimes. I must've been really dumb for a long while," I joked.

We both laughed, and I told Lydia all I really had to tell, and when I was done, she just had to add in that I had to tell her "this "and "that." I swear to you, that girl never fails to make a conversation longer; even though I talk too much, she likes to hear too much.

Lunch seemed shorter than usual that day probably because we didn't run out of things to say whether they were questions or answers! And then, the bell to go to fifth went off. Lydia and I took a decent while getting up, putting our stuff away, and throwing our trash, and a decent while getting to class, which, as I mentioned, was art, because we were so captured by our conversation about Tyler. All we had time to notice was our conversation and our thoughts of how it'd be tomorrow or in a couple of hours when I'd be meeting him for the eighty-second first time. Yes, we were completely being fifteen-year-old girls, and damn right, it felt completely okay. Only, a couple of hours and tomorrow came a little quick…he was in our art class. Yup, he was practically walking alongside us and we had no idea!

Why? Just why did we decide to not get to fifth period early?

I went to a seat in the middle of the classroom and pretty much threw my head onto the table. The middle was the farthest back I could sit and, coincidentally, the only seat I could take that didn't place me right next to Tyler or right across him, so I'd have to face him and his beautiful face.

Another thing, that was also a small class. Why, oh why did we have to have a class together that lacked in numbers?

"Melenium Champion?" our teacher announced.

I raised my head and raised my hand as I tried to look as collected as I could. Honestly, do you think I wanted to be seen totally distressed by the love of my life the very first day he learned and even heard my name? Exactly.

"Okay, Melenium, you'll be sitting with Tyler Everlong."

Well then, I was dead. First thought that came to my already-exhausted mind was *Kill me now!*

"Actually, Mrs. Sally, don't you think that we should stay where we are now?" Lydia said, reviving my life and saving me from reality.

"Why is that…"

"Legend, Lydia Legend. Well, I think that we are all more than capable of making knowledgeable choices of who we sit next to, in order to not only get work done and done well, but also to be next to somebody who may assist us in getting inspired. I mean, after all, this is art class."

"You really want your friend next to you, don't you?" Mrs. Sally said, seeing right through Lydia's quickly thrown-together speech, which I found to be quite convincingly given.

"Yeah, that too."

"All right, Ms. Legend, I don't know if you're shy exactly or just extremely attached to your friend, but I suppose you make some points that are valid enough and the other students seem to agree with you," Mrs. Sally said, looking over to the Fans, whom I hadn't even noticed were there.

I stared at Lydia basically in awe, utterly grateful that she saved me, because my heart was ready to beat out of my chest. Given that she sort of saved herself too because, by the way Mrs. Sally was seating us, Lydia would've had to sit with, guess who, that's right, the one and only Cara Montoya. I asked her before, but she never quite told me. I think that means that she definitely knew she was saving herself too.

After that entire conversation blew over in what felt like the longest five minutes ever, I wanted to hug Lydia like I had never hugged her before! We all had to introduce ourselves, but later we were free to do whatever.

"I am so happy I have you!"

"I know, I know. No need to thank me."

"Seriously, Liv, I was ready to die. I probably wouldn't've even been able to walk my way to his table. My legs went numb!" I admitted.

"It sure did look like it."

"Was it that bad?" I was almost too afraid to ask.

"No worries. I don't think anyone else noticed, but I did because I know you so well. But I had to save you, that's what friends are for."

"You're for sure not kidding. I owe you one."

We whispered back and forth for the rest of class; on top of that, I had to get myself together so I could actually walk my way to sixth period and not have Lydia drag me there. It was only down the hall, and even though she had done it once that day already, I preferred walking.

There it was, the bell to sixth period and hooray for me. I stood up and was actually able to walk to culinary! Guess what, Tyler was in that class too. Lydia and I both noticed, so no embarrassing conversation and no wondering whether or not he heard anything. I was able, luckily, to have had myself put together enough to be okay with the fact that he sat next to me in that class; however, it did leave me a bit shaken to find out that I wasn't going to be able to cook with Lydia the entire year.

We were actually given some things to do, pointless things, but still, so I didn't actually talk to him. But I did smile at him, and hey, that was a big deal for me. Meeting him, every time, was a big deal for me.

A little sidenote here: I really hope that you aim to find someone like that, someone that gives you a special feeling whenever they're around you and such an excruciating feeling whenever they're away. I hope you never settle for someone who just says that they love you; keep going and hold out for someone who makes you feel loved constantly and makes sure you never forget it. I pray that you find someone who feels new to you every day in a way that you fall in love with them always. I hope they explore you mentally, physically, emotionally, and spiritually and, obviously, never get bored of doing so. And I hope they let you do the same. I pray you know how to appreciate them. I pray they know how to appreciate you. I pray you know how to let them appreciate you. And oh gosh, I hope they love you the way you deserve and teach you how to love yourself and how to see yourself as lovely as you truly are, because we all know that most times, the most difficult person to love is our own selves. Just love someone that teaches you every day the deep definition of what love really is.

That was one of the longest sidenotes I've made, but let's move on.

Seventh period rolled around, and I've always loved math; have I mentioned that? And I especially love algebra, so algebra II was sort of a great way to end the day. Guess who came along with me to algebra II. Wow, you're pretty great at guessing, aren't you? Yeah, that's right, Tyler did, and you know, so did Lydia.

While our classes were mostly right next to each other, math class was very far away, almost as far as it could get from the culinary room! I didn't want to be late, and I also knew I wasn't going to last an entire school-distance-walk conversation with Tyler, so I grabbed Lydia and helped her with her stuff so we could get to math not first but less late than other kids.

The Fans actually kept up, sadly, so I kind of figured they knew how long it took to get from one end of the school to the other end without totally booking it, kind of running, jogging, or even doing a little bit of a power walk. Wasn't this going to be fun with a six-pound textbook all year?

And finally, the end of the school day was just about to creep its little head around the corner and tell us that we could go home or anywhere else for the day; either way, we were just about free.

"So what's the plan?" Lydia questioned.

"What do you mean?" I responded.

She gave me a look that meant "Are you really that stupid?" And I had to stay looking at her till it clicked.

"Oh, okay!"

"Yeah, I knew you would catch on." She nodded.

"Umm…I don't really know. Do you wanna stay with me while I go talk to him, or do you wanna meet up at the parent pickup?"

"No, I'm not staying with you! You've been a chicken all day. You have to man up and talk to him on your own!"

"You're right." I took in a deep breath. "I have to be a man." Then I made a questioning face, realizing our choice of words.

"Don't make that face. You get the gist of what we're saying here. So, what's the plan?"

"Okay, well, I guess the priority is to get you out of class before everyone else, because that's a heck of a lot easier than making us two stay behind."

"You know my mind too well," Lydia interjected.

"Yeah, it's a blessing and a curse," I joked.

"Oh, I got it! Teachers usually tell kids they can wait to use the bathroom if it's this far into class, right?"

"Right…but I still don—"

"But teachers, especially guy teachers, can never turn away a girl with…you know, girl troubles."

"So true! Okay, go like…"

"Like, right now, I can't control my issues, Mel, get my stuff though. Please."

It was one sneaky way of getting me to carry her stuff, but it was also a clever way of getting me some time to break the ice with Tyler. Not only would we both be alone, but I would also have more stuff, which in turn would make me struggle with carrying everything across campus, so Tyler and his courteous self would have to offer to assist me, a helpless little thing. Ugh, sometimes friends are just way too lovable!

I finished getting Lydia's things together and all my things as well, which included two textbooks. I hadn't realized that we were going to get the textbooks that day! Luckily, I got everything together just before that final bell.

"Hey, umm, would you like some help with all that?" Tyler asked.

With no control over myself, I looked at him like he was a lifesaver. That was pretty understandable being everything I had on me. After I got over my love strike, I laughed and nodded a grateful thank-you.

"Where'd your friend have to go?"

"Huh? Oh, uh, she had some issues," I said, still a bit stifled.

"Oh!" He nodded and blushed a little, which was adorable. "I get it."

"So, I'm Melenium, by the way."

"Champion, right?"

"Yeah." I laughed a little.

"I remembered from art. Don't worry, I'm not stalking you or anything."

"Okay, I'll take your word for it, but that might explain some sounds I've heard outside my window," I said playfully.

"Dammit! I'm not as sneaky as I thought I was." He played along. "But seriously, cool name. So you spell it like *millennium*?"

"No, but it's obviously pronounced the same exact way. It's like 'Mel-any-umm.'"

"Aww, okay. I get it."

"And your name? I can't just call you 'my stalker' forever. You're cuter than that." Oh damn, did that kill me to say. I have no idea how I didn't just face-plant it right there and then.

He smiled and said, "It's Tyler. Sorry it's not as cool as yours."

"It's all right, no one's is. Not even Lydia's, and her last name is Legend!"

"Oh yeah, my last name is Everlong, by the way."

"That's not too bad. What's your middle name? Or are you one of those people who are weird about telling other people their middle name?"

"No, I'm not. It's Adam," he said.

"That's cool, that's cool. TAE. I can call you Tay."

"Why? What's wrong with *Tyler*?"

"Well, you know…everybody needs a nickname. And nothing's wrong with Tyler. I'm just saying if ever the day comes that you need a nickname, you won't have to search for one, you'll have one. And it's better than just being called Ty, that's too predictable. *Tay* is super similar, but at least it's different."

"All right, I'll give you that. And what's your nickname?"

"Mostly everybody calls me Mel, 'cause I guess there's something wrong with *Melenium*." I shrugged my shoulders.

"Well then, if everybody calls you that, that means I can't. I need something more original. What's your middle name?"

"It's Gabby."

"Okay, Melenium Gabby Champion…I got nothin'."

I smacked my tongue. "I guess you're just not creative enough."

"Challenge accepted! I'll have a nickname for you by tomorrow morning."

"Okay, don't think I won't hold you to that."

"I wouldn't have it any other way." He smirked. We had made it to the school's parking lot by then, so we stopped at the parent pickup before we started to head for his car. "You wanna text Lydia and see if she can help you out with, well, her stuff?"

"Uhh, no, it's okay. I think I got it. Thanks for the help." I hoped I knew what I was doing.

"If you say so." Tyler started to put Lydia's things back into my hands. "Actually, would you, umm, maybe like it if I gave you a ride?"

Ding, ding, ding. My plan worked like a charm! Having a best friend / sister who was wonderfully devious was absolutely incredible sometimes, because along the way, you pick up a few pointers.

"Yeah." I played it cool and acted somewhat surprised. "That would be cool. I'll just have to let Lydia know."

"Of course," Tyler agreed. "C'mon, follow me so we can put all this down."

I followed him to his car, and when he went back to go unlock the trunk for our stuff, Lydia popped out of seemingly thin air to give me a double thumbs-up and gestured for me to text her. And I nodded knowing that, of course, I was obligated to spill out everything that had happened those past fifteen minutes and the things that were about to happen as he took me to her place—all innocent, I promise.

"So am I dropping you off at her place, your place or stopping at her place so you can give her, her things and then to your place so you can get home?"

I laughed slightly. I wasn't too sure if he noticed it or not, but it was so amazing to me that we spoke to each other and got along like we knew each other since the beginning of time, which we kind of did, but he didn't know that. I'm sure you all realized how perfect we got along and acknowledged how adorable and cheesy it was. See, find a love, not necessarily like that, but at least that surreal.

"Just to her place, if that's cool? Gotta hang out with the annoying bestie. You know how it is."

"Not so much, but I have an idea."

"Trust me, an idea is all you need."

"I'll take your word for it, but I'm sure I'll find out one of these days."

We got all our books and backpacks in his trunk then climbed right into his Jeep. As you might've imagined, we just let the radio play as we had a bunch of meaningless yet meaningful conversations. I tried my best not to be awkward, and I would say that I did pretty darn well considering the fact that there wasn't any awkward silences. Anyhow, we did talk about something that's always awkward—why I wasn't too fond on going home.

"Do you spend most of your time with Lydia?" Tyler asked.

"Like you even have to ask, yeah. I obviously do."

"I guess it is pretty apparent. Why is that though? If you don't mind my asking."

"Not really. I'm just more comfortable being around her. Home isn't exactly home, if you know what I'm saying."

"I can imagine! Well, you don't need to tell me your whole life story on the first day I get to even learn your name, so you wanna ask me anything?"

"Something basic, sort of."

"Great, those are the fun ones!"

"Why did you switch schools here?"

"Not-so-basic question with not-so-basic answer."

At that very moment, Mrs. "Tell Me Everything" called my phone. I looked up from my screen with a guilty expression at Tyler.

"Answer it. It might sound stupid sometimes, but you should never ignore a call."

I nodded with a slight smile at how sweet he sounded.

"Hey, Liv, what do you want?"

"Hey, Mel…so how's it going?"

"Can this wait, like, do you honestly need me right now?"

"Oh, okay, I get it. You're making your move. Gotta go, bye!"

She hung up, and I looked up from my screen. "She, uh, had to go, but there was nothing urgent," I said.

"That's good. Now you have time to make your move."

"Oh crap. Please disregard anything you think you heard her say."

"No idea what you're talking about. I heard nothing."

"Thank you…so anyway, you were saying…"

"Oh, right, well, I moved schools because my dad got a letter from my mom. It was for child support or something. The return address was somewhere near this city, so we packed up and moved," he explained.

"Oh wow. I'm sorry I asked. I—"

"Don't be. It feels all right telling you. Honestly."

I smiled. "Good to know. Uhh, you take the next right, then turn left."

"Oh right. We can't stay in this car forever."

I blushed and put my head down, staring mainly at my feet. "Hey, if it's cool, do you think I can turn to you if Lydia ever has any more issues in seventh?"

"I'm already looking forward to it," he responded.

I got mine and Lydia's things and was just about to turn my back when he decided he wasn't done. "And you know, if anything else ever happens, I should probably be the one you call too, so, like, I think I should probably get your number and you should probably get mine."

"Yeah. That seems like a good idea."

"I guess I'll see you tomorrow morning, right?" Tyler said.

"Me and Lydia. We're sorta always together."

"Right. And don't change that, she's probably more than worth keeping if you decided she's your little partner in crime."

"She really is," I agreed.

"Right after first? I saw you leaving science."

"Oh really?" I said, knowing I could've talked to him that morning. "Maybe even at breakfast. Do you get there early?"

"Not so much, but if anything, I can try."

"Well, see you tomorrow," I said.

"Sounds like a plan," he agreed.

I walked into Lydia's house, and obviously, the very second I closed the door, I was attacked and bombarded with questions. I felt like I was Jennifer Aniston in a tell-all interview!

"I see him proposing to you by the end of this semester!"

"Lydia, shut up! He asked me for my number, that's all!"

"And he made a date to see you in the morning and said he'd take you home whenever and wants to give you a pet name! Mel, he basically announced his love for you within thirty minutes."

I looked at her like she was completely out of her mind. "Please tell me you're kidding!" I said.

"You know I'm joking...halfway joking, but still, Mel, that's so cute! He always loves you so much right away, and he doesn't even know it!"

"Those are the key words—*doesn't even know it.*"

"You know, you're usually a lot more optimistic," Lydia suggested.

"I know, and I'm sorry, it's just..."

"I get it. Something came up."

Obviously, something was up, and I couldn't stand how she could tell; even more so I couldn't stand how I knew I couldn't tell her. I had some time; I wasn't going to have to wait too long to speak up about it, right? I didn't know if it would ever even be okay for me to hint toward it. Tomorrow just couldn't've arrived slower.

Chapter 6

"𝓛ENNIE!"

"Huh?" I asked, so puzzled as to what Tyler was talking about.

"Cool, you already answer to it."

"I'm completely oblivious to what's going on! Someone to tell me things!" Lydia said even though she did, in fact, know what was going on.

"Oh, hey. I'm Tyler."

"That's right, the cute one. Mel told me about you."

As if I needed more pressure on myself, Lydia felt the need to add in her special touch. I know friends always have your best interest in mind, but don't you ever just want to backhand them? 'Cause I do—did!

"Shut up, Liv!" I turned to Tyler and said, "I didn't say that."

"Dang, so I'm not cute."

"No, well, I mean, yes, you are. You really are, but no, you're not supposed to, like, know. So no, wait, what? Umm. That's Lydia, Legend."

"Mel, I'm supposed to introduce myself. That way, I can say it like James Bond and be all cool!"

"Well, go ahead, I'm not stopping you."

"No. It wouldn't even be cool anymore," Lydia said, crossing her arms.

"Oh well," I said, knowing it wasn't a big deal.

"Well, hi, Legend, Lydia Legend," Tyler said to make her feel better.

She perked up a little and said hi again to Tyler. "So Lennie, huh? I like it. Plus no one's ever called her that before, so that proves it's creative, at least creative enough."

"Yeah, well, instead of 'Mel-enium,' I figured I could take out Lennie from 'Me-leni-um.'"

"Well, it seems like you got the official stamp of approval, Tyler, so Lennie it is," I told Tyler.

We all smiled and stayed talking through breakfast. Once the bell rang, we made plans to meet up between classes and then at lunch. Biology seemed to have gone by really fast; all we did was take notes, and for the most part, that's all we would do in that class.

Tyler came to meet Lydia and me for nutrition break, and we explained how it was always better to get breakfast than nutrition, because breakfast was always free; besides, the food was all the same anyway.

"Well, I guess I just wasted $4.50," he said.

"Yeah," Lydia and I said simultaneously while grabbing the breakfast he bought for all of us.

"So do you guys grab breakfast even when you're not hungry?"

"Yup. Just in case," I said.

After that little lesson took place, the bell to go to class went off. We agreed to meet up for lunch at our bench. Tyler didn't exactly get where our bench was at, so Lydia and I just suggested he go to the vending machines near the front office; if he got there before us, he'd see us coming, and if we got to the bench before him, we'd find him.

We didn't meet up after second or third period. All of us sort of agreed that it was just too out of our way to make it a daily routine, so the only way we'd see one another in between classes was by complete coincidence. If there was anything big to go down, we'd tell one another at lunch. And if anything seriously big went down or was about to go down, we'd call or message one another. We knew how to get away with that.

I remember once Tyler was extremely starving and so he decided to sneak out of his fourth period at least fifteen minutes early! As you might've guessed, he got caught, and to top it all off, he got caught by the school's meanest security guard. (We never did get along, but I, of course, had my ways of avoiding her.) Anyway he texted both me and Lydia to make sure we got to the cafeteria early, so we could get him one of the good trays, but neither of us remembered to take our phones off airplane mode that morning, because we had a biology test and we didn't want the slightest possibility of our phones ringing. As you probably have guessed, we really quick went to our bench, didn't find Tyler, so we really quick checked our phones, which didn't have any missed calls or messages. So instead of going to the cafeteria, we went looking around for Tyler because I guess that particular day, we weren't that hungry anyways, so we just needed to find the other member of our pack.

By the time we had checked every logical place we could think of (yes, even the cafeteria), the bell was close to ringing. We sort of gave up and came to the reasonable conclusion that if all else failed, we'd see him in fifth, sixth, or even seventh. He couldn't have left; his car was still in the parking lot. We were just about to leave our bench and make our way for art when, just outside the office, we saw Tyler with his head hanging low.

"Hey, Ty!" Lydia said.

"Tay, where've you been? We've been looking everywhere for you."

"I had to spend lunch in the office filing papers because I got caught sneaking out of class."

"How'd you get caught? We taught you specifically how to not get caught."

"I know, but I just wasn't thinking. That's besides the point though, did you guys get me lunch?"

"What?" I asked.

"No, we didn't even get ourselves lunch. Like Mel said, we were just looking for you the entire time," Lydia explained.

"Are you kidding? Really? Didn't either of you get my message?"

I started to get my phone out. "Obviously not, I guess. You probably forgot to press Send or something," I said, freeing Lydia and myself of blame.

Tyler took my phone from me when I showed him how I had no notification on my phone or the message in our thread. "Mel, you have your phone on airplane mode!" he said; looking disappointed, one might call it. "Lydia, I bet you do too, right?"

So Lydia took her phone out, and sure enough... "Yeah. Sorry, Ty."

"Well, like that helps, you guys can't begin to fathom how hungry I am. I didn't eat yesterday and wasn't able to eat at all this morning!"

I took a deep breath and sighed. "Relax, we'll hook you up."

"What do you mean?"

Lydia looked at me and instantly realized what I had realized right in that moment. We hadn't introduced Tyler to Julian. We weren't going to be able to get him a good tray from the cafeteria, but Julian was the next best thing. Heck, sometimes he was even better.

"C'mon, you need to meet someone," Lydia said.

"Well, we're kinda going to class right now."

"Hey, are you hungry or not?"

"Yeah, but I've already been caught once today."

"Don't worry. Lydia and I never get caught, so if you're seriously hungry, we'll at least get something to hold you over for the rest of the day."

"I guess I have no reason to protest," Tyler said.

So I grabbed Tyler's hand, and we all went down to the science hallway; like I said, mostly everyone knew where to find Julian anytime of the school day. I walked in and acted as if I was going to sit down then "realized" I was in the wrong class. That was the way Lydia and I signaled for Julian to make us a sale. While I apologized for interrupting the class, Julian tossed his bag to Lydia. Tyler got two bags of hot fries, Gardetto's, and a king-size Snickers—that was for all of us, of course, because we all missed lunch.

I walked out, and Tyler put the money in Julian's backpack. Not even a minute after I left, Tyler walked into the class and said that Julian had forgotten his bag with him and simply wanted to drop it off. So the teacher pointed Julian out and let Tyler give the backpack back. Tyler whispered a "Thank you," and of course, Julian nodded a "No problem." We told Tyler that we'd introduce them soon because, for obvious and survival reasons, he had to know Julian.

The three of us crept our way to the teachers' lounge, where we indulged in our hot fries, Gardetto's, and Snickers. We also bought drinks from the soda machines in the teachers' lounge. We could've gotten drinks from Julian, but he really only kept drinks in his cold locker, and the drinks he did carry around were all just water and room-temperature green tea—no, thank you.

I guess we could've gone to art class that day, but it's not like we would've done anything anyway if all we wanted to do was eat. We were too consumed with the food we wanted to consume. Anyhow, that was a pretty great day, from what I can remember. It was our first little school adventure/mission as friends for that year and that lifetime.

Well, I'm getting a little ahead of myself; we're not that far into the story just yet, so let's get back to why we didn't meet in between classes.

After hearing that little story, you'll understand why later on it became a bigger deal.

With the school week having had started on a Wednesday, you can rightfully infer that the weekend came pretty quickly. The second week went by smoothly; that was shocking. Did Cara seriously give up torturing me? Yeah, I didn't believe it either. But come week 3, a.k.a. our progress-report week, things took a little turn; depending on how you look at it, it might not have been so little.

Since we were just far enough into our first quarter, we didn't have to go to fifth that day, only to our advisers. We were divided by class and grade, so Tyler didn't get to stay with me and Liv, which was almost a good thing because he was still completely oblivious to what was going on with the Fans and me. Anyhow, that Tuesday, Mr. Lewis gave Carter transcripts to pass out, and this time, no announcement was made, but MC and CM were still all tied up. Leaving me alone for the first three weeks of sophomore year was a questionable decision, but Cara did have a heart, right? If nothing else, she had a busy schedule. I was a target again; I just knew it. Now I had something that I would have to tell Tyler. Great.

I never brought up grades. Lydia knew that I didn't want Tyler finding out about the whole thing with Cara, so she only brought it up when he wasn't around, and Tyler never really cared to talk about school-related things. However, that week was the week that Tyler decided we knew each other for a fair amount of time, and he asked me out! Despite my nerves, I told him that it sounded wonderful and that it would be great on Friday.

By the time Friday came around, I was really excited; I couldn't wait for the final bell to ring and for the school day to be over! The morning was nothing but normal, and it was that, that threw me off and made me a bit suspicious. That morning, I was a bit early, so I did see Cynthia's car driving down the typical road, but I didn't get splashed. Maybe that was all that was planned for that day. Lunch came, and still nothing had happened, so I figured I could let my guard down, at least until Monday. That felt nice because then I could just focus on my date with Tyler. But then we went to art; not too much of a ways into class, both Rachel and Cara got called out. They got an off-campus, and just before stepping out of the class-room, Cara looked at me straight in the eye and winked. One thing I will tell you is that she definitely sent an unsettling feeling into my stomach.

Unsettled, that's all I was. I wasn't on high alert or jumpy in anyway. I didn't gasp at any locker being slammed shut or door thrown open or every dropped pencil or phone vibration. But that didn't mean I wasn't unsettled. The thing was that I very well knew that anything I had coming my way was going to find me; I couldn't stop it. I suppose the unsettling part was that I knew it was coming, and I had the unfortunate privilege of having to anticipate the whole thing. Whether it was harmless, like hiding the extra clothes I had in my locker, or something harmful, such as tripping me down so I could roll down the hill outside the math hallway, I didn't know, but the anticipation I guaranteed was equally torturous, if not worse. Whatever Rachel and Cara were doing, at least it'd be over in a shorter amount of time.

Fifth period ended without any incidents, so we went to sixth period; the same thing: sixth period began and finished with no occurrences that were out of the ordinary. When seventh period rolled around, I felt it, whatever it was, coming. It didn't have to be in class or even in school, but I knew the Fans were going to do something to me that day. I just prayed that they wouldn't screw up or interfere with mine and Tyler's date.

Two thirty-eight came around; we had twenty more minutes until the final bell released us announcing to us that we were free for a weekend. Kathleen and Carter got up and spoke with the teacher; I remember we had a substitute that day. They got permission to leave the class, and I got the directions to leave with them. Of course, they needed my help in particular. Who knows what ruse they fed the substitute?

Before stepping out of algebra II, I stopped and bent down to tell Lydia and Tyler, if I didn't come back before the bell, to wait about five minutes and that was all. I asked that they get my things and we would all meet just outside the music room. They nodded in agreement and asked if I was positive I would be all right; I nodded back. I was sure that Cynthia had some sort of reason for staying behind.

"Melenium, c'mon. We need to hurry!" Kathleen said.

Well, look at that, someone actually learned my name. I wasn't even sure, if according to Cara, that Kathleen or the other Fans were allowed to know my name or the names of the people who didn't exactly have the best social status.

So I walked out the door and took step after step following them. At that point, all the nervousness and anticipation had gone away. I was thinking very thoughtless thoughts and stared down at my feet, not even paying attention to where exactly I was being led. I don't know what exactly made my anxiety go away or even when it went away—by seventh, during seventh, or when I walked into the hall—but it did. All I had to do at that point was get to where I was apparently going, endure whatever I had to endure, then it'd be over. Does that seem settling to you? I guess it seemed settling enough to me.

When the three of us stopped walking, I looked up from the floor to behold that we were in the library. I had no idea what could possibly go on if we were in the library. They seemed clueless, almost innocent.

"So…" I gave a questioning look.

"What?" Kathleen said.

"Well, you guys needed me for something, right?"

"Yeah, just be patient. We need your help carrying some books over to my car, but we need the librarian to get them out for us." Carter explained.

I mouthed a simple "Oh" and nodded my head as if it all made sense. I knew I didn't get dragged to the library solely to assist Kathleen and Carter with some boxes of books. If all they needed was an extra set of hands, then they would've asked one of the guys. The thing was, they didn't snap at me or anything like that, so I wished I could believe that it was all as innocent as it appeared, but I just knew it wasn't.

The librarian came in and unlocked her office, which is where the boxes were, then, out of courtesy, asked if the three of us could handle carrying the books; in turn, Carter cordially replied with a yes. There were only five boxes, so I guess it really wouldn't've been much trouble, because the boxes weren't heavy. But I was still confused on why this seemed so casual. Perhaps they were actually unaware of what exactly they were taking part in, so the only way to behave toward me really was plain and casual.

The three of us each picked up a box and made our way to Carter's car, and I came to the conclusion that I'd reach my fate when I got to her car, but we all got there and all that happened was the three of us putting the books in her trunk. There were two more boxes full of books though, so there must've been something waiting for me back in the building, I supposed.

The three of us all walked back so two of us could carry the remaining boxes and one of us could just hold open the doors. Kathleen and Carter insisted that they carried the books, so I walked only so far ahead opening the doors. When we were just about to walk out the building, I opened the door, and of course, tons of slob were poured all over me! That's right, I was covered in a mixture of maple syrup, orange juice, toothpaste, and what I'm pretty sure was dog fur.

My jaw dropped, and I stood there in disbelief. The bell had already rung, and mostly everyone had walked outside, so of course, everyone saw me covered in all that crap! I wasn't so much embarrassed, but I was indeed angry at the Fans, of course, but also at myself. How could I not have seen that coming? I turned around and saw Kathleen and Carter staring at me, but that was just it, staring. They actually felt guilty? But really what would it matter as I stood there?

Lydia and Tyler were on their way from math class since they'd just finished waiting. From a fair-enough distance, they both stopped, dumbfounded with the sight of the mess I was. Once they snapped out of their shock, they began to jog their way toward me.

"What freaking happened, Mel?" Lydia screamed.

"I've been punked, that's what happened!"

I tried shaking off what I could of the syrup and turned myself around. Tyler, Lydia, and I walked to the gym; Lydia grabbed my spare clothes, and I headed to the showers, while Tyler kept an eye on all our stuff.

"Out of all days, they just had to pick today!" I said.

"Well, that's probably why they chose today, Melenium."

"I guess you're right, but, Liv, honestly, how am I supposed to survive this for the next three years?"

"Well," Lydia began to say.

"And now I'm gonna be absolutely forced to tell Tyler about all this!"

"Well, yeah, Mel. I don't know why you wouldn't have told him in the first place."

"Because, Liv! How am I supposed to explain that four girls hate me with legitimately no purpose and the fifth one hates me because I get good grades?"

She sighed deeply and didn't give me an answer, because she really didn't have one. And I turned the water off and dried myself off. I straightened my hair again, and once I finished, I did as Lydia did and took a deep sigh.

"Do you think…," I started.

"You wouldn't."

"Do you think I could?"

"I don't know, Mel. It's just, you never have before."

"I know! I mean, I've never even thought about it, but do you think it could be of any harm?"

"I really have no clue. I mean, eighty-two lifetimes and this discussion has never come up. Not once!"

"The question is, do you think he'll believe me?"

"And if he doesn't?"

"Ugh! Liv, and what if he does? There's so much to explain, too much even. Where does that leave you? Him? Me? All three of us?"

"Your date is still tonight. If it feels right, just tell him, 'Me and Lydia remember our past lives…all eighty-two of them.' And you know, Ty has always been a real easygoing guy. What's the worst that could seriously happen?"

"Yeah, I guess you're right. I think I have to tell him this time."

The two of us headed out of the showers and across to the gym to pick up our stuff from Tyler. We headed to the culinary room to put my clothes to wash. I was almost afraid that the gunk that covered my clothes was going to clog something.

Francine came to pick Lydia up not too much after I put my clothes in the washer. Tyler and I stayed about another hour to wait for my clothes to finish washing and drying. Then we left for our date and to begin our weekend.

"So, where exactly are we going?"

"Well, I thought I'd get you out of town for a little while and take you to this park I know. It's not exactly Central Park, but it's pretty nice, and there's a spot that's overlooking all the city lights," Tyler said, sounding kind of shy.

"Sounds awesome. Any specific reason why you chose the park?"

"Not really. It just seems like a nice place to get away, and there's never really a bad time to just get away from it all." He looked at me with an expression I couldn't really make out. "And after today I'm sure getting away can't sound too bad, right?" he asked.

"I guess that's pretty obvious, huh?"

"What was all that about anyway?"

"Now that's kind of a long story."

"We have some time to kill, don't we?"

"Yeah, but can we wait till we get to the park? Long story kinda means long night, long enough anyway."

"Yeah, no problem, so what kind of music should we listen to?" As he asked, he turned on the radio, and what do you know, Green Day was playing. That was just perfect.

"Why are you laughing?" Tyler asked, puzzled.

"Oh, just because almost always the first thing I hear on the radio is Green Day."

Tyler nodded and asked if I was a fan. I told him that, that was barely a question; everybody was a Green Day fan. He nodded again, in agreement that time.

The ride to the park was quiet, and I love the fact that it was a long ride, because looking out the window and watching the scenery was astonishing to me. Of course, not the entire ride was silent. I mean, no one can witness a breathtaking sunset and just not talk about how marvelous it was!

We got to the park a little bit past seven o'clock then walked our way to that view overlooking all the city lights. It had been even more incredible than I had imagined it. It was absolutely beautiful.

"So, umm...," Tyler began and stammered when I turned his way, "do you wanna tell me that long story of yours now?"

"And I thought I was the curious one," I said jokingly.

"Is that a yes?"

"I guess," I said, taking a deep breath "But only because you're just so damn persuasive."

"Right, I'm so blessed."

"Okay, just promise to not call me crazy. You don't have to believe me, because it is a lot to take in, but I'm not messing with you, so just try your best to let me finish and not find me insane."

"I promise, but it sounds like I should prepare myself."

"Yeah, you might want to." So I waited about two minutes, letting Tyler prepare himself, but mainly I was preparing myself, because I even thought I sounded crazy! I just had to let it all out. "'Kay, well, basically I have to tell you that I've been reincarnated. Yeah, that's great, right? Not only that, but I've had eighty-two lifetimes, and I remember all of them! It's not like I'm born knowing how to speak, and like every other kid, I have to learn how to use a toilet, but that all comes a lot easier than it does to other kids. And well, because I remember all that, you can imagine the fact that I can remember other things too like world history and algebra II. That helps in explaining how I don't really give too much of a damn about school but I'm still a straight A student! That leads us to me being dead-on tied for valedictorian with that girl Cara Montoya that's not only in all of our classes but also all of mine. Long story short, she takes grades very seriously, so me giving her competition does not, and I mean does not, make her happy. So now that I'm a problem to her being better than everyone, she hates me and is out to get me. And not just her, her little applaud squad too. Oh yeah, and Lydia lived all of those eighty-two lifetimes with me and remembers them all as well."

Tyler looked at me—well, stared actually. It was a blank stare, but it was still covered in so much wonder. I could tell that because of his promise, he was searching for words other than "you're crazy" and words that weren't alternatives for that sentence. I stared back at him, not really having any words to add, nor did I have any sort of way to explain the insanity of the words that had just spilled from my mouth.

"So...you're telling me that you...and Lydia have been reincarnated?"

"Yes."

"And you both remember it all?"

"Well, each lifetime. We obviously can't remember absolutely everything."

"Oh yeah, obviously, because this whole thing is all so obvious." His voice started to escalate, and I knew it had to be freaking him out. He believed me, but he had no idea how. What I was saying was all too far beyond logic. I had to be insane, but I wasn't; that's what made my story insane...or him.

"Okay, I get it." I almost felt a bit of relief. "I'm insane!"

"No, Tyler, no, you're not. I promise. All of this is real and honest and beyond science, but real. I swear."

78

"I'm totally dreaming, right? Or being punked?"

"No! Watch. I can prove it."

"How?" he asked.

"Umm, well, I know that you call tattoos birthmarks, and I know that you think shooting stars are angels on their way back to heaven. If I was crazy, how would I know that?"

He gave me that blank expression again, searching for more words, not knowing what to say. After so long, he palmed his face then looked back up at me.

"So, I believe you, what does that mean?"

"Nothing!" I replied quickly. "At least, I don't think it does."

"What do you mean? Why did you say it like that?"

"You see, this is the first time I've ever told you, the only time you've ever known," I explained hesitantly.

"You mean to tell me out of eighty…"

"Eight—eighty-two."

"Okay, eighty-two lifetimes you've had, and not once did you tell me, 'Hey, Tyler, I'm a reincarnated human being who remembers all of her past lives.'"

"No. It just never came up."

"Of course not! That doesn't just casually slip into everyday conversation, but I'd think that you'd make it a point to tell me. You and Lydia told each other, didn't you?"

"Yeah, but that was different. We both sorta just knew. I mean, we were sisters the first time."

"Great! Oh man, that's just great." He ran his fingers through his hair and breathed in deeply. "Okay, okay, I believe you, but what does that mean? Will everything come rushing back to me in a dream tonight, or do I start remembering things next lifetime just, like, what happens?"

"I really don't know. My second lifetime, I just realized I remembered things that couldn't have been memories from then because I had been too small and I just knew it couldn't've been a dream."

"So I just gotta play it by ear?"

"I guess. It's not like you'll go mad or anything, if that's what you're worried about."

"Good to know, Lennie, good to know."

"This is what I meant when I said it'd be a long night, so I can answer any questions you might have."

"I'm thinking I have too many to ask them all."

"Well, just whatever you want."

"Umm…well, am I always named Tyler?"

"Yes. Everyone is always born with the same first name. You get to choose your last name when you start remembering lifetimes, if you want, because that becomes who you really identify as, but other than that, the rest of your name changes."

"That explains your name and Lydia's. No one just gets cool names like that."

"Yeah, I'll admit, both of our names are pretty awesome."

"And when you die, do you feel it?"

"What do you mean? Like, do you feel pain?"

"No, like, do you get to heaven, or do you wake up there?"

"You wake up there. Yeah, you open your eyes, and there He is. You don't even know how, but your legs manage to work and you just stand before Him."

"I guess I don't wanna ruin anything, but last thing, can you explain what it's like?"

"Hmm…well, it's quiet and peaceful, but booming with the most beautiful sounds. You never have trouble sleeping, and you only ever feel tired when it truly is time for rest. Beds feel as lovely as you would imagine a cloud feeling. The weather is either a comforting warmth or a refreshing cool, always. Sometimes you feel sick, but only so you can get better. Bones break and things of that nature, but only so you can heal. Really heaven is just earth, but minus what the devil threw in."

"Wow. I guess I never imagined that heaven would be what the world was supposed to be."

"Oh yes. And really that's probably the best way to describe it," I said.

Tyler turned his head and watched the city lights, how they were so still. The wind blew lightly, and calmly I stared at him then watched the city lights as well; after I began to watch it all, the lights, the occasional car, the falling stars, the angels headed back to heaven and everything in between. The feeling of living in complete truth—well, almost-complete truth—was nice. Somehow it felt so light. It was as if the omission of one story held the weight of a thousand universes, and by revealing my story to Tyler, all that weight simply faded away into thin air.

The two of us stayed sitting on the hood of the car for a while until another conversation sparked itself in Tyler's mind. That was the conversation that seemed to change, alter, everything in that lifetime. The domino effect, snowball effect, it tumbleweeded, whatever you want to call it—that's what that one conversation seems to have caused that one night.

"So Cara hates you because of your good grades?"

"Yup. That's about it. She didn't even know my name before our transcripts had first come out."

"And you two are completely all tied up despite the fact that you don't really give a crap about school?"

"Yeah, you got the whole story," I confirmed.

"Listen, why don't you just start actually trying in school, like your best?"

"I don't know. I just never cared to. I mean, why would I?"

"Because! Look, she already seems like she's gonna start torturing you now, the least you could do is give her a reason to, you know? Win! If you're valedictorian now by not trying, just imagine what it would be like if you were trying!" he said.

"I mean, I guess you have a point, but—"

"No buts. Me and Liv will even help you. And another thing—"

"What could that be?" I asked, nervous about the proposition.

"In spite of the fact that she is punking you, don't you think you might have a reason to be punking her?"

"You want me to be spiteful basically."

"No, it's not that. I just don't want you to continue to be the victim."

I put my head down and thought about all that Tyler had said, the points he made and how now he actually did sound persuasive. I thought about all the arguments I was willing to throw out at him and what they would probably conclude to. I don't know how long I took, but by the end of it all, I agreed with all of Tyler's propositions.

I peered up at him and shrugged, mentioning the words "I guess we should let the war begin."

We stayed out a bit longer then drove back to town. Our ride back was a lot more talkative. I suppose we did indeed have a lot more to talk about than we did on our way up.

The next day, I called Lydia and went to her house first thing in the morning. Her first reaction when I told her the plan—I guess—was "Heck yeah! This means war!" Honestly, how could I forget a reaction like that? But after telling her everything, I realized there were some more things that we had to go over, just so throughout all this, things would stay on the up-and-up.

I called Tyler and told him to meet us at Lydia's house, that we had to go over some things. While we waited for Tyler to get there, Lydia let out her curious (I would call it nosy) side come out.

"How was the date, Mel?" she asked.

"It was nice, Liv." I paused. "I mean, after I said everything, he actually believed me. How could you figure he'd believe me that easily?"

"To tell you the truth, I wasn't positive if he'd believe you at all."

"I know. I was pretty scared," I confessed.

"So...did he kiss you?"

"Liv!" I felt myself blush very brightly.

"He did, didn't he?" She gasped and smiled widely with so much certainty. "That's so cute! Was it a small kiss or like a really serious one? You know, a kiss where you felt the intensity of all the years you two have been in love?"

I threw my hands over my face and assured my nerves by receiving the warmth that came from my face. I wouldn't say that I would get embarrassed when it came to Tyler, but there was a feeling that I always got in the beginning of our relationships that I can really only describe as pleasantly unnerving.

"It was somewhere in between, okay? If you must know."

We stayed talking, and before we knew it, Tyler pulled up in his Jeep. Lydia nudged me a bit just as he climbed out to tease me, but for the most part, that was the end of that.

"Hey, guys. So, what was it that we needed to talk about?" Tyler asked.

"Gotta ask Mel, my friend," Lydia said.

"So, Lennie, what is it?"

"Well, we're all already caught up on our so-called war, right?"

"Right," Lydia and Tyler agreed.

"'Kay, well, we now have to go over some rules, because we have morals, guys. We're not looking to exterminate anybody or anything like that," I explained, looking at the two of them.

"What kind of rules exactly?"

"Yeah, and why do we need rules? They don't have rules."

"I'm sorry, are we them?" I asked as a response.

"No," Tyler replied.

"That's why we have rules. And as far as the type of rules, umm, they're not anything that render us helpless, but they're restrictions that keep us from low blows."

"So anything that's just straight-up not cool?" Tyler asked.

"Exactly," I agreed. "You guys can add on if you want, but basically what I had in mind was, one, we don't do anything in school. Two, we don't do anything back-to-back, like we can't pull pranks two days in a row. Three, we don't pull anything that's going to get her in trouble in school or might jeopardize Cara's chances of winning valedictorian. We're competing for that top spot, and if I win it, I want to win it fair and square, not because she ended up suspended or anything. And four, we don't do anything that one of us isn't cool with. That's pretty much it. Umm, if either of you have something to add, feel free, or if you think of anything, do not hesitate to speak up, but yeah, that's it."

"Sounds good," Lydia said.

"Yeah?"

"Yeah. Everything is totally reasonable, and for sure, if things seem to escalate, these little rules will keep us in line and in check."

"Nice. And you guys don't have anything to add?"

"Not really. Not now at least. I think you've covered everything."

"Yeah, Mel, it seems like you thought of everything," Lydia said.

"That's so cool. I'm so glad you guys agree, because I just want to stay in line, like you said, Ty. And you know, I just don't want to make her feel so down that, well, I guess just so down that it's too much."

"So that's it?" Lydia asked.

"Yeah, I guess that's it."

Chapter 7

*F*ORTUNATELY, THERE WILL ALWAYS BE people who hold morals true and close to their hearts. Those are the people that really try not to let things get out of hand. Unfortunately, not everyone makes it a priority to not be such a facinorous person! In this case, Cara was the type who didn't make it a priority.

It all really began at the football field, well, more so during the football game, but I'll explain first how I even found my way there.

Being that I was trying to get more involved in school academically and through extracurricular activities, Lydia and Tyler were trying to do the same. So when we could, we were all glued at the hip, and when we couldn't, well, we still kind of were. This time in particular, Tyler decided that he wanted to be on the football team. It was already too late for tryouts, but our school's cornerback had to switch schools, and the team let Tyler have the position. I suppose Lydia and I could've gone out for the cheerleading, but again tryouts were over, and to top it off, the cheer captain wouldn't have dared let us cheer. Guess who it was… Yup, it was Cara. As an alternative, Lydia and I signed up to run the concession stand. It wasn't that bad; it was actually kind of fun. We got into the games for free, which meant we always got to watch Tyler play, and we got the snacks at a discount. Plus whenever people ordered iced tea, after we handed it to them, we got to make our idiotic pun and say "Tea you later."

This one game that was super packed, Cara saw her shot to get me pretty well, I'd say. Since it was so packed as well as so cold, no one took much notice of the cheerleaders, much less if all of them were on the field, so this whole plan started to unravel about ten minutes before halftime.

Lydia and I were at the concession; it was seriously getting cold, so I got up to run into the gym, where I knew our coach always had blankets and such. I guess one of the Fans took notice, and that's when Cara, Rachel, and Cynthia booked it to the gym. I was searching for a good-enough blanket in the weight-room closet, which is in between the two locker rooms we used for games for the boys' team rather than our regular equipment closet, which is in between our girls' locker rooms. Anyway, before I picked out the blanket, Cynthia and Rachel bombarded me. Rachel held me well enough for Cynthia to throw my shoes off and take my pants off, then she tied a pretty damn good knot around my ankles. And Cynthia held me well enough for Rachel to get me out of my shirt and have Cynthia tie another knot to restrict my wrists! The two of them carried me to our home team boys' locker room then left me there. Cara came in right after to throw my clothes and shoes out the window.

"Don't worry. Someone will find you soon," she said with an extreme amount of pleasure in her eyes.

I heard the three of them run back to the field. In the distance, I heard a faint whistle signaling a time-out. I didn't know from which team.

At that time, our team was up, and for the rest of that quarter, Tyler was going to be on the bench, so he sneaked away to go see Liv and me.

"Hey, Liv, how's everything?" he asked.

"Hey, Ty, it's all good, I guess. Just waiting for Mel to get back."

"Yeah? Where'd she go?"

"She went up to the gym to go grab us a blanket. It's pretty cold just sitting here."

"Hmm…" Tyler hummed curiously and somewhat to himself. "Liv, I'm gonna head up to the gym."

"But, Ty, there's not even a full minute on the board."

"I know, but only Carter and Kathleen are down with the other cheerleaders, and I don't think that's a good thing."

Lydia nodded her head, wondering if she should've gone with Tyler, but decided against it and watched Carter and Kathleen instead. Tyler ran up to the gym and didn't see anyone, nor did he find a track of anyone. He went into the weight-room closet and obviously didn't find me, but he did hear something in the locker room. I had been screaming—at least attempting to scream—because I didn't want the entire football team finding me in nothing but my underwear! So Tyler went to find me in the locker room tied up, and as soon as we made eye contact, we heard the buzzer. My heart started racing, and so did Tyler's. Teams usually rush into the locker rooms to discuss everything, so Tyler had to figure out where he'd hide me real quick! The quickest idea, and probably the only logical idea, was putting me in one of the stalls and locking it. Of course, it was one of the small stalls, because with all their padding on, the guys only like to use the big stalls. Tyler made his way back into the main area and just on time too. The team asked him what he had been doing there, and he simply said he needed the bathroom and couldn't have held it any longer than he had, and that was that. The team went on talking about all they were doing right but also about what the other team was doing right and how to stop them.

On their way out, Tyler went back to me and told me how he'd have Lydia come find me. Luckily, she did instead of the coach and the entire team. She had taken a bit longer than I thought she would've, but at least she got there.

"Wow, Mel, Cynthia tied you up really well."

"Yeah, I could sorta tell."

She shrugged at the fact that she stated the obvious. "So, I guess we're at the big-kid games now, huh?"

"No doubt about it," I said, struggling to get my hands free.

Once Lydia got me untied, we both realized something. I didn't have any clothes! The ones Cara threw out the window hadn't been there when Lydia went to go check. Lydia went and got a blanket from the closet to cover me then was my lookout to at least get me to the girls' locker room. I waited there while she insisted on going to figure something out.

She ran down to the field to go find Tyler, but he was in the game. After waiting seven minutes, she asked the coach to call a time-out or take Tyler out of the game for only a minute but that it was an emergency. The other team was starting to catch up, so the coach called a time-out.

"Ty, we have a problem."

"Why? What's wrong?"

"Melenium doesn't have any clothes!"

"The school building isn't open?"

"No. Why would it be open during a game?"

"I don't know, Liv! I'm just thinking out loud here."

"Oh, I know! Your keys are in your bag, right? She'll just sit in your car till the game is over, then you can take her home."

"That's not gonna happen."

"Why not?"

"Because are you not aware of how cold it is right now? She'll freeze. Plus my heater sucks."

"I guess you're right, but what do we do then?"

"Okay, uhh, you go to my gym locker, the combination is 12-46, and it's locker 137. Get my bag, and she can just wear my clothes. I'll drive her home in my football gear, I guess."

"You know, Ty, it's not so hard to understand why Mel is so freaking in love with you every lifetime of ours." Lydia smiled and headed back toward me.

Tyler smiled real lightly then headed back into the game.

Lydia ran to get Tyler's clothes then made sure to put everything back. She rushed back to me, handed me the clothes, then told me what exactly happened. Of course, I was pretty ecstatic that he was just so sweet about it all, and another thing that always made me happy was when Lydia expressed how much she liked him too.

I got dressed and managed to find that good blanket I was searching for, so Lydia and I were still able to see the end of the third quarter. We did indeed have a line at the concession stand when we got back though; a lot of people were looking to buy hot chocolate at that point though, not iced tea, so sadly, we couldn't tell anyone our pun.

It was a tied game by the time the fourth quarter started, so it was definitely a good game, from what I can remember. Tyler got called in until the last three minutes of the game. Still all tied up, he managed to grab the ball on the fumble and score the winning touchdown with only seconds left on the board! Let me tell you now that I was so glad that, that game didn't go into overtime. I was tempted to shut down the concession early so Lydia and I could wait inside, but I was obviously glad I didn't.

Francine picked Lydia up that night so the two of them could pick up Lydia's dad from the airport; he had been in Chicago on business for a few months, actually maybe even just over a year! So I waited patiently outside the locker room for Tyler; since I had his clothes on, all he did was take his pads off and pack them into his bag. The two of us walked to his car and waited awhile so it would be easier to get out of the parking lot.

"So, how are you holding up?" I asked.

"Me? Really?"

"Yeah. That last touchdown must have been a real adrenaline rush, right?"

"It was for sure, but what about you? How are you holding up? And be honest."

I looked down at my feet and played with my fingers, but I finally pushed out the words. "Fine…I guess."

"Hey, I said to be honest."

I let one deep breath in. "As you can imagine, not so great, I mean, that whole thing was pretty brutal, but I'm okay now, I survived. That means all in all, I'm fine now." I shrugged. "I guess."

Tyler looked at me with admiration, I guess you might say, but I didn't understand too much why. I was fighting back tears as hard as I could. I thanked God that I was successful. And I was doing my best to hide my choked-up voice. I coughed every so often so that the times that my voice did sound weak only really seemed like a slight cold.

That broke me a little. I only really saw it getting worse, and that really made me feel scared. So how could Tyler look at me like I had overcome or conquered something? I wasn't anything to admire, far from it actually, the way I saw it.

"I'm just really glad I have you and Lydia," I said.

"No problem. You know that we all have each other's backs."

"I know, but when the going gets tough, it's always nice to be reminded."

"Even after eighty-two lifetimes, huh?" he joked.

"Yup. It's something that never gets old."

For the rest of the trip to my house, we were both quiet. It seemed like that happened most nights; we could find comfort in the silence we shared, the fact that we had two different lives sharing a reality for only a few moments but in two totally different manners. And that within an instant our realities would go back to being divided—it was always so fascinating to me.

When we got to my street, Tyler stopped and put his car in park. I looked at him and thanked him for taking me home as well as lending me his clothes for the night. He laughed and said not to mention it, that it was nothing really. I told him that I'd give them back to him the next day at school, and he nodded in approval.

I looked out the window, then turned back, and reached out my hand. Tyler, in turn, reached out his hand to hold mine. I stayed at staring at our hands, deep in thought about everything really, and I felt Tyler's stare shifting from me to our intertwining fingers. I took myself away from my thoughts, knowing that if I didn't, we would've been there all night. I pulled my hand back and leaned over to kiss Tyler on the cheek, and I told him good night.

I stepped out of Tyler's Jeep and slowly approached my house. You see, I always had Tyler drop me off a block away from my front door so that nothing stupid or unnecessary would happen with my mom. And when he'd drop me off at night, he'd wait with his lights on, watching to see that I got in safely. He'd wait after I got inside as well, still to make sure that I was okay. He only left when I waved to him from my bedroom window.

Since we had school the next day, all I did after walking into my house was start getting ready to go to sleep. I was tired, so I felt like I'd have no trouble that night, but with insomnia, there's really no telling. So I laid myself in bed and stared at the ceiling with all my frivolous thoughts running through my head. My eyelids started to feel heavy after about ten minutes, so after about twenty or twenty-five did I expect my mixture of calm, relief, happiness, exhaustion, fear, and sadness to deliver me to a land of temporary peace, separate from my chaotic reality that was always there when I woke up.

The next day was a Thursday, and I couldn't have wished more that it had been Friday or, better yet, Saturday. I was tired and really just did not feel up to the day, but I got up anyway. I thought about skipping school that day even if it was for only the morning, but I told myself that Cara didn't beat me down, so I had to stop acting like she did. I got dressed in actual clothes, not just sweats, brushed my teeth, and headed out the door. I hadn't been splashed for a few days, so I was under the not-so-safe assumption that all that had stopped. After walking for half an hour, I did, however, have to turn back. I remembered I had to take Tyler his clothes. I was already going to be late, so I decided to take the time to wash and dry Tyler's clothes. Lydia called me when I got back to my place to ask where I was; I told her I was washing Tyler's stuff and that I'd be there no later than second period. After telling me that she'd get the notes and work for me, she asked if I felt okay. I told her I was all right, that I just wanted some alone time to think and just find my calm. She agreed, then we ended our call saying that we would see each other soon.

I thought about things like Cara and school, but mainly I thought about how Tyler told me not to be the victim. In a way, I figured my getting up that morning was me not being the victim. By the time his clothes were done, I was done with my thoughts for a while, and I was out the door again. I put my music on and sang my way to school in absolutely no hurry.

Even though I wasn't in a hurry, when I got on campus and checked the time, I knew I probably should've walked a bit faster, because I went to second period around fifteen minutes late. Luckily, all I had to do was walk into class because that day our teacher really didn't feel like taking notes or anything like that, so all she did was change the attendance record and put that I was indeed present and in class.

"I see you took your time."

"I saw no reason to rush."

"No reason? You mean, other than your best friend being all by her lonesome?"

"Yeah, I guess you could say that," I said to Lydia as I gave her a sarcastic smile.

She gave me a friendly glare then said, "Okay, but seriously, when do we make our attack?"

"Honestly, Liv…"

"Oh, sorry, sorry, I mean counterattack." She sat up straight and looked very content with herself, having used what one might—just might—call battle jargon, or what I will very loosely label war terminology.

"No, Lydia, I just meant not now."

"You want to wait for Ty? We could text him and meet him for next period."

"That's not what it is, I—"

"Yeah, I guess it can wait till lunch."

"No, no. That's not it. I mean, I'll tell you both at lunch, but for the rest of the morning, let's just drop it, yeah?"

"Yeah. Probably has something to do with why you didn't come running to me. Am I right?"

I looked at her basically to say that she could just be patient. Most of the time, well, I guess I'll say half of the time, Lydia is patient, but when she lacks patience, she really lacks patience. For the rest of the period and even that morning, she kept constantly checking her phone for the time and catching glances at every clock in our classrooms! I had to pretend that I didn't notice; if I did, I knew she would've stayed on me about not telling her what it was I was holding off.

By the time the bell rang for lunch, Lydia was so anxious she couldn't help but grab for my wrist and pull me to our usual bench. She said that we didn't need to get lunch right away because she wasn't sure if she felt hungry. Tyler met us there and said he was glad to see I made my way to school. Without any hesitation, Lydia interrupted and told Tyler that he could talk later and that if he wanted lunch, he'd have to go without her and me because there were things we had to talk about. I looked at Lydia, astonished by how impatient she had become at that point, and told her to calm down and be still as I began to explain to her and Tyler.

"We're gonna hold off on doing anything."

"What? So we're just not gonna do anything at all and let them get away with the nasty things they've done to you?" Lydia asked furiously.

"I didn't say that, I said we'll hold off on doing anything."

"But why?"

"Because I was thinking about it, and I just don't wanna do anything drastic."

"But, Lennie, that's why we have those rules set up, remember?" Tyler jumped into the conversation.

"Yes, I remember, but think about it, we could do exactly what Cara did to me and still remain within those boundaries. The rules are definitely important and still in effect, but just because we have them doesn't mean we couldn't still take things too far. We could manage to do something really mean and ugly if we don't calm down first, and I'm not willing to treat anyone that poorly…even Cara."

Both Tyler and Lydia took a deep breath in and admitted that I did indeed have a point.

"Okay, I guess you're right."

"I mean, admit it. When something rotten like that happens, isn't the first and only thing you wanna do is the worst thing you can fathom in your head?"

"Yes." Tyler nodded and agreed almost instantly.

"See. So, we'll wait it out a little then plan our counterattack. I'm thinking next week. Sound good?"

"Good enough…I guess." Lydia pretended to roll her eyes.

Once our little discussion was over, Lydia managed to decide that she was hungry, so the three of us put our stuff down and walked to the cafeteria.

We picked up our trays and walked back to our bench. We spent that lunch talking about random topics, our opinions and our own random stories. Of course, Tyler was learning more about Lydia and me, than we were learning about him, but we were still all hearing new things about one another because as far as that lifetime went, we hadn't known one another that long. The best part was probably telling Tyler about himself from earlier lifetimes. Whenever we talked about things like that, he was always at the edge of his seat, for which I definitely couldn't blame him.

That day in art, we started what was supposed to be our two-day project, but we all knew that Mrs. Sally was going to let us have Monday to work on it and probably Tuesday as well, so a few people didn't bother to start. The project was supposed to be done on poster paper and incorporate calligraphy and a lot of color. I have never exactly been an artist, but I always did like to pretend I was and take a decent amount of time on my work in art. I think that's because it has, for as long as I can remember, made me feel better and calmer, which I've always needed help with.

The rest of the afternoon was normal. We had a normal culinary class and a normal algebra II class. The final bell rang, and although the day wasn't bad, I was ready for that Friday. The three of us chatted to the parent pickup for Lydia and me to wait. Tyler stayed walking to his Jeep, and just before he started his car, I ran to Tyler because I still had to give him back his clothes. I told him that I had washed and dried them. He said it was too bad, that he was looking forward to having something that smelled like me. I was stupid enough to say that they at least smelled like my laundry soap—I have no idea how I found that funny. Tyler gave me a pity laugh and shrugged his shoulders. We kissed goodbye, then I ran my way back to the parent pickup, where I saw Francine and Lydia waiting for me to get my lovestruck self in the car.

The next day was my lazy day at school. Every assignment we got, I just said I'd do it at home, and all the notes we took, I just took a picture of and said I'd copy them at home. The only exception was my art poster. I worked on that all of fifth period and even wanted to take it home, until I remembered everything else I was taking home that weekend.

Francine let me stay over that night since it was Friday. Right when we arrived at the house, Lydia and I put our stuff down, turned on the TV, then lay down to take a nap. After dinner, we stayed up a few hours, and shortly after that, we went to sleep. When I woke up, the only thing I did was open my books. I always woke up too early, and I preferred to have breakfast with everybody else. I didn't want to wake anyone up, but I hardly wanted to do homework, so I held my pencil in one hand, rested my chin on the other, and stared off into space. About an hour and a half had passed by the time I heard anybody wake up. It was Richard, Lydia's dad. He hadn't exactly gotten used to me by then, but he was a very warmhearted person and also very gregarious, so he and I were able to have very natural conversations.

"You're up early."

"Yeah. I have pretty crazy sleeping habits," I said.

"So, you've been working I see."

"Kinda. Actually, not really. I got ready to start, but my motivation is running a little low."

"Don't worry. It's hard to get straight to work in the morning, especially without breakfast, I would imagine."

"I guess so. So why are you up so early?"

"I'm just a morning person, I guess."

I put my head down to try to focus on my books and get some work done. Richard stood where he had been at for only a moment, then looked at me, and said, "Do you feel like having breakfast?"

"Uhh…well, I was kinda waiting for everyone."

"Of course, but they'll be asleep for a while longer. Plus, if anything, they'll think we haven't eaten, and we'll just get to eat more." He laughed.

I laughed a little too and told him that it didn't sound like too bad of an idea. Richard and I made breakfast that morning, but sadly, once we got to sit down and eat, both Lydia and Francine woke up. So we were not able to have a second breakfast, at least not a guilt-free one. On the bright side, though, neither I nor Richard had to cook more breakfast. Lydia was the only one who got to be lazy that morning.

We all sat down and ate, and I got a very bittersweet feeling. It's no secret that it's a sweet feeling to be happy and feel like a part of a family, a real family, a happy family. But the bitter feeling accompanies that sweet feeling because that family isn't actually my own.

On another note, after breakfast, I sat around dreading the work I had to complete, because of my prior laziness. I took a deep breath after a few minutes and got to work. I still needed some motivation, so I put on my music and started with the easiest work I had: copying notes. Starting off easy helped, but I was still working slow since I was so easily distracted. And by the time lunch came around, I was more than ready for a break. I ate slowly, so did Lydia. Then, I stayed on break because Lydia wanted me to. Fine, I won't blame her; basically, it was because I wanted to. I just decided to finish history before dinner and I'd do the rest the next day.

Sunday was a bit different. I still woke up early, but I skipped breakfast and had lunch a little late. All I wanted to do was get my work done. It felt very abnormal to have unfinished work just lingering around when I did have the free time to complete it. I was working toward being valedictorian then, and I had to remember that.

I was all done by the time it was three o'clock, so I still had a good chunk of the day. Lydia and I went to Tyler's to just hang out for a while. When we were ready to go back, it was past six thirty, so I told Lydia that she could just take me home. She asked if I was sure, and I told her that I simply had to. She sighed sympathetically and dropped me off the same way Tyler would—a block away—and waited till she knew I was okay. And I waited for her call so she could let me know she got back all right.

Monday, you already know about how Tyler goes to school starving, tries to sneak out of class, gets caught, can't message me or Lydia, so we finally introduce him to Julian and skip class all afternoon in the teachers' lounge. The next day, though, was a bit more important. That was the Tuesday we officially introduced Tyler and Julian—and Carol too.

"Julian! Carol! Hey, we were just looking for you guys."

"What do you need? If it's drinks, just to let you know, I'm selling blackberry lemonade now, so if you wanna walk down to my locker, you could try those out."

"That actually sounds really good. How much? Just as much as—"

"Liv, hold on real quick!" I said.

"Oh, right. Sorry."

"This is our friend Tyler, Julian."

"Hey, it's nice to meet you. You practically saved my life yesterday," Tyler said.

"That explains why my bag was so much lighter yesterday." Julian laughed. "Nice to meet you too. And you're pretty lucky you get to hang out with two of the coolest girls I know. This is the third," Julian said, pointing to Carol.

Tyler and Carol both just casually said hi, but after that point, the five of us were pretty close.

"Actually, Julian, he is very lucky," Lydia said, putting Tyler and me closer together and placing his arm around me.

"Oh yeah, very lucky," Julian said.

Tyler and I just laughed, while Lydia clapped her hands together and said, "Well, let's go get that lemonade."

We all headed toward Julian's locker, and on the way, I decided I felt like having a lemonade too, then so did Tyler. Typically, Julian gets $1.50 for drinks, $1.25 from casual friends, but for me and Lydia, only a dollar. Since Tyler was with us, it only cost him a dollar too. Of course, we weren't at the very top of the list though. No, only Carol was at the very top. She got everything for free; she even had all of Julian's locker combinations, just in case he wasn't there for whatever reason. That's one huge reason why it was important— well, nice—to be friends with her.

When we went to fifth period that day, I was very excited, because I got to put the finishing touches on my two-day project poster. After class had finished, I told Lydia and Tyler to go along without me, that I'd see them in math; it was a block schedule, so we only had first, third, fifth, and seventh period. Wednesdays were different obviously, only even-numbered classes, but we always had fifth. Anyway, I stayed behind so I could ask Mrs. Sally about my art.

"What do you think?" I asked, holding my poster up.

"Oh, wow, I love it." Mrs. Sally took my poster to look at it better.

"Great." I smiled. "And I actually wanted to ask a favor."

"What is it?"

"I was wondering if you could just give me a grade for this really quick now so I could have it."

"Yes, that'll be fine. May I ask what for?"

"I wanted to give it to my boyfriend. I really think he'll like it."

"That's sweet," Mrs. Sally said, putting my grade into her computer.

"Let me know how he likes it, all right?"

"Will do, and thank you so much." As I walked out, I realized I didn't want Tyler seeing it until after school.

"Actually, can I keep it here until the end of the day?"

"That's okay with me. And don't worry, I'll make sure no one touches it."

"Thanks again, Mrs. Sally," I said and quickly walked out to math.

When I got to class, Lydia and Tyler asked what it was that I had to stay behind for. All I said was that I'd have to tell them later because that day's lesson seemed particularly important, which I guess it might have been, but I didn't pay a tremendous amount of attention. I was pretty excited about showing my poster, probably a little too excited.

The bell rang for us to go home, and I happily pulled Tyler and Lydia the opposite way of where we usually went and told them I had to get something and they had to come. I walked just a bit ahead, and they both figured that it had something to do with why I had stayed behind. When we walked up to the art room, I told them to wait right outside and went in. Mrs. Sally handed me my poster and wished me luck. I walked back out into the hall and ask them both how they liked it.

"Lennie, this is so good!"

"Yeah, Mel, I can't believe you even got it done so fast."

"Thank you, guys." I was smiling really big, about to tell Tyler I made it specifically for him, then Lydia jumped in.

"So, do you know where you're hanging this up, Ty?"

"What do you mean?"

"Well, obviously, she made it for you." Lydia playfully hit his arm.

Tyler turned to me to see if Lydia was right, and of course, she was. She hit the nail on the head, like she always did.

"Yeah, Tay, she's right. I made it just for you!"

"I think it's so cool, honestly," Tyler said, looking at me and down at the poster, which was in his hands at that point.

Personally, I was very proud of that painting. I had done it in watercolors, which I don't find all that easy. Plus watercolors aren't my favorite, but with that picture in mind, I couldn't imagine doing it any other way. It was my own interpretation of the spot that Tyler took me; I hadn't been there in a while, so I had to paint a picture from memory. I was never too fond of my calligraphy, but that time, I had done pretty well. I used red lettering, and it said, "I thought that you should know…" I used the ellipsis because I didn't know too much of what I actually had to say. I figured leaving it ambiguous and up in the air like that meant that I'd get the chance to say everything, even everything I didn't say.

"Okay, you two, I'm heading out. Tyler, you're taking Mel home," Lydia said.

"Why, Liv? Did something happen?"

"Uh, yeah. You and Ty are having one of your 'you're my soul mate' moments!"

"If you say so," I responded.

"Well, it's definitely cool with me," Tyler said.

"See, Mel, he's just dying to have you all to himself."

"Oh yeah, he's basically ready to throw me over his shoulder and drive me away with him so you're nowhere in sight," I said, rolling my eyes.

"That's all that I'm saying."

"I'm glad we can all see it," Tyler said with a sarcastic smile.

So Tyler and I walked Lydia to the parent pickup and waited with her until Francine got there. Tyler explained that he was taking me home for the day, and as always, she just thought it was cute. Lydia went off with her mom, and Tyler and I walked to his car and pondered whether or not we were going somewhere or if he indeed was just taking me home.

"Do you wanna do something?"

"Mmm…I don't know. If you do."

"Well, we'll probably stay stuck in the parking lot if I say 'only if you do,' so I'll just take that as a yes," Tyler said.

"Awesome, so what're we doing?"

"Damn, Lennie, I don't have every answer."

"All right, all right. Calm yourself, Tay. How about we get some ice cream?"

"I like that idea."

We went from the school straight to the ice cream shop, except we took the long way. Tyler always liked taking the long way whenever we went anywhere. On the car ride, we mainly sang songs; honestly, I don't even know if we were singing along with the radio. We were probably just being our own radio station. Even if the radio was playing that day, we were being too loud to hear the actual song anyway, which I typically hate, so it was a rare occasion kind of. It was when we got to the ice cream shop that we actually started conversing.

"You know how Lydia asked where I'm gonna hang my poster?"

"Yeah. You know where?"

"I know exactly where!" Tyler said enthusiastically. "If you want, you can help me put it up, or at least come see what it looks like."

"That sounds fun, right after this you mean?"

"Uhh, yeah. Now is as good a time as ever, right?"

"That's true." I smiled. "I'm almost finished with my ice cream, so we can go soon."

"No rush," Tyler said, "and this should be cool, you'll get to meet my dad. He wants to meet you."

"Ugh. The pressure's on now. I'm meeting the parent."

"Very funny. Really though, he'll love you, absolutely no pressure."

"I'll take your word for it, Tay. Deep breaths."

We both laughed and headed back to Tyler's house. In all honesty, I held my breath and concentrated on my heartbeats the entire ride there. I knew that Tyler's father, Raymond, was a very nice man, but meeting the family was always something that worried me. Meeting family and friends always meant that there was going to be expectations. Either you would have to put up with them, or they would have to put up with you, or both. But something I've come to find is that you can't forbid someone from the other people in their life, because parts of them come from these other people, and you have to keep in mind that you do indeed love all of them, somehow. Anyhow, with Tyler and Raymond being so close, I had to be as lovable as possible!

"We've been here waiting in the car for twenty minutes now, Lennie, do you think you're ready yet?"

"No, not at all," I said, breathing heavily. "But I suppose I'm as ready as I'll ever be."

"Good," Tyler said with a smile on his face.

Opening his door, Tyler grabbed my hand and led me out of his side of the car. I was thinking about how unprepared I was. It wasn't like I actually had the chance to get especially ready, so I knew the best I could've looked was average; I had no choice but to say that average had to, just had to, mean good enough. We walked up to the front door, Tyler and I faced each other, and again I took a deep breath.

"Remember, no pressure." Tyler ran his hands down from my ears to my shoulders and lightly squeezed them.

I nodded, and the two of us walked inside. There really wasn't any reason to be worried; Tyler's dad wasn't even home when we got there. I felt like taking another deep breath, more so a sigh of relief, when I realized I didn't have to feel like the pressure was on until another day. Tyler turned to me and told me that he guessed I got lucky that time then invited me up to his room so we could hang up his poster. I gladly accepted. I was so happy to know that he really did like my art. Right when we walked into his room, he pointed out to me where he thought he'd hang it up.

"You see, right above my dresser there," he said.

"Yeah, it seems like a great place to put it!"

"It'd be perfectly displayed and everything."

"I couldn't agree more." I smiled.

"Cool, do you wanna hold it really quick while I go grab the thumbtacks?"

"Yeah, no problem."

Tyler left the room, and I looked around and started to take in things. For example, I noticed how his room was particularly clean, maybe even a little empty. I thought that perhaps he thought the same thing and maybe that went along with why he was excited to put my poster up. And I noticed how his room smelled very nice. I don't know what exactly I'd call the smell; all I know is that I liked it very much and that it was quite pleasant.

I don't know what I really expected Tyler's room to look like, but I suppose it wasn't too far from what it had been then. His room was quiet, subtle, and modest, kind of like Tyler's character when taken away from the chaos of the world. I think I enjoyed it very much because it seemed so calm, a nice place to run away to when all you wanted to do was pretend like you didn't exist or like everything else didn't. It was a place that let you breathe and didn't let you drown. It didn't asphyxiate you with silent roars of your own personal madness; it was quite the opposite of my room that lifetime.

"Got 'em," Tyler announced, reentering the room.

"Oh, nice," I said, handing him back the poster.

He hung it up, and we both took a step back to look at it and how glorious I had made it.

"I love it," he said, smiling and kissing me.

"I love that you love it." I smiled back.

"So now I have a surprise for you."

"You're kidding. What is it?" I wasn't entirely sure if I believed him.

"No, you're right. I'm kidding."

I clicked my tongue, hugged Tyler's waist, then shook my head as I placed it on his chest.

"Okay, I'm actually not kidding. I do have a surprise."

I stayed with my arms around his waist, looked up at him, and asked, "What is it?"

"I'll tell you if you come with me to the kitchen to get a drink."

"Umm...okay," I agreed suspiciously.

Eagerly taking my hand, Tyler guided me to his kitchen. He poured the both of us a glass of root beer and jokingly said that it would've been better if we had the root beer with the ice cream.

I nodded my head yes and asked, "So what's my surprise?"

"Well, let's go into the dining room, actually."

"You're up to something, aren't you?" I said, turning to face him.

"Kinda," Tyler said. He then turned me around. "My dad's home!"

I was stunned. I'm sure the both of them could see the shock on my face; if not, I'm more than positive me fainting from anxiety got that point across. I wish I could say that I'm playing around with you, but alas, I am not. My words were drained from my mouth, and I vaguely remember Ray giving me what I'm guessing was a different glass of root beer to calm me down as I sat down on the couch in their living room. I could've knocked over the chairs in the dining room, so the couch was the safest bet.

"I'm sorry I scared you so bad," Raymond said with wide, concerned eyes.

"No, no, don't be sorry."

"You're right, it was all Tyler's fault. Tyler, apologize to the poor girl."

I laughed a bit and said, "I guess I am all right, but an apology would probably make me feel a million times better."

Both Raymond and I stared over to Tyler. He stayed quiet for a few seconds, probably wondering if we were actually serious. I knew I was; I just wanted that pointless "I'm sorry" to fall from his confused mouth.

"I'm sorry, Melenium."

"That's better." I smiled.

"So, Melenium, huh?"

"Yeah, but most people call me Mel. I guess you can call me whatever you like though."

"Whatever I like?"

"Well, within reason, like 'What's-Her-Face' wouldn't really be all that nice to hear all the time."

Ray laughed, and just like that, I felt 100 percent okay. From these last few paragraphs alone, I'm sure you can tell that outside Lydia and Tyler, I'm bad at meeting people. But I've had eighty-two lifetimes to meet them, so they don't really count.

"I like her, Ty, she's cute and charming."

"Hear that? Cute and charming," I said, winking at Tyler.

"Yeah, Dad, she's a keeper."

"She sure is, so don't keep her waiting and ask if she wants to stay for dinner!"

"Oh, right. Well, Lennie, would you like to stay for dinner?"

I laughed a bit more at Tyler's banter with his dad then agreed to stay for their welcoming meal, but I also mentioned how I'd have to get home before nine o'clock; after all, I did have school the next day. As lame as it sounds, I did have to respect school nights.

So in only a few minutes, Raymond had dinner on the table. It was leftover ribs from what he and Tyler had the night before; he apologized for that. I told him that it was perfectly all right and that it all tasted great. Somehow we started talking about cooking, which he's very good at, I might add, and I told him that I heavily enjoyed it as well; he told me that absolutely anytime, day or night, his kitchen could also be my kitchen. Throughout dinner, we talked a little about me, which is always uncomfortable for regular reasons, and with me for reincarnation reasons. I didn't exactly think that I should've mentioned that to Tyler's dad being that not too long before that did I mention it to Tyler for the very first time in eighty-two lifetimes! We also just talked about things that families talk about. I had another one of those bittersweet feelings again about the whole family situation.

Dinner finished, and Tyler and Raymond walked me to the door. Ray told me that I had to be sure to come back, that he wanted to see me around more often. Isn't it amazing how you can arrive somewhere for the first time and then, either instantly or when you have to leave, realize that you have indeed found your home? I'm basically implying that in that moment, I had found my home and I had found my family. I didn't want to leave, but I knew that I sadly had to and that stalling was only going to make it harder. After making our way to the door, Tyler and I walked to his car, and Tyler started to take me home.

"Your dad's really nice."

"See, I told you. You had nothing to worry about."

"I guess you were right, but things could've gone a bit more smoothly."

"And I wouldn't deny that." Tyler laughed.

"Anyway! I appreciate how you both made sure I didn't feel any pressure and, you know, made me feel at home."

"Well, personally, I think that was the most at home I've ever felt."

I laughed a bit and asked, "What do you mean?"

"Uhh," he paused, "well, with my mom never being around, my family has always had something missing, you know? And tonight, it was like you filled the void."

"Aww, that's so sweet." I smiled. "I guess I can kind of relate to what having that empty feeling feels like."

"I would imagine you could," Tyler said.

"For what it's worth, I'd say you fill my void too."

"You don't have to say that, you know?"

"I know, but I'm serious. I just never really thought to put it that way."

Then Tyler smiled. I imagined it was because he didn't have anything to say. After just a short amount of time, we drove up to the street that he usually dropped me off at. I told him good night, and he said it back. I opened my door and ran to my front steps. I paused for a moment, then turned back around. I made my way back to Tyler so I could tell him that the next day would be our big day. We were finally going to plan our "counterattack" as Lydia liked to call it. I told him that I would call her when I got inside and that I was sure she'd be ecstatic. I kissed him good night once more, and that was that.

Chapter 8

*T*HE NEXT DAY, I WENT to school, and I found Lydia waiting very eagerly for me. I don't think that she ever looked at any of those plans as revenge, because she isn't a vengeful person, but as more of a game—a rather facinorous game, but a game nonetheless. Tyler was late that day, so I had an excuse to tell Lydia we had to wait until lunch. But once humanities ended and lunch began, the three of us—not only Lydia—raced to our bench. We didn't have to wait in line that day for our food. Tyler had stopped to pick the three of us up some lunch specifically so we could hurry to that moment. That was sort of why he was late that morning.

Our lunch period went by super quick that day, but it was as long as we needed. I guess we were all thinking about suggestions for so long that once our chance came, we had everything perfect as far as our own details went. Excitement helped that day because we all had a lot to say but also the willingness to listen to things we somehow didn't think of ourselves. The three of us discussed it some more on our way to art class and on our way to the parent pickup, but not in class. We didn't want to risk any "overhearing"—eavesdropping— from the Fans to interfere with our plans. I was all willing to play that conniving little game of ours, fair, but something told me Cara wasn't, exactly. She had to win no matter how repugnant things got.

Tyler waited with Lydia and me at the parent pickup; he would've driven us all to Lydia's place since that's where we were all meeting anyway, but by the time he thought of it, Francine was already in sight. As Tyler stopped to say a quick hello to Francine, Lydia and I got in the car and told Tyler that we'd all see him in a bit. He nodded and jogged to his Jeep, and we drove off campus to

Lydia's house, our unofficial official HQ. Lydia got drinks for us, and I made nachos for us while we waited for Tyler, who arrived only about ten minutes after we did. Francine drove kind of fast, and since cops liked to pull over the students, Tyler drove somewhat slowly when he was close to the school.

"Okay, Mom, we'll be in our headquarters if you need anything!" Lydia shouted.

"That's fine. I'll be in mine too, I guess," Francine said.

We all waltzed into Lydia's room. She went straight to her bed. Tyler pulled up the chair to her desk. And I sat right on the floor, comfortably and by choice, so don't worry. We snacked for about five minutes without saying a word to one another. I guess being diabolical really had worked up our appetites. But my little eager beaver came back from her trance and broke the silence.

"So our plan seems pretty clear to all of us, yeah?"

"Yeah, Liv, I think we all got it. Ty?"

"I get that it involves the Halloween carnival and dogs, but…"

"Okay, so let's go over it one more time." I clapped my hands together and continued. "On the night of the Halloween carnival, we'll get Cara away from that little applaud squad of hers, then get her near, well at least close enough to the apple-bobbing stand," I explained.

"And that's when we'll let our dogs go one at a time," Lydia started.

"But that's the thing, Liv, you're the only one of us that has a dog."

"Tyler, we're taking two dogs from the shelter."

"What?"

"The shelter lets kids sixteen and up take shelter dogs for a night or two to see how things go if you tell them that you're wanting to adopt a dog."

"So we're gonna lie?"

"Not entirely. Look, I don't know about you, but I might adopt the dog I get."

"Okay. Umm, continue, I guess."

"Well, Cara hates dogs, so we'll let them each go one at a time, and if all goes according to plan, she'll run into the stand and be drenched in water."

"Yeah, she'll find out what that feels like finally!" I expressed. "And the dogs will probably be all over her after that, and that'll just be the cherry on top."

We all laughed, but I did have one last question.

"I get that this isn't during school, but since it's a school event, do you guys think it's cool that we go through with all this?"

"Well, it's a school-hosted event, but a lot of kids from the high school don't even go, Mel. It's mainly the middle-school kids and elementary-school kids with their parents," Lydia said.

"I guess that's true."

"Wait, if barely anyone in the school goes, how do we even know that Cara will be there?" Tyler asked, puzzled.

"Since it's a school event, that means students can participate and, you know, help out. That's extra credit. And that means Cara's gonna be there."

"Oh yeah, that reminds me, I signed us up to help out too," I mentioned. "Liv, you and I are running the raffle. Tay, you're doing bingo."

With everything worked out and set, all that was left to do was wait for Friday, October 28. That night, we had dinner with Lydia and her parents, and Tyler took me home. The plans left us all pretty excited, so I didn't even mind when I had to sneak into my house. My mom was shockingly home and awake, so I didn't really want to take my chances with all the potential drama.

So we weren't pulling our prank instantaneously; we—mainly me, myself, and I—were willing to take some more of Cara's ammo in the meantime, if she had any. Thankfully, she didn't have any in that meantime. I think she and I came to a common-enough under-standing that if we were playing big-boy games, then we didn't really have much effort to spare on the more petty full schemes.

While waiting, my grades stayed up, even raised a bit. Lydia's and Tyler's did too; we kept an eye on one another. As did Cara's, of course; I don't really know about the rest of the Fans. I might have mentioned that Cara didn't help her friends out much; as far as she was concerned, that just put her more ahead.

The day before the carnival is when our first plot started to unravel. After school that day, Francine didn't come to pick us up. Tyler played chauffeur for the day since he and I had to go to the shelter and pick up our dogs and Lydia didn't want to be left out.

Once we got to the shelter, we all went around looking at all the irresistibly adorable dogs there; there were tons and tons of them. Admittedly, we stayed there for what one might say was too long— three hours. Only about half an hour before the shelter closed did we decide on our two dogs. Mine was a dog named Neptune, and Tyler's dog was a dog named Gadget, and just in case you're wondering, Lydia's dog was named Nestle. She had named him after the water; I have no idea why.

We had to drop Lydia off right away not only because it was somewhat late but also because we couldn't let her parents find out about the dogs, at least not at that point. It'd kind of let them find out about the whole situation, and we couldn't've let that happen. So after dropping Lydia off, Tyler took me home, and I was very tempted to ask if I could take both Neptune and Gadget with me for the night, but either way, Tyler would've said no. Unlike Cara, we adored dogs!

"I guess now we just wait for tomorrow night."

"Yeah. You nervous?"

"Kinda excited mainly. Is that bad?" I cringed.

"Not too bad." Tyler laughed.

"Good." I laughed back. "Okay, well, I guess I'll see you both tomorrow. C'mon, Neptune."

"Night, Lennie. Oh, hey, did you want me to pick you up tomorrow?"

"Oh yeah. That's a good idea so the dogs can be together," I agreed.

"Cool, I'll wait here at the corner."

"Sounds good. 'Kay, well, have a good night."

The next morning, Tyler came with Gadget pretty early since we had to get back to his place to drop the dogs off, but honestly, I was wide awake, ready for the carnival. To make classes go by faster, I worked on any and every assignment I had. The things we were doing in class often enough left me some free time, so that day I managed to get pretty ahead.

When school was released, Tyler and I went back to his place for Neptune and Gadget but had to let Francine take Lydia so she could get Nestle. We did, however, have to make up an excuse as to why we were bringing dogs to our Halloween carnival. Apparently, it's believable that there are dog competitions at nighttime Halloween carnivals.

Lydia and I went with Tyler to run the first hour of bingo, but after about fifteen minutes, we lost patience just sitting there. We weren't allowed to participate in the game since we were volunteers. I figured that we needed to keep an eye out for Cara, so I told Lydia that we'd split up and meet up near the apple-bobbing stand once Tyler was about done, then we went around mainly playing the games we could play—like throwing darts at balloons. We didn't need tickets for those; at least being a volunteer paid off in that way. I spent a decent while trying to knock down the tower of milk bottles, but sadly, I was off my game that night. Just before I left, I ran into this guy named Harold. He was a senior my freshman year; he was one person that actually knew my name then.

"Hey, Harold!"

"Hey, Melenium, it's been a long time."

"It has. So what are you doing here?"

"Well, I figured it was Friday night and I had nothing to do so…" He threw his arms up and flapped them back down implying a "Why not?" "Plus two of my friends are meeting me here after they finish, umm, working." He stammered a bit.

"That's cool. I mean, it is better than nothing, right?"

"I guess." He nodded. "I have to admit, I'm a bit surprised to see you here."

"Oh, I know! I'm becoming a little less antisocial." I laughed.

"And where's your sister at? Lydia?"

"Lydia's not my sister," I half-lied.

"Well, she might as well be. Anyway, is she here?"

"Yeah, she's somewhere, but we decided to meet up in a while, see who else came out."

"Nice, nice. So how are things in school?"

"Same old, same old for the most part. And what about you?"

"No school for me. Couldn't afford it, you know."

"I get that. What're you doing nowadays then?"

"I'm working at this makeup store, kinda far out of town."

"Really? You like it?"

"I know, I know. It seems kinda weird, but it pays and it's really not that bad. Plus, I'm good at selling, so it works out."

"As long as it works." I nodded. "Hey, well, it was cool getting to see you, but I gotta go. It's about time to meet up with Lydia."

"All right. Yeah, it was cool seeing you. Hope you have a good night."

"You too. I'll see you around." And I left off with Neptune to find Lydia and Tyler.

It took only a few minutes to find Tyler because I heard Gadget barking, and once that happened, I found Lydia too by hearing Nestle bark. And they both found me because, as you can imagine, Neptune joined the barking too. Thankfully, the dogs all calmed down quickly.

The three of us got together and just basically ran through things before it was crunch time. Lydia told us how she found Cara near the balloon-dart game and that she had been by herself, so that was already taken care of. We split back up again after deciding where we were all going to be watching from, and that way, we would be able to see one another and watch the dogs too. Just to mention, because I feel I shouldn't have left this out, the dogs were all completely friendly and did not bite, ever.

We were all in place, and Tyler signaled to us that he spotted Cara close to the apple-bobbing stand. We agreed that he'd let Gadget go first, next I would let Neptune go, and finally, Lydia would know to let Nestle go. I watched Tyler and side-eyed Cara. Tyler let Gadget go, and he was off. He ran right to Cara like Tyler pointed him out to do. I counted to ten then sent off Neptune. Cara noticed Gadget basically when he was about to jump all over her, and she tried to chase him away angrily. And while chasing him away, Lydia let go of Nestle, who ran incredibly fast. At that point, Cara was running toward and straight into the barrel for apple bobbing. She was just about to run into the stand when Nestle jumped on her shoulders!

That pushed her over into the water, and she flipped right over, falling down and being soaked in what I'm sure was drool-infested water, because a lot of people were trying to sink their teeth into those apples. And once the water was all dumped out, the dogs were all over her again, covering her in a more direct drool—also known as puppy kisses.

I laughed so hard my stomach was aching painfully. I didn't really notice if Tyler and Lydia were laughing as hard as me, but I'm sure they were sparing more than just small giggles. I pulled myself together enough to run and get Neptune, who had to shake herself off the moment I pulled her away. A few people gathered around to help Cara up, and some people found towels to bring her so she could dry off—maybe a little.

We all got our dogs and pulled away from the crowd, laughed some more, then went a bit farther away from the scene of the crime. The dogs all needed to go inside, so we could dry them some more, because it was a pretty cold night. Before going back out, I went to grab one of the extra jackets I had it in my locker just in case Cara stayed and didn't manage to get her hands on a dry jacket.

It turned out that Cara went straight home—obviously. Rachel stayed back to run the cakewalk we were holding inside; that was what Cara was supposed to do until the end of the night, but under the circumstances, I'm sure she and Rachel got credit.

Tyler, Lydia, and I sold tickets for twenty more minutes just before doing the raffle drawing. During that time, Rachel saw us with our dogs. It wasn't like we were trying to hide from being found out, and Cara probably did add two and two together to figure out that the three of us had something to do with it, but whatever wasn't concluded was then concluded.

I announced the winners of the raffle, and after handing out prizes, the three of us and our dogs were making our way home. We didn't want to be stuck trying to leave the parking lot like all the other people who were going to stay until the end. We all figured what was another half hour anyway, although it was a damn fun carnival for more than just obvious reasons.

We had to take Lydia home first, mainly because she was the closest, but she did have a curfew too. Tyler and I told her good night and said we'd see her tomorrow. Finally, I got to go home to my bed and sleep. I was excited to go to sleep because the night was tiring and I was excited to get to cuddle with Neptune too.

I told Tyler that I'd leave Neptune in his car real quick so I could set her up some more food and water without her getting too excited; he nodded, and I ran inside.

"And where the hell have you been?" I heard my mom ask.

"What do you care?" I replied with an attitude and turned on the lights.

"I care when all my damn things are gone."

When I turned around to the now-lit living room, I saw everything had been stolen! Not one thing seemed to have been left. I turned to face my mom, and she was still staring at me like she was expecting some sort of answer out of me.

"Well?"

"What do you want me to do? You could've stayed home too, you know," I said.

"I want you to shut your mouth and start figuring out how you're gonna replace all of my things!"

"Yeah, right, like that's gonna happen. And you're too much of an idiot to have even thought about calling the cops!" I started yelling.

I started for my room to see what might've been taken from in there. My mom had no intentions of letting me to my room, so I bumped her shoulder out of the way, but she grabbed my hair and threw me back in front of her, and I fell. I got back up and decided to just head to the door and go back with Tyler. Again, she had no intention of letting me by. She grabbed at my arm. I threw her off and pushed her away from me. I had never actually gotten physical with her before, so both she and I were a little stunned. But quickly she looked me in the eye and hit me in the mouth, busting my lip. I looked back at her and saw that there was no remorse in her face, then I turned around and headed back to Tyler's Jeep in tears and with my lip bleeding profusely.

"And where are you going now? Back to your little friends to go whore around, right?" she screamed.

"Screw you!" I shouted and continued walking.

"Yeah, screw me! Just remember, Melenium, you're nothing without me, and because you like to act like such a dumb-ass, you better know that you can't come back here!"

"Don't worry, I won't!"

By the time I got close enough to the car, Tyler had climbed out and ran up to me because he had come to notice that I was crying. He pulled me into his chest and held me for a while. He released me a bit and cupped my face with his hands. Already aware of my answer, he stared at me and asked if I was okay. I wasn't all that capable of getting words out in that moment, so I just weakly shook my head no. He pulled me back into his chest and asked quietly if I would like it if he took me home with him. Remaining as close as I could to him, I nodded my head. He let me go and gestured for me to climb back into his Jeep so we could go.

When we pulled up to his house, all the lights were off. His dad didn't see much reason in waiting up; he knew Tyler would come home. We all went straight to his room—that included Gadget and Neptune. The dogs were good and didn't instantly jump on the bed, but I could tell they sure wanted to. Tyler went to find a pair of pajamas for me before doing the same for himself. I was very comfortable wearing flannel pajama pants and a simple Coldplay shirt. He asked me if I'd prefer that he sleep on the couch, but I told him that I'd feel a lot better if he slept with me, so we both lay down and made ourselves comfortable. Within seconds, Neptune and Gadget were on the bed, finding their precise places.

Tyler had his arm wrapped around my waist. Tucked in next to him, I felt completely secure and calm, but the excitement from the past hour had also left me completely awake. I kept my hand on Neptune, petting her, staring out the window at the trees swaying in the light wind that I couldn't quite hear from inside, so it wasn't like that was keeping me up at all. And I guessed he got somewhat caught up in the night's commotion because it didn't take too long for Tyler to reveal that he was still up as well.

"Hey, Lennie, you up?" he whispered.

"Yeah, still am. What's wrong?" I asked, my voice also hushed.

"Nothing's really wrong, I'm just real awake. My eyes don't seem like they want to close right now."

"Mine either, but I don't wanna keep anyone up."

"Don't worry, we'll stay quiet," Tyler said, still with his voice at a soft whisper. I let out a soft giggle and didn't really continue the conversation we had started. I wasn't sure how to.

"Hey, umm, can I ask you something?"

"Of course. Ask away."

"Uhh…well, have we, like, ever gotten married?"

And there I was, a bit more awake. I definitely hadn't expected that question. "Well, never married. But we have been engaged before."

"A lot of times? How come the wedding never got to come around?"

"Kind of a lot of times, but only because I've lived eighty-two lifetimes. I think we've been engaged forty-eight times, so more than fifty percent of the time. And we never got around to the wedding because, well, because each time life just sort of happened."

"Do you mean death just sort of happened?"

"Basically, yes."

"Wow," Tyler said, taking in a deep breath. "Well, do you think you want to try again this lifetime? It might be that eighty-two is our lucky number." He smirked.

I rolled over to face him. "Is that you proposing?" I asked.

"What? No. When I propose, it's gonna be amazing and romantic."

"If you must know, I would for sure say yes and would love to take our forty-ninth shot this lifetime." I smiled so widely as I confirmed my answer.

"Good to know I have my future wife already in my life."

"Yeah, good to know I have my future husband."

I turned back over on the bed and adjusted myself again so that perhaps at random I could fall into a slumber. I did, however, quickly realize that I still was not going to fall asleep all that soon. So I placed my hand on Tyler's leg and began to shake him a bit. He then asked me if anything was wrong, and of course, all I told him was that I wasn't ready to go to sleep. For the next few hours, we had stayed up talking about anything that really came to mind. I asked if often a time he experienced déjà vu; he said that he did often enough but not even close to every day. He asked me a compilation of questions that had to do with either dying or being dead in heaven, but he also told me to not answer a ton of them because he didn't want to spoil anything. The two of us also talked about things that I didn't have to have lived eighty-two lives to discuss. For example, we talked about whether or not we wanted kids, how many we'd have, and what their names would be. And I mentioned how we would definitely have to travel because I loved to witness how the world always changed so constantly, but also how some things never did change. Then Tyler added in that it wouldn't just be us two, that Lydia had to of course come, which I of course concurred.

We remained talking till six in the morning, I think it was. And afterward, oh boy, did we sleep. We slept until at least one o'clock in the afternoon, and we really only woke up because the dogs were whining to go outside to use the bathroom. Luckily, both Neptune and Gadget were house-trained.

Tyler went to take the dogs out, and I stayed in so I could call Lydia, since I had three missed calls from her that morning and I don't even know how many text messages! I told her everything that had happened the night before and that I spent the night at Tyler's. All she asked was if I was going to keep staying at Tyler's or if I was going to end up moving in with her, because if I needed to, it would be fine. I told her that I didn't exactly know, but I didn't really want to think about it right then. She dropped the conversation, said she'd be right over, then hung up before I could even say, "Okay, bye."

Tyler came back inside right away. I supposed that the dogs really had to go that morning, since they went that quickly. I could see that he came in with a very curious look on his face. It was a look that seemed like he wanted to ask a question but didn't know if he could.

"What's on your mind?" I asked.

"I, uhh, don't think I should ask."

"Why not? You should know that we can talk about anything."

"Okay." He licked his lips and looked down at the floor. "Do you ever want to die?"

"What?" I asked, taken aback.

"Do you ever want to die, like just not want to be here? And do you ever want to stay? Do you get any sort of say-so ever?"

"Whoa," I stammered a bit. "Well, I've never been asked that before."

"It's okay if you don't wanna answer. I was really just thinking out loud. I'm sorry."

"No, no. Don't be sorry. You're coming to know me better than ever. I don't ever really want to die. I mean, sometimes I feel like going home or not existing, but I calm down and...," I took a heavy breath, "breathe deeply and think about all the pretty incredible things here on earth. And there are times that I sort of feel like staying, like how sometimes you don't want a TV series to end, but I know that I have to go, which is why I'm okay with the fact that I don't get a say-so. I don't need one. God knows what He's doing." I smiled.

"He knows what He's doing definitely, but you never get the slightest of urges to just say 'Can I stay?'"

Knowing where he was coming from, I shook my head at Tyler with a smirk on my face.

"Do you wanna know how I got a hold on this whole concept of death even when I feel like there's so much that's unfinished?"

"Yes!" Tyler said, very excited as if it were the answer to a question that he had been asking all his life.

"Okay." I laughed a bit. "It's this one poem that He told me. He said to never forget it, so I'm telling you now to listen closely and never forget it."

> I promise not to fight when You call me home.
> And for right now I will freely roam.
> I am not too sure of what I know,
> But I promise to believe in my time to go.
> I will not take what is not completely mine,
> And I will not argue when You say, "It is time."

Chapter 9

$\mathcal{A}$ KNOCK AT THE DOOR SUDDENLY broke the silence that had arisen between Tyler and me after I recited the poem. Tyler turned his head and nervously announced that he'd answer the door and let Lydia in.

"So how are you holding up, Mel?" Lydia asked right away.

"Believe it or not, I'm actually pretty all right."

"Honestly?"

"Yeah. It's almost relieving that I don't have to go back to a place that never even felt like home. I was just forced to call it that."

"I believe you when you say that it wasn't exactly a healthy place to call home, but are you sure you're all right?"

"Positive," I said. "So let's start off our weekend, yeah? Even if it is almost two o'clock!"

We all got up and ate what Tyler and I called breakfast and what Lydia called lunch. I guess leftover pizza is really any kind of meal. Sluggishly, the three of us made our way to the TV to watch old Disney Halloween movies—the best kind. Of course, there was a marathon, so we basically had our plans for the rest of the day, or until something more interesting came along, which was unlikely.

Come evening time, I'd say six-fifteen-ish, Raymond pulled up to the house and opened the door exclaiming that he had made it home. More than likely, he only expected Tyler to be there, so Lydia's car probably was a peculiar sight to see when he came within reasonable distance of the house.

"Hey, Tyler, who else is here? Is it Mel?" he shouted.

"We're all in here, Dad!"

"And yes, I'm here, Ray!" I added in.

Raymond made his way into the dimly lit living room and said a courteous hello to me and Tyler and then noticed a brand-new face. "Hello…"

"Legend, Lydia Legend, but you can just call me Lydia, or Liv."

"Okay, Lydia. I'm Raymond, but you can just call me Ray."

"Sounds good. Although every once in a while, I'll probably call you Mr. Tyler's Dad. Hopefully, that's not too bad," Lydia joked.

"Nope. Not too bad at all."

"Lydia is Melenium's other half. They're practically attached at the hip," Tyler pointed out.

"Really? I never would've guessed." We all looked at Raymond curiously.

"Well, it's just because she seems to be doing a fabulous job at meeting me, and, Mel, we all know how that went with us."

"I don't know how that went! How'd it go?" Liv shouted with an excessive amount of curiosity.

"Okay, so…," Tyler started.

"Tyler, shut up! We're not going into that story!" I yelled with an extreme amount of volume.

Ty mimed zipping his lips together as I pointed my finger at him sternly with a harsh look on my face. I turned to Lydia and told her to not ask Tyler anything about that happening; she pinky-swore that she wouldn't.

If there was one thing I knew about Lydia, it was that she would never break a pinky promise, so I left the room to take all the dogs out again. If there was a second thing I knew about Lydia, it was that she loved loopholes and that she loved to find them. I couldn't believe that I had left one so obvious for her! While I was out in the yard, Tyler didn't say a word about how I met his dad, and Lydia didn't dare ask him to, but she did certainly ask Ray to tell her every detail about the fool I made of myself that day when I first met him.

I went back into the living room with only a light puddle of laughter to hear. I gave an all-knowing stare to Raymond, and out came the roaring ocean of giggles that I expected from that story that I honestly hoped I would never have to relive. I gave in; a smile formed onto my face, and I gestured for the three of them to give me their hardest sniggering cackles, which easily enough they did.

Once they were through, we watched what was left of the final *Halloween Town*. I didn't pay too much attention to that one since it was my least favorite of the series. It was arguably late, and Lydia had to be getting back to her house. Completely unaware of my situation, Raymond asked if I'd like to spend the night there; he mentioned that it'd be quite pleasant and no trouble at all. I still wasn't all that positive of what my living arrangements were going to be, so I just nodded my head yes and told Lydia that we would see her the following day and to leave without me. I made sure to remind her not to say a word of my circumstances to her parents, at least for a while, because I still had no answers for whatever questions they might've had. I didn't really believe that they would judge me negatively; they knew I was a good kid, but I was still in an uncertain predicament, to put it lightly.

Lydia easily agreed and told me not to worry in the least bit and that indeed we'd all see each other the following day. That night, there wasn't any dinner to be had. I think it was because Lydia and I were so unexpected. So Ray offered Tyler and me any of the leftovers that were still in their fridge. Tyler said yes; I politely declined but asked if I could get something to drink. Raymond headed to the kitchen, and I followed Tyler to the dining room basically so I could watch the two of them eat and make humorous conversation, or so I thought.

I knew from the night before that Tyler had brought up marriage and engagement, but it wasn't like we were engaged then or had been in a very serious relationship for ten years at that point, but Raymond still very much so considered me part of the family, and it was nice. At the same time, it was also kind of nerve-racking—that coming from the girl who faints when she meets the parents. Well, since I was part of the family, Ray really wanted me to be there when he told Tyler that he'd heard from Tyler's mom a bit and that he'd be leaving pretty soon to see if he could find her and maybe make things okay again.

"You mean, we're gonna be leaving in the middle of the semester?" Tyler asked, not so outraged, but heavily confused.

"Not exactly. You see, Ty, you're right. You are in the middle of the semester, and junior year is a major year. You can't just leave."

"But you can?"

"I can't just give up on her, Tyler." Raymond paused and gave a heavy-hearted look into Tyler's eyes. "I gotta find her," he said more quietly.

"So what, you're just gonna keep on looking for her the rest of your life? The rest of my life?"

"No! I couldn't do that. That'd be like me giving up on you, and I hope you realize that you're more important. But, Ty, if I can find her and make things okay, then maybe we could actually be a family again."

"Dad, I get where you're coming from, but you're just gonna leave and stay gone?"

"Don't take it like that. I'll be home at Christmas—that means most, if not all, of Christmas break, spring break, and summer. And I promise I will definitely be here to see you graduate."

"And after that? Is it that we're leaving?" Tyler added emphasis on the "we're."

"Probably not," Raymond said after a heavy sigh. "I know you have a life here, son, and I would never want to be the kind of dad that makes you abandon your life. So after graduation, I'm done."

"Are you sure? I mean, I gave up waiting because I didn't want to be hopeful for something hopeless. But if you don't find this situation hopeless, I don't want to be the kind of son that makes you give up hope."

"I'm sure. But at the same time, there's always room to just see what happens."

They exchanged smiles and solid stares. In that case, words wouldn't work; there were things that words just couldn't say. Everything was understood, so it didn't need to be said; nonetheless, I sat there as if without a voice, motionless. I did not want to interrupt the volume-less conversation, so I remained patient. It did not take long for the two of them to reacknowledge my presence and bring me into their conversing.

As long as the subject was loaded with the matter of handling family affairs, I thought that perhaps then would be as good a moment as ever to bring up what had happened between my mother and me the night before. For whatever reason, I just really thought that Tyler's dad should know.

There was really no beating around the bush, and there wasn't any sort of way that Tyler could help in explaining it, so I dived right in and began with how and why she hit me. I also mentioned that my household was always a violent environment.

It was Tyler's turn to sit silently; well, it was kind of his and his dad's turns, because I was the only one speaking. Ray was paying a lot of attention, but I remember Tyler being pretty much captivated. He knew what had happened, but I suppose me telling the entire story over and in more detail captured more of him.

Once I finished, the two of them remained silent. They stayed staring at me. I began to feel awkward, so I lowered my head and aimed my eyes at my twiddling thumbs. I imagined that both of them wanted to speak out and say something, but face it, what words are really appropriate to break that sort of silence? Eventually, I spoke up.

"I appreciate it, Ray, that you didn't immediately point out my fat lip. I know that it's remarkably obvious."

"I don't think it's as obvious as you probably see it."

"I hope it's not." I smiled a bit and removed my hand from covering my whole mouth.

"You finished your entire drink, Lennie, you want some more?"

"No thanks, Tay. I'll just wait for you guys to finish."

"You know, Melenium, I know that it's not the most traditional of questions, but would you ever think about staying here?"

"Dad!" Tyler screamed.

"I'm not trying to say that she has to," Raymond started to say to Tyler then turned back toward me. "It's just that obviously, you're not going back, and I want you to know that you're welcomed here. Plus, when I leave, I'm sure company would be welcomed, right, Tyler?"

"Of course."

Shortly after that, that conversation was wrapped up. What wasn't exactly dinner continued with lighter-subject talks. For letting me stay the night, I offered to wash the dishes for Ray, but he wouldn't hear of it; instead, he told Tyler he had to wash them that night. The fact that I indirectly gave Tyler an additional chore made me laugh a bit, when I was out of his sight, of course. I told Ray that I was honored by his suggestion for me to stay there but that I wasn't quite positive, so I added in that I'd have an answer for him the next day. Then I went to the kitchen to tell Tyler that I was going to sleep and that I'd see him in the room.

I took about fifteen minutes to get ready for bed, and by then, Tyler was finishing up getting ready as well.

"You know I really do hope that you don't feel like you have to stay here."

"I know, and I don't feel a need to say yes," I said.

"Not that it wouldn't be awesome to have you living here, because I'm sure it would be," Tyler stammered.

I sat on the bed and stared at him while he rambled on for a bit. I just nodded my head and listened until, finally, I hushed him. I told him that I understood what it was that he was trying to say and said that if he was comfortable, I thought I'd like to stay with him. He seemed to have been taken aback, but he instantly told me that it would be delightful if I stayed at his house.

He smiled, and I smiled back—bigger. I felt like an idiot, but honestly, I couldn't help it. I knew Tyler's dad had the next day off, so I decided to tell him the news—hopefully, good news—the next morning when we were all up. Knowing that the next day would be glorious, I went to sleep with Tyler beside me.

Chapter 10

$\mathcal{W}$AKING UP THAT MORNING, I felt marvelous, especially excited. But everyone was still asleep. I've always known myself to wake up pretty early most mornings, so I got up and paid no mind to the time. I figured waiting to have breakfast would only be fair, so I whipped out my phone and played around as much as I could until it all started to feel frivolous. I checked the time, and it was past eleven thirty! I raised my eyebrows in astonishment, thinking that this couldn't possibly be a regular routine.

I went back to Tyler's room and shook him a bit to gently wake him. He moaned, wondering why I could possibly be bothering his sleep. I told him the time, assuming that would get him up. It didn't.

"'Kay, I'll be up in a while." He lazily groaned.

"How long is 'a while'?" I asked after pondering the thought for a few seconds.

He didn't answer, so I just left the room again. I called Lydia to see what she was doing, because even though she was never as much of a morning bird as I am, I knew she had to be up.

"What? They're still asleep?" she hollered.

"I know, and I'm out of things to do. I can't stay quiet much longer."

"Wanna come over?"

"Can I? That'd be so cool."

"Yeah. You know my parents don't mind."

"Okay, let me just get ready, and I'll be right over."

We hung up, and I got dressed real quick. When I was ready to run out the door, I went to Tyler's room to tell him I was leaving. I sat down on the bed and started to shake his leg again. He slapped me in the face with his pillow, and I let out a small shout as I fell off the bed. At the sound of my shriek, he jumped up and got out of bed. I wished that I had known that was one way to get him to wake up.

"Oh my gosh, are you okay?"

"Yeah. Don't worry, your pillow's not that hard," I joked.

"Sorry. I guess it was some sort of instinct."

"It's fine," I said, getting back up. "I'm going over to hang out with Lydia. I guess I'll be back later, 'kay? Unless you wanna get ready real fast and come?"

"Uhh, what are you guys gonna do?" he said, rubbing his eyes.

"We'll probably go shopping since I don't have any clothes anymore."

"Oh, right. I think I'll hang back. I mean, I have more time with you than she does now, so…" He shrugged and laid his head back down. I went to kiss him, smiled, and headed for the door. "Oh, wait. When my dad gets up, do you want me to tell him, or do you want to tell him?"

"Uhh, you can tell him if you want to. I don't want it to seem like I'm imposing or anything."

"You know you're not. He offered. But I'll tell him, I don't want you fainting again."

"Ha ha, very funny." I rolled my eyes and left.

Francine let Lydia use the car that day, so we left within no more than ten minutes. She was so excited because this was the first time that we got to leave the house alone with the car. In all honesty, I think it's just that Francine didn't feel like taking us anywhere, and you'd be ridiculous if you thought that Richard would. He didn't really do shopping. He got all his clothes as gifts. He told everyone that if they ever wanted to get him anything, it had to be clothes. Luckily, almost always did his friends and family get him something he liked. If not, Francine returned it and got the money, after which he then made the exception to shop…online.

Anywho, we left right for the mall and went to a store that had just been added to see if it was going to be another go-to place of ours. To our luck, it definitely was! It sold not only clothes that were in season but also some clothes out of season. Obviously, the in-season stuff was in front and was more in stock. The only reason I bring it up is because I am one of those irrational girls that wear sweaters or hoodies with short shorts, and that store totally let me be that insane girl.

After that one store, we went to the food court because that was just what we always did once we finished with the first store. We went to six other stores after that. We really should've only gone to three more, maybe four, but Lydia likes to window-shop. She has a shopping problem. You could probably guess that we spent quite a while at the mall.

Once we were leaving, since it was already kind of late and we wanted to sort through clothes, Lydia asked me to stay over for dinner. Naturally, I agreed and said yes. I called Tyler up to let him know that there was a chance I'd either be home late or end up staying the night because, well, it was Lydia. I knew the sound of his smiles; he smiled and simply said, "Okay, I love you." He didn't mind at all, and I figured part, if not all, of the reason was because he wanted some one-on-one time with his dad. It definitely was going to be something foreign for Tyler to be away from Raymond, not to mention for that long.

I hung up the phone and let Lydia know that there was no problem with our plans. When we got to her house, the two of us got all our new clothes down and went straight into her room to sort them out. Dinner was already almost finished, so I suggested that we sort out what I would be taking with me first. About twenty, maybe twenty-five minutes had passed, then Francine was calling for Lydia and me to get to the table, that we had already been served.

We stood up from the bed and made our way to the table. I can remember that night we were having macaroni and cheese mixed in with ground beef and sour cream. I was somewhat hesitant to try it for the first time, mainly because I had never—out of all my lifetimes—tried sour cream before. To me, it didn't sound too good. But curiosity struck, and I dived right in. It turned out that I had been truly missing out because I ended up absolutely loving it! I loved it so much I had seconds and I really wanted to ask if I could have thirds.

Throughout dinner, there was not a moment of silence, from any of us really. As soon as Richard was done eating, he went to put his dishes in the dishwasher and checked how much food they still had left.

"We still have a good amount of macaronis, Melenium. Do you wanna take any home with you so Tyler can have some?" Richard asked.

"What?" I questioned, real confused.

"Oh, right, Melenium, I was gonna offer you some to take home tonight, unless you're staying the night, of course." Francine stared, waiting for my response.

I looked puzzlingly at Lydia. Her head was down with her eyes focused on her plate. She didn't appear shocked or even a little taken aback. I couldn't believe she told her parents without even consulting me.

"Melenium?"

"I'm sorry, I just didn't know Liv had told you guys about me moving in with Tyler and his dad," I said, shaking my head back into focus.

"Oh yeah. When she mentioned how bad things got with your mom, we knew you obviously couldn't go back for your clothes, so don't bother about paying us back or anything."

"Yeah, Melenium, we're just sorry we didn't take you in before this all happened," Richard announced from the kitchen.

"It's all fine," I said. "But if it's all right, I think I'd like to go home now."

Lydia groaned out her mouth and nodded as she just finished up her plate. She got up and said she'd get her shoes on and we could go. Richard brought me the macaronis and said he was glad that I liked them so much. I just smiled and put my head down. I thanked them both, said good night, and went to wait near the door. Lydia came with a bag with my new clothes inside, and we got into the car.

"So you had fun today?"

I looked at her with no reply then rested my head on the window.

"Left you pretty tired, I guess."

The entire drive there, I was silent, and she was silent. She hadn't bothered to turn up the volume on the radio, so I basically listened to static the whole way home. She pulled up into the driveway and tapped on my shoulder. I looked at her hand and then up at her.

"You slept this whole time, Mel. I think you need to go to bed. I'll ask Ty to help me get down this stuff."

"I wasn't asleep, Lydia," I said quietly.

"What do you mean? You didn't say a word on the way here. Are you just real tired?"

"No, what I am is pissed off!"

"What're you talking about? Why?"

"Because, Liv, you told your parents! Honestly?"

"Yeah, and?"

"And that's mine and Tyler's freakin' business. You can't just carelessly tell people!"

"Mel, it was just my parents. It's not like they're gonna judge you for it or tell anybody."

"You should've been the one not telling anybody, Lydia!" I shouted. "I mean, you told them I moved in with Tyler, why I moved in with Tyler, and why I needed these new damn clothes!"

"I didn't think you'd make this big of a deal out of it."

"It doesn't really matter how big of a deal you thought I'd make out of it. The point is, it wasn't your business, therefore, not your business to tell."

"All right, fine. I admit it wasn't my business, but it's not like I did anything that's actually wrong."

"What? You honestly believe there's no blame for you to take here? Why don't you just tell them about all my lives? And while you're at it, tell them about all of yours too. Let's start from our first life. You know, how we were sisters and how you liked to copy every single thing that I did."

"That's not cool."

"No, I guess it's not, but neither was you spreading my business. Not asking me if it was okay and not even telling me they knew— that's what's not cool. Do you know how awkward that was?"

Lydia stared at me like she was angry but also like she was sorry. I grabbed my bag, opened my door, and rolled my eyes, knowing she didn't get the point I was making. Halfway to the door, I turned back around to her car. I opened the passenger door back up and angrily told her I still wanted my macaronis.

I stomped inside and, with frustration in my voice, told Tyler and Raymond hello. I put my bowl on the dining room table and treaded my clothes to mine and Tyler's room.

There was no doubt that something was upsetting me; the debate between who was going to find out what that something was, was being held as I got ready for bed and went back into the living room. I could see from my peripheral vision that once I sat down, Tyler and his dad were exchanging looks. Finally, Raymond asked me what it was that I brought home. It wasn't exactly the question I expected, but I mumbled that it was leftovers that Richard sent. Raymond told Tyler to go put it away. So he left the room, and I sat there with my arms crossed with Ray.

"So what's wrong, pretty girl?"

Uncrossing my arms, sitting straight up, and turning toward him, I yelled, "Don't you just hate it when you trust people with your business and then they go around telling the world? I mean, she thought I was being dramatic—can you believe that? I think my feelings toward this are completely valid. I mean, it wasn't her business at all!"

"I'm guessing you had a fight with Lydia, right? She told someone what? About you having to leave home?"

"Yes!" I shouted then realized I should've calmed down. "She told her parents that I lived here and why and why I needed the new clothes."

"And you just feel like she disrespected your privacy, right? Because you told her, trusting that she wouldn't say a word."

"Exactly. The worst part is, she's not even sorry. She doesn't think she did anything wrong."

"Trust me, Mel, she's sorry. It's just that she doesn't know why, but she is sorry she hurt you."

"I wish I could believe you, but I think I need to hear all that from her. Thanks though."

Raymond nodded and told me that he knew he could do a better job at making me feel better than Tyler and that was why he had to tell Tyler to leave. We both laughed and returned to watching TV.

Tyler came back into the living room, and we all stayed watching the television, and I started to fall asleep. I think I ended up passing out for a moment, but I woke up and pretended to still be asleep so I could hear everything. There wasn't much to hear, being that Ray said he was "gonna hit the sack" and told Tyler he should do the same. Tyler stood up and stretched, took a deep breath, and started for his room. Before he could make more than three steps, Ray asked him what exactly he thought he was doing. Tyler looked at him, confused.

"You're not thinking of letting her sleep on the couch, are you?"

"No! Of course not." I heard Tyler say. I could tell he wasn't about to forget me. "I'm just gonna make her spot on the bed."

"You better be," Raymond said as he walked to his room.

It was maybe two minutes later that I completely shut my eyes and felt Tyler pick me up. I had to try pretty hard to keep myself from smiling. It was also difficult to keep my body limp as he went to lay me down. After doing so, he covered me with the blanket and walked over to his side of the bed. He kissed my head, but then he also whispered in my ear.

"I know you're faking it."

I released all the laughter I had been holding in, and once I finished, I asked him why he still carried me to bed.

"Well, because everyone loves it when somebody covers them or carries them to bed. It helps to remind us of when we were little kids, which is always nice because we all miss being kids. And I know you've gotten to have eighty-two childhoods, but I also know that that means you've gotten eighty-two lifetimes to miss your childhoods. If I can give a bit of that back to you for even just one night, I'd be honored." He was blushing somewhat at that point. "Plus, I also feel like you'd do the same for me." He smiled and shrugged.

I stared at him as he stared at the ceiling then would catch a glance of me then would stare back at the ceiling. Finally, he shifted himself from his back over to his side so he could stare back at me. It was almost as if we were having a staring contest. When the silence was becoming too loud for me, I moved my head forward and kissed him gently on the lips for perhaps five seconds. I pulled away, and I smiled and bit my bottom lip to savor the taste of him. And I swear to you, he tasted like everything I love: calming sunsets, roaring waterfalls, and the view of lightning bolts.

"What was that for?" he asked.

My heart started to beat so fast that it almost hurt within my vibrating bones. My lungs were emptying out faster than they were filling up. It was almost unreal to me. It felt like I had a plethora of things I wanted to say, but I was basically unable to speak. With my heart racing so fast, somehow my mouth and my breaths came together to utter the three most important words in the English language.

"I love you," I said as if it were my first time saying it ever.

Tyler grabbed my hip and pulled all of me closer to him so that every part of ourselves was touching with no space in between, seemingly even our souls. And he kissed me, not so gently. He took hold of my chin and brought my lips to his. I remember that kiss lasted longer. We breathed heavily, and that was how I can recall it not being so gentle. It was filled with far too much passion to be gentle.

My hand was placed over his chest, and I felt his warmth turn into heat. It was such a quick change in temperature it was like throwing something toward the sun at light speed. His heartbeat, like my own, rose as if it was what was being thrown. We remained gazing into each other's eyes for a few moments, but then...

"I love you too," he said, "so much." And I had the honor of feeling how much he meant it.

He kissed me again. The intensity of that night escalated from bad to spectacular, and honestly, I don't even know how. All I know is that, that night was the first time in a long time I actually felt like I belonged, like I was safe.

Chapter 11

BACK TO SCHOOL WE WENT. Tyler driving me wasn't weird, but it sure felt weird knowing that it was just going to be us two, and I didn't know for exactly how long. I felt empty, like something was missing from me. I just so happened to know that, that something was a someone and that someone was Legend, Lydia Legend. I passed by our regular spot; normally, there she was. But instead of going to her, I coldly passed her by without even thinking of looking back. Tyler and I went to a different part of the school altogether.

I put my stuff down, and Tyler did the same; but I sat down, and he stayed standing. He told me that he was going to talk to Lydia for a bit. I swallowed hard and nodded him the okay. I told him that I wouldn't dare try to make him give up a friendship over feelings that I knew would fade. I was going to forgive Lydia. I knew I couldn't live without her. Partially, it was because I never had to before.

I almost told him that I wanted to go with him. I guess the reason I didn't was because I wasn't ready to be the same girl I always had been: the girl who just got over everything. I was telling myself that my feelings weren't valid, that I wasn't allowed to be sad, angry, or hurt all the time, so I always made myself get over it, whatever "it" was. I wanted to stay angry forever, but at the same time, all I wanted was my best friend. I wanted to hug her tightly and admit that I was sorry for getting so mad about something I could forget. Perhaps it was just my pride. It was almost like, if she wasn't willing to be the one who admitted her apologies and hug me tightly, then it was only right for me to stay angry.

Only minutes went by before Tyler came back, and as soon as he did, the bell to go to our first period rang. I took a big breath before standing up and gathering all my stuff. On our way to class, Tyler asked me how exactly I saw this working. I told him that all three of us just had to find out. I didn't have to feel bad though, because it's not like I told Lydia that she couldn't talk to Tyler or that he couldn't talk to her. I knew that I'd prefer that he talk to her more because I knew I could handle not having anyone to talk to. After all, Lydia was my little sister; I still wanted her to feel more secure.

The morning had passed, and I went to the math section of the school. I told Tyler that he should hang out with Lydia for at least the first half of lunch, and I told him that they could hang out at our usual spot. While I was walking to the math section, I put in my ear-buds, but after I put them in, I went awhile without actually putting music on. Just before I was about to turn my music on, I heard some laughs that I thought I could've lived without.

I looked up, and I saw all the Fans. With all the havoc that had been going on those past few days, I completely sidelined my whole situation with them. In all honesty, I almost forgot they existed. Cara looked at me and rolled her eyes. I was surprised she didn't tell me anything, but I supposed it wasn't really out of the ordinary. The only real contact we had was her screwing me over or me doing the same to her, and with that being said, that never really called for the exchanging of words. When something bad happened, we just always knew it had something to do with the other.

I took my sight off her and stared blankly into my lap as I mind-lessly waited for Tyler to find me. When he came, he tapped me on my knee and said he was sorry if he took long. I responded and told him that I didn't really mind. Sometimes I wasn't sure if I meant it, because being left alone with my own thoughts was sort of a scary idea.

The afternoon was just as the morning was; I talked only to Tyler, Lydia talked only to Tyler, and Tyler was stuck in between two girls who just didn't feel like swallowing their extreme amounts of pride. At the end of the day, Tyler walked Lydia to her car then came to his Jeep, which I was already inside of so we could both go home.

Come Wednesday, being without Lydia still hadn't become any sort of routine. I'd say it got worse because that sudden void we created still wanted to be filled by what it didn't have to be missing in the first place. I thought about making my apology, but still, my pride stood tall. I spoke to Tyler and even Ray about how being without my other half did have quite an unpleasant feeling. They both said that she and I were probably being driven crazy but that we both also were too stubborn to give up our stance.

The next day, I got out of school early. That whole week, our school was volunteered to help out at the animal shelter and relieve some of the full-time workers. Thursday was the day that Tyler, Lydia, and I signed up for. What a shocker, it was also the day the Fans signed up for. Since I felt like thinking things over, I volunteered to take some of the dogs walking while Tyler and Lydia helped with the grooming.

I knew this one trail that started at the school, led through the dog park, then ended back at the shelter. Tyler let me take his Jeep to get to the school. I knew I'd have to walk back, but at least by then, I wouldn't be walking five dogs. Since Tyler told me that they were taking advantage of the day and grooming Gadget and Nestle, I decided I'd take Neptune on a real nice walk with the other dogs.

When the dog park was within sight, I let the dogs off their leashes. They all ran straight to the park. Neptune stayed more toward me, and the other dogs stayed mostly together, so it was really easy for me to keep track of all of them. But of course, something had to happen. I guess I really should have seen that coming. When I ran over really quick to clean up after one of the dogs, I turned around to see Neptune gone! I checked to see that all the other dogs were still fine together. Being that the walk back to the shelter wasn't going to be any longer than twenty, maybe thirty minutes, I took the time to look for Neptune while still letting the other dogs play. I found her after about ten minutes, but then another shocker—I couldn't seem to find the other dogs. I spent a solid forty to forty-five minutes looking in the park. I finally came to the conclusion that I was in full-on panic mode and needed other people's help to find these four other dogs.

On my power walk back to the shelter with Neptune, Neptune kept pulling me and barking. Finally, I let her lead me to whatever spot I figured she wanted to pee in. Guess what, turns out she was my angel because she led me to three of the four dogs I lost in our walk to the shelter. And just before we walked into the shelter, there was Cara with the fourth dog I was desperate for.

"She had tons of fun on her walk. It's a good thing I was there at the park though. Otherwise, she would've had to walk alone or, worse, with you."

I glared at Cara heavily. I had no intentions of speaking to her, only of taking the dogs back to their kennels, because it was already way past my planned volunteer time. I grabbed for the leash in Cara's hand, but she quickly pulled it away. I gave her an annoyed look then. And she was quick to respond.

"I didn't hear you say *please*."

"May I please have the leash so I can walk Bruce back to his kennel?"

"That didn't sound very nice, but since I know how to be respectful, you can have it."

By instinct, I said "Thank you." I didn't care enough to take it back, so I just kept walking. I think I heard her say, "Now you're getting the hang of it." I took the dogs to their kennels, made sure they had enough food and water, then started to leave. Only the boss was there getting everything ready to close up. That made me figure that it was a good idea to call Tyler and see where he was. He picked up quickly and instantly asked where I was and where I had been. I told him it was a long story and that I'd tell him everything when we met up. He was still at the school waiting for me. Lydia kept him company apparently during my overtime. She had just left home when I called. Of course, he offered to come get me so we could get home faster, but I told him that I had found some more frustration that I needed to walk off and that he could just meet me halfway at the park. We hung up, and I tried to think about things that didn't have to do with Lydia or Cara. Sadly, when I got outside, Cara came from behind me with a bucket of ice water and dumped it on my head!

"What the heck is your problem!" I screamed.

"I don't know what you're talking about," Cara said, slightly laughing.

"Ever since the day you learned my name, you've been at my throat."

"That's because ever since I learned your name, it's like you've been at mine."

"How do you figure?"

"I know you're the one who planned what happened at the Halloween carnival."

"That was me getting back at you for what happened at the football game, not to mention all those times you purposefully drove through that puddle to drench me on my way to school."

"Fair enough, but still, you are not going to steal that top spot from me." She sounded very serious.

"I'm not trying to! All I'm doing is, going to school and putting my best efforts into my work."

"Then why is it only now that you do all these extra credit events?"

"Because," I paused, "because now I actually have people to do these things with and friends that tell me I should try in school!"

"Whatever. Either way, you're not taking my spot."

"I'm not trying to compete with you, Cara, and if the stunts that you pull are your way of trying to coerce me to give up in school and not give a damn, then it's not gonna work. You can make my life suck a little or a lot more than it has to, but whoever gets number one will get number one because they earned it. It might not even be either one of us. Think about it, Cara, who's number three?"

I walked away, still completely soaked. I wasn't really thinking anything. I wasn't thinking if Cara's pranks would get worse, more constant or if they would stop. I wasn't thinking about Lydia or if she felt sorry at all. I wasn't even thinking if Tyler needed me to hurry so we could finally just get home.

I was basically mindless. I was cold and dripping wet. I'm sure anyone who saw me wondered why on earth I was walking anywhere as I was. All I knew was that after that long day, I was ready to start a new one. And I was so glad that it would be Friday!

"Before you ask, don't, because I'm pretty positive you already know the answer," I said to Tyler as I climbed into his Jeep.

"Cara dumped water on you?"

"No, it rained," I said sarcastically. "Of course, she dumped water on me—ice-cold water, to top it all off!"

"Do you want my jacket? You know, just so you can warm up."

I shook my head and told him that I just really wanted to go home, so he put the car in drive, turned the radio up, and we headed to the house. I was still pretty much mindless, and I still really didn't feel like talking, not even to Tyler. I was glad that he understood. I always appreciated that with the relationship we had, we didn't have to fill the air with conversation. When we got home, I took a shower and just went to sleep. I was feeling too fed up with everything. In the meanwhile, Tyler ate, spent time with his dad, took a shower, and got ready for bed. We didn't have our usual "before bed" talk, so it did take me a long time to fall asleep. But I was still asleep before Tyler got to bed. It took him longer to fall asleep that night too.

The next morning, I woke up extremely early, as in four in the morning! I didn't want to wake Tyler up for my sake alone, so I tried to fall back asleep. The fact that, that was not going to happen quickly made itself clear. I stayed, staring out the window, creating imaginary situations in my head. But after about half an hour, I started remembering things, a lot of things from other lifetimes. There are some times that those are the memories that aren't so good. Thankfully, not too long after, Tyler started to wake up on his own. It was then that we had our "before bed" talk.

"You feeling better?"

"Now that you're awake? Yeah, I guess."

"I'm guessing you can't sleep."

"Nope. Not at all. I miss Lydia."

"Wow! It took you way too long to admit that," Tyler said.

"I know. Shut up."

"Don't even worry. She misses you too."

"Really?"

"Oh yeah. She admitted it Monday."

"Then why hasn't she said anything? Why didn't you say anything?"

"I wasn't supposed to. Lydia strictly told me, no spilling any secrets. Even though I'm pretty sure it was no secret. As far as why, she hasn't said anything herself, I don't know. Pride?"

"Probably. I mean, that's my reason."

"So does all this end today?"

"I think so," I said, still with a groggy voice. "Is it cool if I hang back from school today?"

"Yeah, it's Friday, and we have no tests. I'll pick up any of the important work if we get any though."

"Okay." I turned myself over and stared at the ceiling. I was silent again, but this time, in a special way. It wasn't in one of those loud silences or one of those comforting silences; it was one of those dire silences. The kind that even feels empty like there must be someone dying to say something that hasn't been said. "Tyler, is it okay to keep secrets?"

"Umm, I think that there are always variables that need to be filled in before you can really decide. Sometimes it's okay, but you need to understand that covering and omitting the truth can't continue forever. Eventually, things just can't be secret anymore."

I breathed for a while. I thought his words over, whether what he said was supposed to be only an answer or if it was all meant to be advice.

"Do you think you'd be upset if I told Lydia about your mom or about this situation with your dad? Like, do you appreciate that I didn't tell her, or did you expect me to keep it between us in the first place?"

"I don't know. I think that, yeah, I probably would've gotten upset with you. If you didn't consult me at all, I'd have every right to I think. And I did trust and expect you to not let Lydia know, but I do still appreciate that you knew how to handle what was my business." He kissed my cheek, and I lightly smiled. "For what it's worth, I think the way you felt in this situation was completely valid and you weren't overreacting." Again I smiled. "And you know what, I'll let Lydia know everything going on with me, 'kay? This way, you don't have to feel like there's division between you two. That's part of what's been bothering you, isn't it?"

I nodded, still not wanting to use my voice. He just said he knew it. But did he? I dug my face into his chest and tried to calm myself down. It helped when the sun started to come up. I looked at the time and realized that Tyler was going to be late. All he said was that it was okay, because it wasn't like he'd be missing the whole day. I was having a small anxiety attack, and I didn't really want Tyler to know, so I told him he had to hurry and get up.

He put up a small fuss, but I got him to give in, thankfully. I threw the blanket over me; for some unknown reason, I always did that when I had anxiety attacks. I found that strange, because you'd think that if I was hyperventilating, I would want as much access to air as possible. It was instinctive. It always helped.

I stayed in bed wondering if I actually wanted to apologize. I didn't feel like I had anything to apologize for; perhaps I did overreact. After hours of thought, I concluded that I had to talk to Lydia to receive the apology I felt I deserved. And then I'd give her the apology she deserved. We both had to understand what it was that was wrong, then all would be fine, because like I mentioned, I didn't want to be the girl who just always caved in.

School was out, and I called Tyler about three times. He hadn't answered at all, so I left a voice mail and sent him a text message. I was about to start worrying, but he quickly replied back to my text. He said that he was talking with Lydia and that he'd be home soon. It was five o'clock when Tyler texted me again and said that he was on his way. Shortly after, I heard my phone ring again. I assumed it was Tyler, but to my surprise, it was Lydia. All she said was that she would be over that night.

Chapter 12

I RAISED MY EYEBROWS IN SHOCK and stared at my phone for a few more seconds. It rang again. Tyler was asking if I wanted him to pick up anything.

Within twenty minutes (perhaps even less than that), I heard him drive up and come inside. I walked to the door as calmly as I could, half expecting Lydia to be with him. When I saw him alone, I asked if he talked to Lydia or knew that she was coming over. He said that she barely said a word that day, that she was staying really quiet and didn't say anything about coming over. With that in mind, I texted her back and told her that it was okay and that I'd stay up. She didn't reply.

Ray came home maybe an hour after Tyler had and the three of us all helped with making dinner that night. I didn't really feel like eating, but I hadn't eaten all that day, and I knew it was only best. I served myself a good amount and just ate slowly. I think all of us were tired that night because there weren't many laughs and only limited conversation.

By the time dinner was over, Tyler and Ray went to watch TV, and I offered to wash the dishes. And once I was done, I went to mine and Tyler's room to read a bit. I was never the best reader (I stuttered a lot), but I liked it. It helped in letting my imagination run wild. I read to myself very quietly; that way, if the doorbell rang or if there was a knock at the door, I'd have not the slightest chance of missing it, and I kept checking my phone. I trusted that Lydia was coming. I didn't doubt her, so I didn't call her.

I finished four chapters, and Tyler had already lay down, so I decided that I'd go to bed.

"Finally," Tyler whispered loudly.

"You know, you could've just gone to sleep without me."

"That's nearly impossible, and you know it."

I smirked and made myself comfortable. "She didn't come," I said.

"You sad? Do you wanna call her?"

"Maybe in the morning. For now, let's just talk."

"Okay. Well, guess what."

"What's that?" I asked.

"I told Lydia pretty much my whole situation."

"Really? How did that go?"

"Yeah. Uh, it went well. She promised not to tell anyone."

"Good." I laughed a bit.

"I told her that you knew as well and that, that was part of what made you feel bad. Keeping it from her, I mean."

"And what did she say?"

"She just nodded her head, said that it made sense and that it helped to explain why it bothered you so much when she told her parents about me and you."

"Maybe that's why she wanted to come over?"

"Maybe. Oh, she doesn't know how long this has been going on. If she asks, you don't have to lie, but if she doesn't, try not to bring it up, okay? I just don't want her feeling weird about my dad."

"I know. I won't. Let's just get some sleep. It's kinda late."

"Sounds good." He kissed me. "See you in the morning, beautiful."

He turned over and closed his eyes. He fell asleep from what was probably a long day. It's never easy trusting people, and it's even more difficult when you decide to trust someone new all at once. Tyler didn't know Lydia like I did. All he knew was that he should've and that she knew him.

I, however, couldn't sleep. I could only stay up. For whatever reason, I couldn't shake the feeling that a promise had just been broken. Lydia never broke promises, especially the ones she made to me, so why wasn't she here? I started to get sleepy, and my eyes started to shut despite my wanting to stay awake. Suddenly, the most cliché thing started: I heard pebbles tapping my window! How lovely was that?

I opened my window, and there Lydia stood. I smiled, but only inside; my pride still wanted to be at least slightly angry. She waved her hand, motioning me to join her outside, so I did. She brought nice hot coffee. When I got close enough, Lydia stretched out her arm and handed me my cup. We sat and sipped our coffee in silence until, finally, her voice joined in with the soothing constant sound of the night's breeze.

"You know I love you, right? And that I'd never intentionally hurt you in any way, especially emotionally, right?"

I looked her in a way and nodded my head and let my voice join in the sound of the wind as well.

"Yeah. I know that, Liv. Of course, I do! And you know that I love you possibly even more than that, right?"

"Yes!" She smiled brightly. "So I just wanted to tell you in the best way that I could that I'm just so completely sorry." She threw her arms around me, and we hugged. I even felt her tears on my shoulder, along with mine rolling down my face. "I know that it was dumb of me to not even think that you'd be uncomfortable with people knowing. And I know that you don't really care, but it's the principle."

"Liv, it's fine. I forgive you." We let go. "I'm sorry too, because I know that I did overreact and that was dumb of me too. Honestly, this past week, I've missed you so much!"

"Really? I mean, without Tyler, I don't think I would've made it. It felt so empty not having you, and I just felt so guilty!"

"I know what you mean. I felt guilty just for being mad," I admitted.

"Well, this is our first fight in Lord knows how long. I'm sure we saved up some guilt somehow."

"This is true." I laughed. "So tell me, why did you come so late?"

"I don't know. I had a whole lot to say, but I guess I just really didn't know how to say any of it. Finally, I just said, 'Screw it, I'm going.' Then, I realized the time. That's when I decided to bring the coffee with me. Somehow I knew you'd still be up, even if just barely."

"So I'm sure you heard about what happened with Cara."

"Yeah. Ty told me. He said that's why it was even more important for us to make up. Because we couldn't get her back if it wasn't the three of us."

"He's right. It probably would've been something real stupid."

The both of us laughed. I think the two of us were extremely ready to forget about our fight and being mad at each other when really we just wanted to make up almost the entire time.

Lydia stood up and said that she had to get home but that she would be back early in the morning so we could finish talking. After a few days, we did indeed have a lot to talk about. I finished my coffee, but even with all that caffeine, I slept soundly knowing that she and I were on good terms again.

That morning, Lydia got to the house somewhere between six and seven o'clock. She called me, and we went to the park because she knew that Ray and Tyler weren't exactly early risers. The two of us just took our turns speaking and listening as the bikers and joggers passed us by. We were talking as if nothing ever happened; I think it was because we decided silently that it was a stupid and it really didn't need to be discussed any longer. We went back to mine and Tyler's house. It wasn't any shocker that Tyler was still asleep. So we took Neptune and Gadget for a small walk up and down a few blocks. That only took a solid hour. By the time it was a bit past ten, Lydia and I decided to wake Tyler up and started jumping on the bed.

"All right, all right. I'm awake!" he shouted.

"Finally. We've been trying to wake you up for, like, forty minutes."

"You're lying," Tyler said, rubbing his eyes.

"No, seriously," I said. "I even tried motor-boating you three times!"

"What?"

"It's true, Ty. I even tried once," Lydia said.

"Now I know you're lying."

"Think about it, Tay, we couldn't just yell. We didn't wanna wake your dad up."

"For my sanity, I'm just gonna tell myself you guys didn't."

"Okay, whatever makes you happy." I shrugged.

"But we totally did!" Lydia said.

We dropped the subject, stopped teasing, and got Tyler to get ready so we could go hang out. We went to our outlet mall first. None of us liked many of the stores there, but every once in a while, we would go in and out of shops to mess around and try on hats and sunglasses, because one good thing about all the stores was that they were all affordable.

Once we finished, we went to an ice-cream shop that was just as good as Dairy Queen, maybe even better because, like all the stores, it was cheap. After we were done with our ice cream, we went to our actual, more expensive mall. And since we already had ice cream, the first thing we did was eat. The three of us agreed on Chinese food. We then spent about three hours browsing through things we couldn't quite buy. Finally, our day was just about ready to end, so we went to Lydia's house to talk about our new plan on how to get back at Cara. Since Lydia and I went to sleep late and woke up early and Tyler woke up early for Tyler, we called it quits after only an hour. We didn't have any ideas, well, not any good ideas, so it made sense to pick up our "meeting" on another day.

Come Monday, we had the most random snow day! With nothing to do, I called Lydia to come over. Surprisingly enough, by the time she came, Tyler was actually awake and had gotten up! He was probably just used to getting up early on weekdays. With Lydia there, we all made our way to the dining room, and I made breakfast. Yup, I really know how to make cereal. At least after that, I whipped up the three of us some hot chocolate. Finally, Lydia decided that she had something for us to do that day—well, something for her to do and for us to tag along: buy her makeup.

It might not have been ideal, but Tyler and I figured it was better than just watching TV and movies when the TV signal gave out. So we got into Lydia's car, made Tyler drive, and went to a special makeup store called UR UR Beauty. Lydia almost never went there, but Christmas was close enough, and she wanted to figure out some things to ask for.

An hour passed, and Lydia found colors she could "definitely pull off" but wanted to ask an employee for an opinion on a certain eye shadow. She found someone who was willing to do her makeup and for free, since it was a slow day. She told Tyler and me it'd take about forty-five minutes. The both of us sighed but told her to go ahead. She then got pretty excited.

I turned to see if looking around could keep me occupied, and I was shocked to find Harold working at the store. I forgot he worked there, but I knew conversation could keep me busy and he'd have time on such a slow day.

"Hey, Harold."

"Hi, Melenium. Crazy to see you here."

"Yeah, I know. I'm mainly here for Liv. Oh, and this is my boy-friend, Tyler."

"What's up, man? I'm Harold."

"Nice to meet you," Tyler said.

"So how's work today?" I asked.

"I mean, I needed a job, and since they only had girls, the man-ager wanted to hire a guy. I'm that guy, so it's pretty nice every day."

"Cool, cool. Is it easy?"

"It's not that bad," Harold responded.

"Maybe I could get a job here. Are you guys hiring?" Tyler asked.

"Uhh, I don't think we're hiring until spring. There are a lot of employees who like to take off for the summer and a lot of people who only wanna work over the summer."

"That'd be cool. I was mainly thinking seasonal anyway. And if I like it, I could probably work senior year too since I won't have all seven classes."

"Well, I'll definitely put in a good word for you, man."

Tyler smiled and then turned to me and smiled even bigger. I had no idea he wanted a job, but I figured the extra money would be nice, and having something to fill up his time while Lydia and I were still in school all made sense. After about twenty minutes, Harold told us to go with him to hang out in the back. Lydia took over an hour, but time seemed to fly by. When she finished, Lydia found us, and we all told her that her makeup looked great. That was all that she needed to hear before she was extremely tempted to buy everything she wanted to ask for, for Christmas.

It was no wonder Lydia only went to that shop occasionally; it was massively expensive! But I suppose it was worth it because, even though I didn't know much about makeup, I thought it looked the highest quality than any makeup I'd ever seen, in any life of mine. Lydia liked it so much that she decided to sleep with it on so everyone in school could see it. She got a lot of compliments the next day being that it stayed the exact same overnight.

She was upset when she had to take it off, but Lydia just knew that she'd be getting some more of that makeup soon enough. Because of the snow day, the week was short, and it really went by fast. Sadly, we still hadn't come up with a plan to get Cara back for stealing the dogs from me. At least not until late Saturday morning.

Without even enough patience to call, Lydia sped her car to mine and Tyler's house and started banging on the front door. I ran to go see what could've possibly made her so excited. As soon as I opened the door, she ran in and called Tyler to come into the living room. She told me that she had an idea—in her exact words, a "brilliant idea."

Tyler stayed in bed, of course; it was only eleven. So Lydia yelled for him again. Once he finally decided to yell back, he told her that we had to go into his room. Lydia made her way to his room, but it was only to pull him out of bed, not to let him know her plan.

I stayed in the living room patiently, while Lydia tried to get Tyler up. It took about fifteen minutes, but finally, the two of them came to the living room. With no hesitation, Tyler went to lie on the available couch. Surprisingly enough, Lydia didn't smack him. He was awake and out of bed; I guess, since she was so excited, that was good enough.

She started by telling us how she thought of her idea and how she couldn't believe how she hadn't thought of it sooner or that we— me and Tyler—hadn't thought of it at all. Then she started to rant about how she knew she had to tell us right away. Finally, Tyler told her to just get on and tell us the plan.

"All right, all right. Have some patience," she said. "So remember how we went to UR UR BEAUTY the other day?"

"Yeah, and?"

"Well, the girl that was doing my makeup told me that the makeup she used was only bought by a few people around here, since it was so expensive. And she said that they only get shipments of it in every few months because it's not exactly flying off the shelves but that it's always just enough so they never order more, like ever."

"Okay, but still. I don't get where you're going with this."

"Well, I noticed that all week Cara was wearing that specific makeup, and then I thought about it and she only wears that makeup, no other kind, and that's the only store that sells it. So we can ask Harold to save the next shipment for us. This way, she won't have her precious makeup."

"Wait. We said no school pranks. Doesn't this plan kinda cut into that rule?" I asked.

"Not really. I mean, it's not like we're humiliating her or anything."

"Nor are we trying to. I mean, you saw how she didn't wear makeup the day we volunteered at the shelter. Without makeup, she's still gorgeous," Lydia said.

"I guess that's true. Okay, I'm in."

"Me too," Tyler said.

"Cool, then it's settled. Only thing is, the makeup comes in an amount that's supposed to last pretty long, and since she has money, I'm sure she has enough to last the rest of the school year. Heck, maybe even the summer."

"I mean, that's fine with me. It means we'll get her back and we won't have to focus on plans for a while."

"Sweet. So her first day of junior year will be less than perfect."

"About how long till we give it back?" I asked.

"I don't know, about a week," Tyler responded.

"That seems good to me."

"Then like Lydia said, it's settled."

We all seemed content with that whole deal out of the way. Tyler tried going to lie down in the bed again, but after Lydia woke him up, he just couldn't do it. I made us all coffee, and that at least helped him wake up fully.

Thanksgiving break and Christmas break passed quickly and quietly. I wasn't sure if Cara thought about what I had said and decided to stop focusing on making my grades drop. Maybe she had for a while; maybe she was just busy coming up with ways to really get at me, or perhaps she was finding out who ranked third in our class and had to coerce him or her into not even attempting to rank number one. Either way, I heard nothing from her or her applaud squad.

Summer started approaching faster and faster when our first and second spring break were over. Thankfully, my GPA stayed the same. One day I checked in the office, and Cara's GPA did not stay the same; it had risen. She wasn't second anymore. We were dead on tied for first.

Finals came around, and I was lucky enough to not be so nervous. I had a bad habit though: I never studied. It just wasn't in me to go back and find the things that, at some point, I already knew. I figured that when test time came around, it would come to me. Plus, more than half the time, our tests were multiple choice, so I could get lucky, and in math, we typically received partial credit.

I did help Tyler and Lydia study though. That probably helped me out a lot more than I'd ever admit. I'd like to think that almost always, things just sort of clicked for me.

After finals, I realized that I had another somewhat bad habit in me. I never went back to check my work. I never reread questions or redid problems in math. Sometimes I was the first kid in class to finish a test, but I was almost never willing to be the first kid to turn anything in. Sometimes I even made myself last, just so at the end of it all I could avoid teachers telling me to go back and check my answers. I thought that what I did the first time had to have been the best, so with all the time I had left, I sat there and pretended to check my work!

I'll admit it, I was damn prideful. And that pride got me in trouble. On the last day of my sophomore year, my final test scores dropped me from valedictorian to salutatorian.

I know that I didn't really want to compete with Cara grade-wise, but I was still upset. I wasn't going to go insane and take extra online or summer classes, but I was definitely going to step it up come junior year. I didn't exactly know how I was going to step up my game. All I knew was that I had to be a lot more than just average.

Chapter 13

ABOUT THREE WEEKS INTO SUMMER vacation Tyler, Lydia, and I went back to UR UR BEAUTY and told Harold about our whole plan. Apparently, Cara was one of the only girls who bought that brand, so keeping it from her wasn't going to be all that difficult. Harold knew that Cara wasn't exactly the nicest person, so he agreed to help us pretty quickly. When the shipment of the makeup came in, all he had to do was keep from selling it to any of the Fans.

It was a week before the first day of our junior year, and that was when Cara caught onto our not-so-devious revenge. We were at the dog park with Neptune, Gadget, and Nestle when Lydia spotted Kathleen, and right behind her, raging, was Cara.

"Give it to me."

"What are you talking about?" I said sarcastically.

"You know what I mean, my makeup!"

"How did you guys even get it?" Kathleen asked.

Lydia looked over to Kathleen and told her simply, "We have our ways." Cara turned her attention to Lydia and told her that we had to give it back to her "or else." Of course, she was mainly threatening me rather than the three of us in our entirety. I didn't exactly feel threatened at all; therefore, neither did Lydia or Tyler. Cara had been taking shots at me for months at that point; why should I have felt scared? What could she possibly do that was so horrible? Also, it wasn't like it was going to torture me for any longer than a day.

"You know what, Cara, you get it as soon as we find it, 'kay?"

She stared at me with a glare that spoke volumes. And all I did was smile and walk away. Not far behind Lydia and Tyler followed, but I also felt Cara staring at me in disbelief of my audacity.

In all honesty, I was in some disbelief myself. I never spoke without reservation like I had right then. But I had nothing more to say to her, and I'm sure she had nothing more to say to me, nothing that I didn't already know or that she hadn't already said just in an altered arrangement of words.

I expected Cara's conniving imagination to come up with an idea to really knock me down on the first day of school. Every room I entered and every sudden noise I heard caused my heart to beat at least a little bit faster, but would you believe that nothing happened? All that fearful anticipation was useless!

She probably wanted me to worry about it all day, right? She knew that I would be expecting my just desserts that day. Of course, how could I have missed what was so obvious? The anticipation is always worse; it's what eats away at you the entire time, what punishes you before the punishment. So by the end of seventh period, I let the terror of it all slip away, because nothing was going to happen that day. Cara also probably thought that if she did anything sneaky, it would ruin her chances of getting her makeup back. It probably would have, but I like to tell myself otherwise.

Come that Thursday, still nothing had happened. Cara was wearing this sort of cardigan with a hood; she had been wearing them all week. With the way they were styled, they seemed to be getting a lot of attention. I hoped that the attention from her clothes helped her gain some confidence and made her realize that she seriously didn't need that makeup that she had been yearning for all week.

I guessed she only had so many of those cardigans to hide in, so early Friday morning, I decided to give Cara her makeup. To be nice, Tyler, Lydia, and I even paid for it. I slid myself behind the front desk that morning to find a combination. I was able to find Cynthia's the quickest, so that was the locker I placed the makeup in. And just for sport, if you will, I wrote a note for Cara that said, "Hope you found that you really don't need this."

The entire morning, I caught no sight of Cara. I thought perhaps she missed school that day. Come fifth period though, I found her looking ever so glamorous as I was used to seeing. It was obvious she got her makeup back. Just before the bell rang for sixth period, she came up to Lydia and me and told us that we should be glad that we gave it back when we did. I don't believe that she actually had some brilliant plot up her sleeve, but I guess all I can do now is be curious. I don't have the opportunity anymore to gamble with her possible—probable—bluff.

On Saturday, I was thinking that maybe Cara wanted to get me then, but then I realized she only took her shot when we were in school or when it came to school activities. I could consider my weekend absolutely stress-free. On top of that, I knew that all the Fans would be at the school the whole weekend.

You see, each year, the senior class was able to vote whether they wanted to start late or finish early. I thought that starting late was the better of the choices. Younger friends or siblings could tell you about new security teachers, coaches, or principals. You had more time to brag about the fact that you were required to do nothing. And it meant that at the end of the school year, you weren't obligated to take exams earlier than everybody else; therefore, you didn't have to study while everybody else wasn't because they had exams exactly when you did.

That year, the seniors voted on starting the school year late, so volunteer underclassmen were setting up the gym to welcome the up-and-coming senior class to their final year in high school. I thought about volunteering for setting up, but I decided against it. I knew that I was missing out on some extra credit, but I figured I would just volunteer for cleanup crew. That would be just as good. Who knows if Cara had pulled something that weekend?

Either way, it was a good thing that I didn't volunteer. That Saturday, the three of us had basically nothing to do, but we all agreed that that day didn't feel like a do-nothing type of day. So we all thought it'd be cool to just take a drive. We had no place to be but everywhere to go. The only thing we had to do that morning was decide whose car we were going to take. Through the entire day, only once did we stop to eat, and that was when we were on our way back home.

Lydia remembered that there wasn't really much to eat at her house. Her mom rarely answered her phone, so she decided to call her dad to ask if maybe he thought it'd be a good idea to bring some food home. So Lydia dialed Richard's number, and seconds later, he picked up. I didn't hear their whole conversation, but I know it started off normal enough. He told Lydia yes, he did indeed want her to bring food home; it sounded a lot better than just seeing what he could salvage out of the little they had, which he planned on doing that night. She said "all right," but just as she was about to say we'd be home soon, Richard told her to stay on the phone but not to say a word, only to listen. Of course, because Richard's tone changed so fast Lydia nervously asked what was happening. Richard just repeated to stay quiet. It was quiet, then she could hear her dad climbing out of his car. It got quiet again, then suddenly, there were three gunshots; they were even loud enough for Tyler and me to hear.

Very quickly Lydia started shouting, "Daddy, Daddy! Are you okay?" I asked if we should call 911, and she nodded her head. Tyler already had the number dialed, so when he saw her nod, he pressed Call. I gave the police her address since Lydia was too choked up to speak. The cops said they were on their way; as were we by the time I got off the phone with them. Tyler was trying to calm Lydia down, while I spent what seemed like countless hours trying to get ahold of Francine.

When we were minutes away Lydia's block, shockingly, Francine got ahold of us by calling Tyler's phone. She said that the battery on her phone was out, and Tyler's number was the first and only number that came to mind at the moment when the receptionist asked her if she'd like to use his phone. She also said that wherever we were, we could make our way to the hospital; the ambulance seemed to have gotten Richard there in an instant, which I'm sure we were all grateful for.

Tyler turned us around and rushed to the hospital, taking all the quickest routes he knew. Tyler kept focused on the road; meanwhile, I paid my attention to Lydia. I noticed how she wasn't crying that heavily anymore like she first was at the restaurant, but tears were still calmly falling from her eyes, running down her cheeks, to her chin, then into her lap. I noticed how she didn't seem to be hyperventilating, but she was still taking heavy breaths, and they were still rather shaky. But mostly I noticed how the call between her dad and herself was still going. She made sure her phone stayed pressed against her ear. Every so often, she'd check to see that the call was continuing or that she had a good signal so there was no chance her phone would hang up. The entire drive, Lydia seemed pretty out of it, and by that, I mean "out of her mind with worry" or "just extremely and undeniably focused on her call," but for the lives of me, I could not tell. It seemed to me like she wanted, maybe even was desperate to hear her dad's voice come through the phone. All she needed was to know that he was alive. Francine would've told us, but sadly, at that time, she knew only as much as we did.

It took about an hour for us to find out how Richard was doing. First, they let Francine see him, then Lydia went in with her mom. Tyler and I waited only a short while—maybe twenty minutes—until Francine came into the waiting room to tell the both of us that we could go into the room and talk to him. She mentioned that she didn't want to pull Lydia away from her dad.

I would imagine that even if Francine asked Lydia to come get us, she wouldn't have. Lydia was always extremely close to her parents, but especially her dad. Richard was in the Army for a few years, so from when Lydia was three to when she had just turned eight, Richard had been away with the exception of some holidays.

Not to mention that Richard was a businessman; there were times when he'd have to be gone for months on end. Lydia was constantly missing him. Plus, in our first lifetime, Lydia and I didn't have a dad. Our mom definitely never made up for it. We yearned for affection; because of that, the both of us developed a lot of separation anxiety. I honestly believe that Lydia got it worse because I made it worse having had run away.

Lydia was sitting on the bed, holding her dad's hand when we all walked in. Richard smiled, said hello and that he was glad we were all there, but really we just wanted to know what and how all this happened. If they wanted to ask, they would have by then, so I didn't expect Lydia or Francine to question that night's happenings. I knew Richard longer and better than Tyler, so that meant he didn't have to ask; I did. As respectfully as I could, I asked Richard to tell me—us—everything.

He started to sit up, took a deep breath, then began to explain. He looked none of us in the eye but mentioned that it really began when Lydia called him. He was just getting home when he heard his phone ring; thankfully, he decided to stay in the car as he spoke with her. Out of nowhere, he caught sight of the light of three flashlights! That was when he told Lydia to stay on the phone. He knew that more than likely, things were going to get ugly, and he needed someone to know if the paramedics needed to be called. He didn't take a whole bunch of time to think; rather, he instinctively grabbed his gun and slowly got down. Richard explained that he loaded his gun with two blank bullets just to shoot and scare the burglars away but also had legitimate bullets just in case. He knew that he could load his gun quicker than humanly perceivable, so he guaranteed himself he'd be all right. He approached the door with plenty of caution and opened the door almost hesitantly. Shooting the two blanks he had, Richard quickly turned on the hall light. He saw no one near him, so he loaded his other bullets but hoped he'd have no need for them. He went near the living room, where he stunningly heard the shot of a gun other than his own, and then felt the instant pain of the gun's bullet. Richard was careful not to lose grip of his own weapon so there wouldn't be any way he'd be deemed helpless, but he did lose his chance to catch even a glance of any of the three boys that intruded his and his family's home.

Richard looked back up and looked around his room at the four of us. I think he was searching for something more than just a look of concern and empathy. Obviously, I was concerned for his well-being. I mean, the man was in the damn hospital for heaven's sake! And clearly I empathized with him, but I had something else in the expression I gave him, and I'm sure he could tell. That's why he turned his attention back to me. I expressed curiosity, and of course, I had another question.

"Where'd the bullet hit?"

"It hit me in the left leg," he said.

"Left kneecap, to be exact," we heard an entering voice say.

It was Dr. Gomez as I remember it. She seemed very nice, and she was great at her job. I think she learned to be so kind because she started off as a pediatric doctor. I only know that because she turned out to be Carol's auntie, and Carol and I were close enough. Anyhow, Tyler tried to continue the conversation.

"Is it bad?"

"Actually, before getting into anything, I'd like just to speak with just the family, please."

Tyler and I nodded and made our descent back to the waiting room, which we both found pretty stupid being that we were practically family anyway. We thought about eavesdropping, but that sort of seemed ridiculous to me, so we played by the doctor's rules. We sat down, but I quickly stood up and started pacing because I was unbelievably nervous. I figured that it was always bad when doctors ask people to leave the room, so I definitely got freaked out. Tyler tried calming me down; it helped a little, but thankfully, Dr. Gomez came in and told us that we could go back in and that "the family" would tell us, so we rushed to see what they had to say.

"Is everything okay?" I asked.

"How bad is it?" Tyler asked right after.

"Umm, well, they have to keep him for five days to really be able to completely say," Lydia said.

"Are you guys gonna stay here?"

"Yeah, we want to, but my mom's leaving to get us clothes and stuff."

"Oh, well, she doesn't have to do that. We can go get your things," Tyler offered.

"Are you sure?"

"Yeah! And I'm sure Lennie won't mind, right?"

"Of course not, we'll go right now if you want," I offered.

"That would be so great. Thank you!" Francine said.

So we left to get everyone's things, but when we got to the house and turned the lights on, we noticed not the sweetest of things. The house was indeed robbed! It was really only the living room, but the office Richard had was missing a few things, and finding out that possessions of yours have been stolen is never nice. I supposed the only positive side was that the bedrooms remained untouched. Tyler and I stayed talking about the matter back and forth for a while; we didn't know if we should tell the family that their things were stolen. Finally, we decided to call Richard and ask if he told Lydia and Francine. When we asked, he said he'd forgotten altogether but that it'd only be best to tell them.

We took our time packing everything. We stopped by the hospital gift shop to get Richard a get-well-soon gift. We wanted mostly to give them more time alone. When we finally got to the room, we saw Lydia standing out in the hall. She looked like she had been crying some more.

"What's wrong, Liv? What happened?"

"They don't know if my dad's going to be able to walk again."

Tyler and I looked at each other pretty shocked. I went to hug Lydia, and then Tyler joined in. Lydia started crying more; I could hear her breathing heavier as she pulled me in harder, wanting me to hold her tighter.

The two of us had a rule when it came to hugging: never be the first one to let go. I'm sure that makes you think about how we ever come to let go, but that really only becomes effective when we can tell that it's needed, that the other person will let go when they're ready. How can we tell when the rule is necessary? I don't really know, but out of all our eighty-two lifetimes, I'd say we've done a pretty darn good job.

This was one of those times that the rule took effect. Lydia just hugged and cried, and personally, I didn't mind at all. And thankfully, because I'm sure it didn't hurt, Tyler didn't either. I guess he, somehow, learned about our rule, or the rule is just obvious, which I hope it is. I'm not sure how long we stayed in that hallway, but eventually, Lydia let go. Her tears stopped falling, but as you can imagine, she still didn't feel that fantastic. I asked Tyler to take all the stuff into the room, and he did. I sat down with Lydia on the floor, and shortly after, she laid her head on my shoulder. Tyler came back out and sat down with us on the opposite side of Lydia and rubbed her back and shoulder. We all sat there quietly for at least an hour. I was sure—and I guess Tyler was too—that there was nothing that we could say that would make Lydia feel even an ounce better. The only thing she wanted was to hear Dr. Gomez say that Richard Legend was 100 percent completely fine.

I don't know when, but at some point, Lydia fell asleep on my shoulder. I checked to make sure Tyler wasn't asleep, because I'll admit that after such a long night, I felt pretty exhausted. I'm sure all that crying tired Lydia out like I can't even imagine. I whispered to Tyler to get up and to lift up Lydia so we could go in and lay her down. He picked her up, and I opened the door. Francine was already asleep on the foldout bed that was in the room, so Tyler laid her down. I went to go ask for a blanket for the two of them.

Once I covered them, we left home. It was late, or early some might say, so Tyler and I didn't even take the time to change into our pajamas. Tyler wasn't the only one waking up late that day, but again he woke up later than I did. I called Lydia a couple of times, but she didn't answer. I ended up figuring out that she fell asleep pretty late too, so more than likely, she was still passed out. I thought about making breakfast, but going back to sleep sounded better to me, so Tyler and I slept until about one forty-five!

Chapter 14

*S*INCE WE GOT OFF TO a rather late start in our day, Tyler and I didn't go to the hospital until four o'clock that day. Richard was napping when we got there. Lydia seemed a lot better. She rested, calmed down, and was able to process that everything was going to be all right, somehow. We stayed with her, and after about an hour, Richard woke up. He told us that he was still feeling pretty tired but that he did feel a lot better than he did the night before, which we were glad to hear. Tyler and I stayed another hour visiting with Richard. We might've stayed longer, but we both figured that since he mentioned how tired he was, he was hinting that he really wanted to mainly rest.

Before leaving, we spoke with Lydia and asked her if she wanted us to say anything to her teachers or if I just needed to pick up her work. She thought about it and decided that she only wanted me to get her, her work. Thankfully, our teachers weren't very nosy; we knew that I wouldn't be interrogated before they gave me the work I'd have to give to her.

The next day, I didn't so much feel like going to school. I knew that Lydia seemed fine, but I still felt like she needed me by her side. I told myself that I'd go to the hospital after school and that Lydia, Richard, and Francine were all right without me there, but I still dreaded my morning. Tyler tried brightening up my morning with loud music. It worked until it was time to get in the car and actually go to school. He picked me up and got me out of the door. I didn't fight him because I knew I had to go, but that didn't mean I wasn't still resilient about going. Sadly, my pouty lip got me nowhere.

In history, we did what we always did: take notes. I just sat there and took pictures of what I was supposed to be writing down, but don't worry, I listened. I figured I could write down my notes while Lydia was doing the same. Aren't I an amazing friend? In chemistry, our teacher was very late, so we barely had a class. Trigonometry was next, then yearbook, which was always fun, or at least not bad, so by the time my afternoon came around, I was feeling okay. Tyler and I called Lydia during lunch, and she said her dad was still supersleepy. She was glad that we called and was even more glad that we were going to see her after school.

Obviously, we felt peculiar when the three of us weren't together. I think that everybody felt it strange when we weren't all together, especially when Lydia and I weren't together. I know that Tyler and I were boyfriend and girlfriend, but Lydia and I were best friends. To some degree, I feel like that's a bigger deal.

After getting off the phone, Tyler and I went to the cafeteria and shared lunch. He wasn't very hungry, and I ate slowly, so we knew it'd take up the rest of our lunchtime. Typically, I would start our conversations, but that day, I was pleasantly surprised when Tyler brought up wanting to go shopping for new shoes. Somehow, that conversation led itself to the topic of dresses. And of course, that would lead me to talking about prom. I caught myself after it was too late to take it back. I didn't want it to seem like I fully expected Tyler to ask me and take me since it was finally my junior year. Thankfully, he didn't feel like I was being pushy at all. Even more thankfully, he still asked me to go! The bell rang; we stood up, and as he handed me my backpack, he very calmly asked if I wanted to go with him to the dance. It's apparent that I said yes, isn't it? It made me smile till my face hurt. I was probably blushing, which never failed to make me feel stupid.

Seventh period came around, and I got there; later Tyler did. It was my genocide class, I'd imagine that he wasn't in a huge rush to get home; however, he could've left early, and that day, he stayed the entire school day. We were far into class, and he walked in very nonchalantly. He held up a note and went over to our teacher's desk, calling her over so she could speak to him. It only took a minute, then he came over and sat in a seat right beside me. I asked him why he was there, but all he told me was that he'd tell me later. We were in the middle of a lesson, so I just let that be the end of it.

I was hunched over with my cheek resting against my fist when the bell to go home rang. I threw my bag over my shoulder, ready to walk straight out the door, but then Mrs. Rose called Tyler and me over to her desk. She said that she had a box that she needed to take home that afternoon in the gym, and she was wondering if the two of us could help her get it and take it to her car. Without hesitation, Tyler agreed. I didn't really mind, but all I could think about was how this meant we were going to be late to the hospital.

We went walking to the gym. Even though I wanted to get to the hospital, I was in no hurry; however, it seemed like Mrs. Rose really was. She stayed walking a significant distance ahead of us. I asked Tyler if he thought we should walk faster and catch up; he just shook his head and pouted his lip "no."

I stared at my feet as we walked, but I lifted my head when Tyler held the door open for me. I saw that Mrs. Rose took a left after walking in, which led to the bleachers, instead of taking a right, which would lead downstairs. So I did the same and turned left toward the bleachers, and I saw a bunch of seniors spelling out the word "prom" and a question mark! My jaw dropped, and I turned right around to look at Tyler. He was bent on one knee with a corsage in his hand.

"Lennie, will you go to prom with me?" he asked.

"Yes!" I said almost instantly.

Never in a million years would I have said no, so even if that uncelebrated invitation was all I got, I would've been content. But despite the fact that prom-posal season was far away, I was ecstatic that Tyler made such a big deal out of asking me. On top of that, it turned out that Mrs. Rose had recorded the whole thing. That's why she put such a distance between us and herself, so I wouldn't catch on.

Tyler stood back up and shouted, "She said yes!" All the seniors started clapping and cheering. I, on the other hand, started laughing. It wasn't like we had just gotten engaged or anything; still, I thought it was priceless.

Tyler got his phone from Mrs. Rose, then we went to the car so we could make our way to the hospital. The ride there was full of smiles. I mean, how could it not've been?

"So were you surprised?"

"Yes! I honestly had absolutely no idea."

"Good, 'cause I only had two hours to have the idea and gather enough people to make it happen."

"You seriously just thought of asking me at lunch?"

"Yeah. I hadn't even thought of prom until you brought it up. And I figured that since you brought it up, I had to ask you, which I did, but I had to do it in a cool way."

"So why didn't you just wait until it was closer to prom?"

"Because it wouldn't have been as exciting. Plus, that would've made it, like, sixty percent more cliché."

"Well, it definitely was a huge surprise to me!" I laughed. "I can't wait to let Lydia know!"

"Actually, I thought we could hold off on telling Lydia."

"How come?" I asked.

"Because I know for a fact that you'll want her to be there. She's your other half. And I know that she'll definitely want to go, so I thought we should ask her to go with us."

"Aww. That's so sweet."

"Plus, she's had a pretty rough week. That's what made me want to ask her in some sort of extravagant way."

Tyler turned to me with a smile on his face and saw an even bigger one on mine. It was noticeable that I thought it was a wonderful idea. I knew that it was going to be at least somewhat difficult to not tell her what had happened that afternoon, but it would be worth it to make her surprise that much more gigantic!

She texted me when we were in the parking lot, and I almost blew it by texting her that I had a video she had to see. So I had to spend ten minutes looking up funny dog videos till I found one that was good enough. I walked into the room watching my phone as if I had been glued to it for hours; that made the whole thing a little bit more believable.

When we walked into the room, we told Francine hi and asked Richard how he was feeling then. Not so surprisingly, he said that he was feeling pretty good. He couldn't get up from his bed still, but he wasn't quite as tired as he had been the day before. The man was a soldier; of course, he was going to heal quickly and tell everybody he was even better than he actually was. Lydia asked for the video that I told her she just had to see. Once I showed her, she laughed so hard, harder than I thought she would've, and she watched it over and over.

Our typical amount of swift conversation passed before I remembered that I had to give Lydia her work. She probably remembered and didn't say anything. Just because she did well in school didn't mean she necessarily liked it. So I ran out to Tyler's Jeep to grab my backpack then went back. We stayed long enough for both me and Lydia to take down the history notes and for Tyler and me to try to explain that day's trigonometry lesson. When we were finished, it was close to nine o'clock, so we left for the night.

I told Tyler that he could take a shower before I did because he was always faster, even when I only took my "quick" showers. While he was in there, I started folding and hanging all our laundry. When he got out and I got in, he was sweet enough to finish what I had started. We started to have dinner, and I realized that he had a football game the next day and we were playing at home.

I contemplated in my head for a while what I was going to do, since considering the team our school was playing, the game was probably going to run long. I was staying quiet and had my thinking face on, so Tyler asked what I was thinking so heavily about. I told him that I really wanted to go to his game but that I felt bad about leaving Lydia alone. I knew there was no chance that she'd leave her dad to come watch the game with me, so I felt like I had a real ultimatum. Tyler told me it was okay if I missed his game. He understood that I wanted to be there for my best friend.

That was part of the problem. I did want to be there for my best friend, but I didn't want to hang out at the hospital, at least not more than I wanted to be at my boyfriend's football game. I decided finally that I was going to go and watch Tyler play. I didn't exactly know how to tell Lydia, but then Tyler told me that I was making way too big of a deal out of the whole thing. I knew he was right because I had a tendency of doing that. He said to just simply call her and tell her that I wasn't going the next day.

So I called her; when she answered, she said that she was just about to call me. I asked her why, and she said she wanted to ask, if it wasn't too much, for me to record Tyler's game! She knew the team that we were playing was really good, so she expected a close game. I told her I would and that that's what I was calling her about. All she said was that I was ridiculous to think that she'd get hurt or offended over me wanting to go to my own boyfriend's game rather than spend three or four hours with her at a hospital mainly to give her schoolwork. When she put it like that, I figured I was being kind of ridiculous.

After getting off the phone with her, I went to mine and Tyler's room, and he was already uncovering the bed to go to sleep. I supposed it wasn't that early and that he did need sleep, so I decided to just brush my teeth and go to sleep as well.

Monday was officially over; Tuesday was going to be ours when we heard our alarm go off. And Tuesday wasn't much better, but at least it wasn't Monday. At least that's what I thought. That specific week, Monday took the cake—the whole bakery—compared to that Tuesday.

Both Tyler and I got ready for the day. We could've gotten to school early, but we both thought it would be better to have breakfast at home. I actually had enough time to make the two of us blueberry waffles.

By the time we got to school, we were in pretty good moods; we didn't even care that there was really only time for us to hurry to our classes.

The bell releasing us from third period rang, and some boy, whom I really didn't even know, told me that I had to go down to the football field. I didn't think much of it, so I just nodded and thanked him for letting me know. I guessed that since it wasn't announced over the intercom, it was Tyler being rambunctious. Perhaps he just felt like being unpredictable that week. It made enough sense to me and my senseless mind.

I took the time to put all my things away and even stopped by my locker to pick up and drop off certain things. I walked to the football field in no rush at all, so when I got across campus and it came within sight, I chuckled a bit. It became clear that this was Cara's counterattack, as Lydia would've called it. The sprinklers were all on and on their heaviest setting, and a hose was running as well. I kept walking to see if I would find Cara or any of the other Fans utterly disappointed that they weren't able to get me back soaking me with heaps of cold water. As I got closer, the content little smile on my face washed away as I came into the realization that the water was completely flooding the field! It was game day; I couldn't let that happen, so I dropped my things and ran as fast as I could to turn the sprinkler system off and disconnect the hose.

I was breathing extremely hard when I had accomplished doing so. I sat on the bleachers to calmly catch my breath. Looking up at the field, I realized that the water had to have been running for longer than just a few minutes. The field was completely flooded and probably wasn't going to be ready for the game that night, especially considering how cold it was that day. A lot of the water had the potential to just freeze, and the rest was just going to lie there because there was no chance it could soak into the ground.

When I was about to get up and leave, I noticed that our principal was standing close beside the first set of bleachers. She gave me a glaring look like she was expecting an apology, but mostly some sort of explanation. I took a deep breath knowing for sure that this was Cara's plan. It was a good one; I had to give her that. I walked over to the principal as prepared as I could've been to take the fall for intentionally flooding the football field and indirectly—arguably directly—ruining that night's game. I was going to claim that it was me who had pulled that ludicrous stunt, but only because it was highly unlikely that the principal was going to believe that it wasn't me. It was also an unofficial rule in the little game Cara and I had going. We had to take our hit and whatever backlash was to follow.

She did nothing more than tell me to follow her to her office, because clearly, she had to talk to me. Fifth period had already begun at that point. Because I was the only kid around was probably the biggest reason behind why there was no reason to believe that it wasn't me who flooded the field. My phone went off; I checked it, and I saw that Tyler was asking where I was. I was supposed to have gotten the message fifteen minutes before that, but my phone was spectacular enough to ring as I was getting in serious trouble.

"So, I suppose you're gonna say it wasn't you."

"Huh?" I questioned as I turned around and saw the principal walking back into her office.

"Well, I'm sure you didn't plan on getting caught."

"You're right about that," I said.

"So you aren't denying it?"

"No. I'm not. And I'll take whatever punishment you feel I've earned myself."

She seemed surprised by how, perhaps, classy my demeanor was. If nothing else, I'm sure other kids had little to nothing to say at best, if they weren't trying to avoid the punishment coming their way. After taking the time to realize that no confrontation was going to have to take place, she sat down and assigned me my discipline. It wasn't just detention or several detentions, no. I didn't get off that easily. I wasn't even lucky enough to get suspended for a few days. Nope, the trouble Cara put me in was harsh. My detention consisted of me having to tend to the field at least once a week, cleaning the cafeteria or the gym daily, and helping in the library at least twice a week, all that for the remainder of the school year! If you ask me, that seems like way too much, even if I had done it.

I had nothing to say, so I took a deep breath in and annoyingly sighed it out as I got up and left. I went to pick up my things, which were still right where I had dropped them, and then headed for my fifth period, English class. On my way to class, I finally replied to Tyler's text message. All I told him was that it was a funny story and that he was going to love to hear it. Talk about sarcasm at its finest.

Being that I still wanted to be there for Lydia for the rest of the week, I knew I'd have to go back to talk to the principal to see if I could start my punishment the following week. Luckily enough, in all seriousness, she agreed to that.

During fifth and seventh period, I was angry enough to just stay quiet and just stare off into oblivion, looking as if I was being good and knew what was going on. When seventh period ended, I snapped back into reality. I stayed in my desk, and Mrs. Rose asked why I was staying behind. I told her I was really just waiting for Tyler. Since he was the one who always picked me up that year, it made sense. So Mrs. Rose left the room to get I-don't-know-what, and I sat there waiting for my bundle of happiness to bring me at least a glint of light to my now-awful day. Finally, my phone vibrated; it was Tyler telling me that he was in the parking lot.

I got up from my desk and left the empty room. I climbed into his Jeep and threw my head onto Tyler's shoulder and groaned loudly.

"Ugh!"

"What's wrong? What happened today?"

"Nothing good. I got caught flooding the football field."

"What? Are you kidding?"

"Sadly, no, I'm not," I said, rolling my eyes. "It wasn't actually me, obviously."

"Obviously."

"But Cara came up with quite a plan, and now I might as well have done it! I don't know what they're doing about tonight's game either." I looked at Tyler, upset.

"We're playing at the other team's school, and next time, we're gonna play here, since it was supposed to be the other way around."

"Well, at least there's still a game."

"Exactly. Don't worry, everything's fine," Tyler said and kissed my head.

"Ha, umm, no. Everything's not fine, because for the rest of the school year, I have to help in the library, cafeteria, and/or gym and tend to the field!"

"Wow. That's harsh."

"You're telling me. When she told me all that, I was like, 'Damn, are you on your period or what, miss?'"

We both laughed. Tyler shook his head as if to say I was too much, then he put the Jeep in drive, and we headed toward the other school. We got there pretty early, so we just sat in the car for a while, finding things to talk about, listening to music and things like that. Eventually, our school's bus arrived, and Tyler went to meet up with his team. I went all by lonesome to the bleachers and waited for the game to start.

It was kind of cloudy when the game started, but thankfully, it didn't rain. I remembered that Lydia wanted me to record the game for her, and I didn't want to chance getting my phone wet; after all, it wasn't waterproof. As the clock wound down, halftime came. Nothing too major had happened, but the score was still extremely close, so I hurried to the concession stand in hopes that I could also hurry back.

I got back to my seat just as the game was starting back up. The second half of the game was already proving itself better than the first when our running back intercepted the ball at the other team's twenty-yard line and ran all the way to the end zone, scoring us a touchdown and putting us ahead by four! The rest of the game was back-and-forth because within a few plays, it was all tied up. On one of the last plays of the game though, we had a fumble. Everyone in the crowd was sure that, with only a minute left, we'd go into overtime. But we got the ball back! We ran down the clock till it was fourth down and decided to go for the kick. Basically, the game was in our kicker's hands. I would think that he felt the pressure, but I couldn't tell because he kicked the most beautiful field goal I've even seen in my lifetimes!

Needless to say, we won that game, and everyone from our school was ecstatic. I was pumped up seeing how well everyone played, but out of nowhere, I saw Cara. We made eye contact, and she just waved at me. She knew fully that every piece of her plan fell right into place.

I wouldn't say my high completely left, but it did drop. So I went to the car and waited for Tyler.

Chapter 15

$\mathcal{W}$EDNESDAY WENT BY RATHER FAST, faster than I had expected it to, which, in retrospect, I was thankful for. Tyler went to pick me up early, so I sneaked out of class about twenty minutes before the bell. When I climbed into the car, I let out a big sigh. He asked me if my afternoon was hard or chaotic. Surprisingly, it wasn't. I left Cara alone like I always did. And she left me alone rather than taunting me about the prank she pulled. It wasn't like her, really, to not make fun, especially of me, but I guessed she might've figured that my punishment was enough.

I told Tyler that we wouldn't mention anything to Lydia until her dad was out of the hospital and she was back at school. He completely agreed with me with not a single argument or question. With her dad in the hospital, Lydia had enough to focus on. Plus, I didn't want her worrying about me for any reason. So when we got to the hospital, the first thing I did was pull out the work that was assigned that day. Lydia huffed then took the work from my hands. She went to put it down on the table in the room then turned back to me and asked if we could watch the game. I had almost completely forgotten about it, but I quickly nodded yes.

We all watched the game on my phone. Seeing it over, it was still exciting for me. Watching the game rather than playing, Tyler still found it exciting enough to pay mind to. And experiencing it for the first time, Lydia thought it was very exciting! Since I recorded some of the time-outs and calls that the referees made, we stayed at the hospital for almost two hours just gathered around my phone. After it was all finished, Tyler and I decided to leave a bit early, partially because I knew that we didn't really leave Lydia much time to do her work. Lydia was a good student, but she procrastinated more than you would believe, so with Tyler and me as distractions, I figured it was a good idea to go.

Thursday was pretty much the opposite of Wednesday; it dragged on and on. I felt like it was never going to end. It was the day that Richard was getting released, and we were going to find out whether or not he'd be walking anytime soon or again at all. By the time second period came around, I felt like I should've been in sixth! And when the lunch bell rang, I was begging Tyler to just take me home, or more so to the hospital. He just had to say no. Man, do I remember how much I wanted to kick him in a certain area and just steal the Jeep. But I'm too nice; I didn't.

Think about it, if I was that anxious, imagine how bad Lydia and Francine were. I probably can't begin to imagine how Richard felt either. Lydia didn't call me or Tyler during lunch, and she didn't pick up either of our calls. After lunch, Tyler decided to stick around so we could leave right when the last bell rang for the day. During my afternoon classes, I tried texting Lydia multiple times, but she didn't answer. That only made me more anxious. Tyler tried texting her too, and the same thing: no answer.

Mrs. Rose let us out early that day. I'm not sure if it was for me or not. She was pretty good at being able to tell when something was wrong. Either way, I ran to the front office to get Tyler, then we sped off to find out what had happened with Richard at the hospital. When we were only a few minutes away from the parking lot, Lydia texted Tyler, saying that they were already home and that we had to go to her house.

She didn't say anything else, and she didn't use any emoticons or emojis, so there was really no telling if we were going to hear good news or really bad news. I texted her back on Tyler's phone to tell her that we were on our way. But also I asked if everything was okay; again, she didn't reply.

Tyler made a quick U-turn and started for Lydia's house. We started talking about what we thought the news would be if it turned out that everything was fine; we had so much to tell her, and we could all go celebrate the fantastic news. If it was bad, Tyler and I knew where we were staying for as ever long as we had to. Lydia would tell us that it was okay if we left but would put up no fight if we insisted on staying because there was no doubt about it—she needed us. And we needed her. We needed her to be all right, and if she needed us to be shoulders to cry on or anything else, that's exactly what we'd be.

Tyler pulled into the driveway and turned the car off. We looked at each other with worrisome eyes. I held Tyler's hand. He kissed my hand gently and told me that everything was going to be okay. I opened my door and slowly got out. Even more slowly, I walked to the front door and knocked. It was silent for a few seconds, but then I heard footsteps approaching to answer the door. Who better to answer it than Richard?

He was okay! He was up and walking—in his words, "perfectly fine." I wanted to jump on him and hug him tightly with all my enthusiasm, but I stopped myself figuring that probably wasn't the best idea. He could support his weight, more than likely not his weight with the addition of mine. So I jumped on Tyler and hugged him with all my enthusiasm. I had a smile on my face that stretched from ear to ear. I calmed down enough to go inside and give Richard a more appropriate hug. Lydia ran up to me happy as ever and hugged me probably tighter than I hugged Tyler! That made me even happier. She might not've been crying the whole time, but I knew she was carrying a heavy heart those five days. The same for Francine, who was ecstatic as well. We all felt like a huge weight had been lifted from our shoulders. And in honor of Richard's recovery, the five of us went out to eat at Richard's favorite restaurant. It was one of my least favorite places, but despite that, I and everyone else had an absolutely wonderful time.

All of us stayed up almost the entire night. Lydia's parents fell asleep just after two o'clock, and the rest of us passed out just before five in the morning! I woke up about two hours later. I stayed staring at the ceiling for over an hour, thinking about only God knows what. I'm guessing I thought about how tired I was and then other random stuff. I eventually pulled myself together, got up, and made coffee. Once the coffee was all done, I tried waking Lydia up, but she lazily told me to leave her alone and let her sleep. Then, I tried waking

Tyler up, and he just smacked me in the face with a pillow. I swear he enjoyed doing so.

Since I was already up and moving, I decided to take Tyler's Jeep and drive to Starbucks to get coffee from there instead. If I wanted homemade coffee, well, I already made coffee at Lydia's. By the time I got back, Tyler was starting to wake up, and Lydia was awake but refusing to actually get up. I told her I made her coffee; that almost worked, but she needed me to take it to her before she moved from being so comfortable. I took her the coffee I made, then sat down, and drank my Starbucks coffee. I explained that she would've gotten coffee too if she had woken up with me. She just pouted and drank the coffee I made her, slightly less happy. Tyler walked in with the coffee I brewed, and he finished preparing, wondering how and why I bought coffee from Starbucks. I told him I took his Jeep, and he got after me a bit, but really I knew he didn't mind that I took the Jeep; he only minded that I didn't get him coffee.

It was somewhat late in the morning, so I decided that I wasn't going to school that day. As you might've guessed, that helped Tyler and Lydia decide that they weren't going either. Francine probably would've made Lydia go, except Lydia didn't do any of the work I took her. All she had done that week was copy the notes that I copied with her! I would've made her go to school, but I wasn't going, so I didn't want to force her away from me because we had already spent so much time apart, too much time apart.

Later on in the day, I decided that instead of being Lydia's distraction, I had to be her motivation; otherwise, she'd never get her work done. Francine made us all lunch, and that's when I told Lydia that she had to start working. She put up somewhat of a fight by whining and complaining, but with Tyler on my side, she gave in and agreed that she had to get things done, and then was as good a time as ever.

Ever since freshman year, we didn't get too much homework, a lot less than we did in middle school, so we were able to get a lot of work done on Friday. On Saturday, we only had to do three assignments, all of which were pretty simple for me to explain, so I knew that if Lydia had any questions, I could answer them.

Lydia didn't ask about Cara at all over the weekend, so Tyler and I omitted what happened entirely, that weekend anyway because we had to tell her. She was the best at plotting. Though we didn't tell her about Cara flooding the football field, we did mention something else: prom! Tyler showed her the video once we were done working on Saturday, and she was so excited. She was a bit hurt that we didn't tell her right away, but she understood why. And she didn't say anything about wanting to tag along, but Tyler and I both knew she wanted to go. She did mention, however, that I had to let her help me pick out a dress, an absolutely perfect dress. I was sure to clear an entire day within the month, and I told her that if we didn't find one that day, we would just look everywhere else! No matter what, we would find it. Of course, she didn't know then that we would be looking for two perfect prom dresses and that one would be for her. She had to wait a little while to find that out.

One thing Lydia didn't have to wait too long for was finding out about what happened with Cara. I mean, how could I keep it from her? My punishment wasn't exactly voluntary, and after maybe two days, it wouldn't appear that way either. I had to elucidate why I was in so much trouble. So come Sunday, I told Lydia my long story about how I got caught flooding the football field on game day.

"Damn. That freakin' sucks."

"Yeah, Liv, I know it freakin' sucks. I don't really need to be reminded."

"Well, it does suck," she said. "You either caught our principal while she was on her morning period or just on a really, really bad day."

"Or both," I said.

"Or both," Lydia repeated.

"I think it was both."

We laughed and stayed talking about how bad my situation was. Eventually, the topic switched over to how badly we needed to get Cara back and how good of a plan we had to come up with. I completely agreed, probably more than Lydia even thought.

Going to school on Monday felt exactly like that: going to school on a Monday. I know that I had done it thousands of times at that point, but that doesn't mean that at any point I came to find it delightful. I went to my morning classes, and during lunch, I went to check out the field. It wasn't flooded anymore, but it was still a muddy mess, and they left it that way just for me! I skipped out on sixth period to help clean the cafeteria that day. I couldn't skip sixth period every day, so I had to figure out exactly what I was going to do for the rest of that year to simply just not fail! I decided to clean up the cafeteria or gym before classes. Tyler was nice enough to drive me; of course, I had to provide compensation. I would sneak him into the teachers' lounge every morning so he could sleep some more on arguably the most comfortable couch ever! I helped in the library during lunch. And I would tend to the field after school on Fridays. On those days, Lydia was lovely enough to take me home, so Tyler wouldn't have to make the extra trip.

Three weeks went by, and I was getting impatient. I was eager to ask Lydia to the prom. Part of my impatience had to do with the fact that none of the three of us could come up with a plan good enough to get Cara back. My punishment was severe, so we had to come up with something seriously good. Too bad coming up with something seriously good was the hardest part.

On one of the days that I was helping in the library, Lydia and Tyler came racing up to me. They had news; I wasn't sure if it was good or bad, and they were awful enough to make me wait to find out. Because for whatever reason, they just had to debate who got to tell me. Finally, Tyler had enough and started to tell me something about a concert. But then, Lydia interrupted, not wanting to let Tyler be the one who delivered the news, and finished it off by explaining that the lineup consisted of a few of our favorite musicians and that tickets were going on sale just before two o'clock, just before seventh period started. Tyler and I had prepaid phones that didn't have internet, and Lydia's phone was almost out of battery. Would you believe that out of all days, that was the day Julian missed school? He would've definitely had a charger for Lydia. By the end of lunch, Lydia gave Tyler her phone to see if he could find a charger so when the tickets went on sale, he could order them. There was a guarantee that the show was going to sell out. The venue where the concert was taking place wasn't exactly Madison Square Garden. Long story short, Tyler didn't find a charger. And when we got to Lydia's house, we checked Ticket Master, and the show was sold out!

That day was pretty rough, honestly. I'm sure that you've missed out on a concert that you were dying to go to and then felt devastated after. Right? Well, that was the feeling.

Because it was such a rough day, Tyler agreed that we could do our prom-posal for Lydia the next day. I came up with the plan. I didn't plan it as quick as Tyler had when he asked me, but I feel like it was rather extravagant and special. It was enough to make her cry, but we're getting to that.

The next day, I was as anxious as ever, because like Tyler, I was waiting till the end of the day to surprise her. It was pretty difficult for me to wait the whole day, but I did it. Seventh period came around, and Tyler texted me, saying that everyone who helped him was willing to help us. They were going to leave class and gather in our commons area at two thirty-five; that meant we had to leave five or ten minutes after that. I don't think I took my eyes off the clock for longer than thirty seconds. Once it was two forty, I got up and asked Mrs. Rose if we could go ahead with my plan. She said yes but that we had to stop asking people during her class jokingly. I left to the bathroom real quick to tell Tyler we were going. I went back to class and told Lydia that I needed her help getting something from the front office. Luckily, she didn't feel the need to ask what it was. We started walking toward the office; when we got to the end of the hallway, Lydia saw our sign that said "Will you go to prom with us?" looked back down and saw Tyler, then turned around to look at me. Tyler and I put our arms out and asked her, and that's when she started to cry and said yes.

Tyler and I went to hug her, then Tyler lifted her up, and I shouted, "She said yes!" And again, everyone cheered as if we had just proposed to get married. I can't really remember the rest of that day, but I know it was a fun day for all three of us.

Lydia was on such a high after we had asked her to prom that she became even more determined to think of a way to get back at Cara. She came up with more than just one plan. The thing was, those plans were just a little too good and too devious that I turned them down. And we, of course, all agreed that if not all three of us were on board with the idea, we had to come up with a different one. Eventually, though, Lydia came up with something absolutely perfect! She would listen to the radio every morning before school and found out that one station was giving tickets away for the concert we were all dying to go to. But they were only giving them away that day. We had Tyler miss a day so he could call in every hour. Luckily, he didn't really mind skipping school. Well, we didn't win the tickets, but we still had full intentions on attending the show. Because, guess who else missed that day—Carter, Cynthia, and Rachel. And guess who was a lucky caller. Carter was a lucky caller. So if Carter won five tickets to the show, then we just had to find a way to make those tickets ours.

The concert took place on a day that we had school, so I guessed that the Fans would come to school then head to the concert after the final bell. Guess who was 100 percent correct—me! We definitely had to get the tickets by morning, so Tyler, Lydia, and I were on a serious mission. Cara was basically the leader of the Fans, so Tyler was sent to search all her things. Carter won the tickets, so we sent Lydia to find out if she had them. And if Cara and Carter didn't have them, then one of the other Fans had to. I made a total random choice and decided to go through Kathleen's things. If Rachel or Cynthia had the tickets, then we would have to find them after lunch, which was risky because in those moments, we didn't know if they were staying all day. It was so fortunate that I went through Kathleen's things, because I found all five tickets in her science folder. After I found the tickets, we had to leave, but we had two extra seats available, and we didn't want to let them go to waste, so we thought of the two coolest people we knew in the school: Carol and Julian. They were both ecstatic that we invited them to come with us. So the five of us sneaked off campus and went to what I'd truly call the concert of a lifetime.

Cara obviously found out that we took the tickets. She was livid, for lack of a better word. And boy, did I expect to be gotten back real well, but hey, I just figured it was worth it.

Chapter 16

$\mathcal{W}$E WERE ALL BACK FROM Thanksgiving break, which meant that we all had to start thinking about one thing: finals. I was somewhat paranoid about what Cara might've planned to do to me and when she was going to do it. But I had tormented myself before with worrying every second of the day about what might happen, and I knew it wasn't worth it. Whatever was going to happen was going to happen. Plus, there was a good possibility that Cara would leave me alone for the rest of the semester. She had finals to focus on.

And of course, I had to focus on my finals as well. I was glad that Tyler, Lydia, and I helped one another because without them, I probably never would have studied. That's right; for the first time, the very first time ever, I willingly studied! It was just as much of a hassle as I expected it to be, but I was definitely grateful that it wasn't more of a hassle. I needed to ace my finals with flying colors, and with all the reviewing I was getting done, I knew I could do it. And I did! Tyler and Lydia also got phenomenal scores on their tests. And for the semester, we all got straight As. I was pretty proud of all of us, but soon after my spirits we brought down. I went to the counselor's office to see how everything panned out once the grades were averaged out, and I was still second, behind Cara. But Christmas break was close, and I knew I still had time, so it didn't get to me too badly. With one semester to go for the year, I had to keep my mentality focused on the fact that I wasn't beaten yet. And I would have to do the same for the next year.

Come January, Lydia, Tyler, and I were excited and freaked out. In a matter of five months, Lydia and I would have finished eleventh grade and move on to twelfth grade, our last year of high school, for that lifetime. And Tyler would be wrapping up his high school years. He was nervous about leaving, but he was ready for his graduation. He didn't plan on going to college right away. He wanted to take a year off. I guessed that he was waiting for Lydia and me to graduate as well, but he insisted that, that wasn't the case. It gave me something else to look forward to at least. We would all be able to start together, stress out together, then graduate together. I had no idea what would fill the gaps in between, but I was still very eager despite the level of time it would take.

My time was occupied though. Since football season was over, Tyler had already started working part-time at UR UR Beauty with Harold, and while he was working, Lydia and I were planning his graduation. Graduating is a big deal; we figured the party had to be a big deal too. That's why we started planning months in advance. I also was thinking about prom. I was pretty lenient about most details like what restaurant we'd go to before. But I made sure I had a say in when we'd get there and when we'd leave. I've always been pretty hung up on getting a place too late and not staying long enough. Oh yeah, and on the side of both those things, there was school.

There was a day in February that Julian asked Carol to be his girlfriend! The fact that they weren't already a couple at that point was pretty shocking too. It was probably pretty shocking to everybody. But I still found it to be adorable, partially because only days later, the two of them would celebrate their first Valentine's Day together. I'm a hopeless romantic; I basically live for things like that. Not too long after that, Carol found Lydia and me during one of our morning classes and called us out. She wanted to ask us if we would take her dress shopping with us whenever we were going. We both said yes in less than a heartbeat. Julian hadn't asked her to prom at that point, but she knew that he was going to. We all knew he was going to. That same day, Julian found Tyler just before he left for the day to ask him if he could go suit shopping with him. And as Lydia and I had done with Carol, he told Julian yes.

About two weeks later, we girls went to go find dresses that were perfect for prom. Lydia wanted a short dress; Carol really wanted a long dress. She told us that she had had a vision in her mind for quite a long while. And I was kind of open-minded to just about every-thing. It wasn't a wedding dress, so I didn't need to find a dress that made me cry. Carol found a stunning green dress that was indeed lengthy in the third store we visited that day. Lydia found a light-blue dress in the same store, and yes, it was short; however, she wanted to be absolutely positive it was her dress, so she didn't buy it. We later had to go back for it. I didn't find my dress until we went to the last store we planned on going to, the last store we could go to! I felt bad, but Lydia and Carol told me to be picky. I ended up choosing a short-long navy-blue dress with white accents on it. I loved it so much, and honestly, I still love it.

By the time we were heading home, it was just before eight o'clock. Thank God our local stores stayed open late during prom season, because after buying my dress, Lydia still had to go back for hers. We got to mine and Tyler's house so he and Julian would know what to look for the next day when they went looking for their suits. They were cutting no corners either. They were buying their suits, not renting them, so they had to know exactly what it was that they wanted and what to match, being that they both wanted to comple-ment us girls.

When everyone went home, Tyler made dinner for us to eat. It was something light, but enough so we could talk about our days. I did most of the talking that night, and I figured it was because I was the one who went out. But I also wanted to hear about what Tyler and Julian did for an entire day. He didn't talk as much as I did, but Tyler told me that he and Julian talked about plans for prom and told me that he helped Julian make a plan on how to ask Carol to the dance! I couldn't wait to find out what they decided on doing, but Tyler said he wouldn't tell me till morning. He spilled out to me that I would get to help though, so my patience was able to run a little bit longer.

The next day, Julian dropped Carol off at mine and Tyler's house at noon, then the two of them left to go and get some suits that were bound to be extraordinary. They came back around five o'clock, not with their suits, but with photos of their suits. The tailor had to make some adjustments, but from what we could tell, the suits were going to be nothing shy of fabulous! Julian's suit was a fantastic emerald suit that also included some black. And Tyler's suit was an intriguing navy-blue suit with striking accents of light blue, which, if you ask me, completed the suit and brought it together. Of course, I had to like Tyler's suit better; it wasn't completely bias though, only mostly.

Once everyone went home that day, Tyler and I went to the living room to watch TV since we ate with the others. We paid almost no attention to what was on. Tyler told me about his day only a bit; mostly he told me about how Julian was going to ask Carol to prom. I wanted to know almost everything because I've always loved surprises. And Tyler was always great at them, so I knew this prom-posal was going to be fun!

Mrs. Rose told us to stop with prom-posals in her class, so we were making this happen in sixth period, which Lydia and I had with Carol. Our teacher helped obviously. In class that day, we got in groups and had to solve puzzles that would spell out the name of song titles from certain artists. It seemed normal enough, so no one thought anything of it, including Carol. Then our group got to the "special" puzzle. Julian spray-painted that puzzle with glow-in-the-dark spray paint, so when we solved it, it would read "Will you go to prom with me?" when we turned the lights off. Carol took a little while solving that puzzle and didn't want much of our help, but once she finally finished it, we turned the lights off for a moment. When we turned them back on, Julian was right in front of Carol. She didn't give much of a verbal response, but when she ran into Julian's arms and hugged him for what might've seemed like an eternity, the entire class was pretty damn sure her answer was yes. I thought it was one of the cutest things I'd ever seen, especially because Julian couldn't stop blushing. And Carol cried a bit too.

The day of prom was wonderful! The five of us got together early in the afternoon to get ready like we had never gotten ready before. We were close to everyone being ready to leave for the restaurant, but Lydia needed quite a bit of time. It wasn't because she had so many things to do; it was simply because she was just slow when it came to getting ready. When she finally finished, we took a few pictures. Thankfully, Tyler's dad had a timer camera, so we were able to take a couple of photos with all of us in them. Walking out of the house, we were going to climb into Lydia's car, then suddenly, Julian ran out and pointed straight down the block. He surprised us with a limo! I knew we weren't going to be the only people who rented a limo for the night, but to me, it was amazing that we were included in the group of people who got their own limo. And it was prom; we had to go all out and enjoy every minute. We arrived to the prom at just close to eight thirty and didn't get home until just before three in the morning. I can't quite remember what we did once we left the dance, and no, it wasn't because we went drinking, but I'm sure it was something magical. Everybody stayed over at mine and Tyler's that night.

For the rest of the year, Julian and Carol would hang out with us whenever they could. They were in a lot of clubs, so often enough, they were busy doing something. Due to my punishment, I made the decision to not join in any teams or clubs that year. Lydia and Tyler didn't want to make me feel left out at all, so they made the same decision. Of course, though, Tyler did finish off his last year of high school football earlier on that year.

Even without extra curriculars, ending the year was indeed busy and stressful. I was trying to give Tyler the best surprise graduation party in history. That meant that I had to invite a lot of people, the right people too, because obviously, no one wants annoying company at a party that only comes once in a lifetime. Tyler got along with pretty much everybody in his class, so I had to invite the entire senior class! I also had to be sure to let everyone on the football team know. Then I had to remember to invite the kids that became Tyler's friend in any other way and, lastly, the members of his family that I could get ahold of. Actually, Raymond took care of that, so I did get some help. Lydia helped me in planning how we were going to leave the gym, so everyone could set up for the party. That took a while. Food was a process too. I mean, just think about how much food I had to order to get all those people fed! It was difficult, but I did it. How I had the time, I don't even know. How I didn't get caught is an even bigger curiosity of mine!

The day of graduation started off great. I woke up just feeling in my bones that the day was going to be epic! Surprisingly enough, and luckily enough, Tyler got up almost right after I had. He was beyond enthusiastic about the entire day. He really just could not wait any longer. We showered and got ready rather quickly. I thought about having Lydia do my makeup since it was such a special event, but Tyler said he liked me better fresh-faced, and for some unknown reason, Lydia put up no argument. So we drove to pick up Lydia then headed to the school. We stayed near Tyler so that if he wanted photos with any of his friends, we could take them. And as you probably guessed, we were in some of those photos.

We got to the school pretty early, so we were able to take kind of a lot of photos, but Lydia and I did have to leave early so we could grab the best seats possible. Tyler was set to sit relatively close to the stage. That was good for us because that made it easier to get photos and videos of him walking up to the stage and him being handed his diploma. We met up with Raymond about twenty minutes after we found seats. A lot of people had already come, so it was a good thing that we arrived as early as we did.

The graduation had begun. Only the principal made her speech before all the names were called. All the speakers would make their speech afterward. The two guest speakers and the valedictorian would go first, and last to speak would be a student from the graduating class who volunteered and was then elected by the class. That year that student was Tyler.

I couldn't pay full attention to the other speakers' speeches because I was anticipating Tyler's so much! He didn't let me hear it or read it, not even the rough draft. So my curiosity sparked a large increase in my interest to hear it. I have always loved surprises. I guessed that was why I wasn't allowed to get a single hint of his speech.

When the principal called Tyler up to the podium to speak, the crowd roared. Plenty of people cheered for him like there was no tomorrow. I was clearly one of those people. I was captivated the moment he began.

"Good afternoon, everybody. My name is Tyler Everlong, and I really wanted to let my classmates know that we're escaping free from our small world of high school into this enormous world of reality. And I wanted to mention how many times we were all gonna fall, fail, and mess up but that there will always be someone to help us up and help us move forward. But for the most part, I think they're all smart enough to know all of that, so I really want to tell you all what exactly went on during our four years of yearning to be alive.

"We learned. That's easy to assume, isn't it? Yeah. But we learned all these things that you probably can't even guess. We learned about science, not just about the elements and the science behind how they combine. But from each other we learned the science behind why we were so willing to fight for a hand to hold. We learned English, not just alliteration and juxtaposition, but also what silence meant in different situations. And what 'I'm fine' really meant coming from, well, everyone. We learned math, but not just how to add equations. We learned how somebody telling you that your hair looked good, that your shirt was cool, and that they wish they had your skin tone added up to equal you realizing that you are a lot more than what your bullies have made you believe you are. And also that a C-, a teacher telling you that you're not trying hard enough, and not having a table to sit at for lunch could and would cancel out positive vibes you had and would only leave you trying not to hyperventilate while crying. And we learned a lot of history. We learned that April 9, 1865, is when the Civil War ended, but we really learned that a civil war goes on within most of us every day, between our minds and our hearts. We learned each other's history, why our project partner didn't want a new dog, and why the kid beside us in art always would draw on himself. And I think we really learned ourselves and what it took for us to survive and that we accomplish so much by surviving.

"It's truly amazing. Sometimes in a day, all we do is breathe, and I believe that that's okay, because there are days when even breathing is hard. I know kids that had days that they simply did not want to, but they did. That's surviving, that's having courage and bravery, that's accomplishment. We've all broken things down to survive. Like in football, we know getting to the end zone will be tough, so we break it up into first downs. The other end of the field could be seventy yards away, and before we know, it will be second and goal, and then we'll have scored our touchdown.

"School has taught me that taking a journey is surviving. And being patient is difficult because all you ever want is to just be at your destination. But I found out it's the journey that molds you and makes you worthy of your destination. In order to get where you're going, you have to become better. That's why school is, arguably, so long. Because we all take those deep breaths and think 'Let's get this over with.' And after those days are done, we're smarter, we're better.

"We just have to survive Monday. We just have to survive till Friday, till winter break, till spring break, till summer vacation. Seniors, we've survived all that, and today we've scored our touchdown.

"I really hope that we can all stand back and truly acknowledge that we are better today than we were four years ago. And we are going to be better four years from now than we are today. We all have loved ones who are gonna help make that happen.

"I have my dad, and I don't know what else to say other than that he is the greatest man I know and is the greatest example of what a man should be. I have the wildest, most admirable best friend. She's a legend, and her name is Legend, Lydia Legend. And I have my beautiful girlfriend who is a champion among championships. Her name is Melenium Champion. And umm, Lennie, will you come up here?"

I was shocked, but I stood up and ran to the stage.

"Melenium, you make me better. More importantly, you make me want to be better. I look at you, and I believe in love and miracles and magic. I love you. And I think I'm going to need help in being better forever, so will you do me an honor? Melenium Gabby Champion, will you marry me?"

Chapter 17

I CUPPED MY HANDS AND COVERED my mouth. I was in awe as I stared at Tyler down on his one knee. It felt as if we were the only two people in the gym. And as tears gently rolled down my face onto the biggest smile my face had ever worn, I was almost completely speechless, but somehow, I managed to say yes. Then Tyler stood back up, we threw our arms around each other, and he lifted me off my feet and spun me around. He put me down, kissed me, and yelled into the microphone, "She said yes!" And that's when the audience really roared!

Tyler ended his speech, and balloons fell down as the seniors threw their caps up. We all went outside so Tyler could take photos with all his friends and family. People started to leave, and it seemed like the grounds were clearing up, so I figured it was time to get back into the gym to surprise Tyler with his party. But Lydia beat me to it. She had us follow her so she could grab something she "forgot."

When she opened the doors, I was ready to turn around and yell "surprise," but I was surprised myself. Tyler really was as well. It seemed that Tyler's surprise graduation party was also my surprise engagement party! There were two banners hanging from the railing: one that read "Happy Graduation, Tyler!" and a second one that read "Happy Engagement, Melenium!" And Lydia was basically behind the entire thing. Once she found out that I wanted to throw Tyler a party and that Tyler wanted to propose, she figured that mashing the two surprises together would be incredibly perfect. I couldn't really blame her. It was perfect. It was the most perfect day I've ever lived. And that really says something.

After the party ended, we went to a couple of parties of friends that also graduated that day. We stayed busy the entire day, so we were honestly back-and-forth once our party was over. But it was so great. When Tyler and I finally got home, we were unbelievably tired; however, for some unknown reason, we both just did not want to go to sleep. So we turned on the TV and lay down, thinking that would make us sleepy and might even allow our hectic day to wash over us and we'd both harshly pass out, but that didn't happen.

Of course, it didn't, right? I don't know why it would.

Tyler and I got up and grabbed a few snacks then went back to our bedroom. We turned music on to play in the background. We sat up right on our bed, and we talked. It really seemed like everything that day was particularly extravagant to talk about, then again maybe it always seemed that way with the two of us; either way, we never got bored or annoyed with each other. If anything, we would somehow end up intrigued. There was never a moment when we were at a loss for words. I guess we both just talked too much; luckily, we both knew how to listen very well.

It didn't take long for the topic to turn to our engagement and our wedding. Tyler tossed around a few ideas, and me, well, I tossed around more than just a few ideas. They were solid plans. C'mon, I had lived eighty-two lifetimes by then. You can't believe that within that time, I hadn't planned at least most of my wedding—there's no way! And I had never been married before, not even once, so I had plenty of time to imagine and daydream. There were some things that, perhaps I'll admit, were too grand to request. One of those things for example was to have trained dolphins jump in the air straight after the words "You may now kiss the bride" were said. But for the most part, Tyler liked my plans—I mean, ideas. At the end of it all though, we agreed that the most important part was who was there to help make that day so special. I definitely did have a ton of people in mind, but I was positive that if Tyler wanted certain people to be there, they belonged there. And we agreed that we didn't want to wait too long for our special day, so we made the date only a couple of days after I would graduate.

We finished that conversation for the night, but still we were not tired. We were more awake than ever. Tyler asked me to tell him some stories, some of our stories.

"Can you tell me about the first time we met?"

I took a deep breath and let it out as I thought back to that time.

"Wow. Umm, let me see. Oh! It was great because we were both little. I had been at the public pool all morning trying to teach myself how to swim, but I just wasn't getting it. So I sat at the edge with just my feet in the water. You came up to me all of a sudden and asked me if I was okay. And of course, I said yeah, that I was fine. For whatever reason, you asked me if I needed sunscreen." We both laughed. "I told you yes because I really didn't have any. I didn't even put some on that morning! So I followed you to your bag, and you introduced me to your parents. That's when they asked you what your new friend's name was, and that's also when we decided to learn each other's names. You gave me your sunscreen, and then I obviously proceeded to put way too much on, so I had to share and made you put more on. Then we walked back to the pool. You asked me if I wanted to race to the other side of the pool then jumped in. I turned, trying not to get splashed in the face. It didn't take you that long to notice that I didn't jump in with you and stayed on the outside. You swam back to me and got out of the pool and asked me why I didn't jump in. I looked down at my feet feeling embarrassed and whispered to you that I never learned how to swim. You didn't look shocked, but you stared at me for a little while. Then you stood up really straight and asked me if I wanted you to teach me. I nodded vigorously, so excited that I was finally going to learn how to swim, something I had been trying to learn for so long. It only took you, like, two seconds to push me into the deep end of the pool, and once you realized I was pretty much drowning, you jumped in and pulled me out. I punched you in the arm and slapped your head as hard as I could and yelled, 'What'd you do that for?' And you shrugged, telling me that, that was how you learned. I thought you were lying, so I started to walk away, but you grabbed my arm and told me that I should still let you teach me. Just like that, I gave in. We went into the pool, and you tried explaining to me what to do, and you had me watch you, and you tried showing me how to swim underwater so that maybe it'd make swimming above water easier. It took almost all day, but I eventually got it. And before you had to leave, we had that race. I'm not gonna lie, you won, not by much though."

Tyler smiled at me; he seemed out of it, but he was just awfully happy. I'm sure it was strange to believe that that was a story of him and me.

"That's crazy. No matter what, we always act like we've known each other forever, don't we?"

"Yeah." I chuckled. "I guess chemistry is just something you can never really fight."

"I guess. It's so insane how you can think back that far and remember all that."

"Trust me, these are just things I'll never forget. I'm positive there are plenty of happenings that will never come back to my mind."

"Still, it's mind-blowing. Hey, can you tell me the first time I made you smile?"

"Now that is something almost impossible! When you taught me how to swim, I'm guessing."

"No, I mean, like, after you had been crying or upset."

"Hmm, well, here's a good one." I waited for Tyler to get real comfortable as he gazed at me with this endless wonder. "It was summer break, and again we were still little. Some kids were outside playing. I watched them ride scooters, skateboards, and bikes, and all I wanted was to do the same thing even if I had to do it all by myself. But I didn't have any of those things, so I was pretty much ready to give up. I saw that after a while all the kids on my block were gone, so I went outside. I drew on the pavement with chalk and played hopscotch, but I still just wanted to ride one of those scooters, skateboards, or bikes. I think about it now and find it strange, because I didn't really know how to skateboard or ride a bike, and every time I rode a scooter, I'd hit my shins, which hurts, very badly. But I was determined anyway. I walked down the street and noticed a bike just sitting there in someone's driveway. I thought to myself, 'I'm not stealing it, I'm only borrowing it. And I'm gonna bring it back. And this kid isn't even using it, so no one will ever even notice.' I made my case, and then I took the bike. I walked it over to my house as happy as could be. Then I got on the bike and took off—well, that's what I tried to do. Finally, I fell and realized that riding a bike wasn't exactly as easy as I figured it would be. I tried again, and I fell again. And I tried another time, and I still didn't get it, but I at least caught myself before I fell. I got fed up and decided this whole riding-a-bike thing wasn't worth it, so I walked the bike back to where I found it, and what do you know, the kid who owned the bike came right up to me.

"That, Tyler, was you.

"You asked me why I took your bike, and I told you it was just because I didn't have one. You told me that I could still borrow it if I wanted, and of course, since I was so frustrated, I said no thanks. That's when you told me that you saw me fall, all three times. I felt my face get hot, so I probably started blushing hard. You laughed. My reaction was just to apologize for taking your bike, then I wanted to go home, but you wanted to teach me how, so I stayed. You showed me how you rode the bike, explaining that I didn't have to pedal so fast and that I should really focus more on where I was going. Mostly you told me I shouldn't've been so afraid.

I hopped on your bike again, and you held me while I pedaled slowly. Then I gained some confidence and started to go faster. I told you to let me go, and the very second you did, I hit the ground. My hands were scraped, and my left knee appeared to have torn right open. I bled, not an unbelievable amount, but enough for me to weep quietly and want to quit again.

You helped me up and insisted that I keep trying. You said that if I went home, then I would've completely wasted all your time. I certainly didn't want that, so we walked to the end of the block one more time. I threw my right leg over your bike, and I started to pedal again. You were running alongside me, so I had it in my head that you were still holding me up. Out of nowhere, you were running ahead of me. I snapped that I was riding a bike all by myself. I was stunned. You stopped and shouted, 'Keep going!' I made it to the end of the block, dropped the bike, and ran to you overjoyed. I was so gratified I couldn't stop jumping, clapping, and smiling. I thanked you over and over again. And for the rest of the summer, your bike was our bike."

"That's awesome." Tyler laughed. "You stole my bike, and later on, we fell in love."

"The ultimate fairy-tale love story," I said.

"I really like hearing all of these stories from you. It almost feels real. I mean, you tell them so vividly and with such passion."

"Well, they're some of my favorite memories. I miss them, so that's probably where the passion comes from."

"You like remembering all this?" Tyler asked.

"I do. And I like talking about it with you since I've never done it before."

I yawned and saw Tyler staring at me with curiosity.

"Can I hear one more?"

"Ugh! Tyler?" I moaned lightly.

"Last one, I promise. Then we can go to sleep."

"Okay, but this is the last one."

"Of course," he agreed as he gazed, waiting for me to begin.

"One lifetime, you and your family moved around a lot, and I met you when we were in about second grade. You moved that summer, but you came back when we were starting freshman year. I was fourteen, and you were fifteen. We started dating, and you would walk me home almost every day. A few months had passed, and I went to school crying. I didn't wanna talk about it, but that day, I told you I didn't want to go home, so you took me home with you. That's when I met your family. I don't exactly know why, but they didn't like me very much.

"They wanted us to break up, so we did, but not really. You just didn't take me home with you anymore. And you didn't talk about me to any of your family members.

"After so long, things got really bad for me at home, so I ran away. No one knew for about three weeks, because my parents didn't care and I made sure you knew where I was. The school reported me missing, of course, because they couldn't get ahold of my parents.

"I knew I couldn't stay with you, and I hadn't met Lydia yet, so I stayed in shelters. But once I was reported missing, since I was underage, I knew I'd get caught and I would be taken somewhere, somewhere away from you. That led me to what I guessed I should've done in the first place. I started sneaking into your room at night. Both of your parents worked, so on weekends, I got to stay there all day. You would bring me up food after breakfast, give me lunch when you got home from school and dinner when you would start to do homework and go to sleep. You started doing your own laundry, so you could also do mine. And the sweetest thing, I think, is that you would teach me everything you had learned that day in school so that I wouldn't fall behind in grade level. Sometimes I was even able to assist you in what you didn't fully understand.

"Sophomore year ended, and your family was going to move again. We had no clue on what we were going to do. I just asked you where you were moving to and told you that I'd find my way there. You were still worried, and so was I, but I had to assure you that I would and everything would be okay.

"I went walking on a day that your family took you to your aunt and uncle's anniversary party. A lady pulled over on the side of the road and asked me what I was doing all on my own. I was pretty upset, so I told her basically everything. The story brought her to tears, and she sympathized with me. So much so that she bought me a one-way airplane ticket and offered to drive me to the airport.

"You were astonished when I told you the story, and we were both so overwhelmingly ecstatic that we didn't even care how much noise we made in your room.

"We moved, and basically, everything stayed the same. You fed me and stayed teaching me. When I turned eighteen, I signed up for GED classes and passed without any trouble. You graduated high school, and we both went to college. You went for a degree in fitness, and I went for a degree in biology. Only a few months into college, we got our own place, and it seemed like all of our problems were gone. We left them all behind us."

He stayed watching me like he wanted me to keep going, like he wanted me to tell him all about his own life and all about our lives. It was like I saw him yearning for something I could not give him, for this memory he didn't have. He was longing to remember it all, like

I did. And I was so sorry, because I really wished I could make him remember it all too.

I glanced at him with tired eyes; his were bloodshot as well. Throwing my hands down onto my lap, I got up and cleared my spot on our bed. He did the same. We lay down and began to fall asleep.

"Hey," he said.

"Yeah?" I responded.

"Isn't it remarkable?"

"What is?"

"I've known you for lifetimes, and you still spark a flame in my heart every time you smile."

I didn't really have anything to say as my heart filled with this comfortable warmth, so I turned over and kissed his back. His words were sweet and honestly made me feel content. But as I turned onto my back, I thought a sad thought. He craved something only God could give him. And I wasn't sure if He ever would. He wanted memories of times he lived, but not from the life he was living. It saddened me to think that he would only dream of things that were not real. And he couldn't remember anything. He could only imagine.

Chapter 18

IT DIDN'T TAKE VERY LONG for Cara to pull another stunt to get me in a heap of trouble once our senior year started. It was mid-September, and Tyler had a doctor's appointment that day, so I chose to let him sleep and I walked to school. I ended up getting to school late because of it, but I didn't find it to be a big deal.

I went to my locker and found it a mess. Clearly, this was Cara getting back at me. I felt too tired to deal with anything that day, but I had no choice but to deal with it. So I walked over to my locker, dropped my bags over to the side of it, and made my way over to the girls' bathroom to grab as many paper towels as I could. I collected a few washcloths and placed them under cool water so I could wash off my locker, which I forgot to mention was covered in eggs! Once I cleaned off the front of my locker door, I opened it. To no surprise of my own, I found the inside trashed. There were miniature trash bags filled with eggshells, egg yolks, paper towels, and gloves. And outside the trash bags, there were empty and half-empty cans of black spray paint. I knew this prank was going to go farther than just screwing up my locker.

Whatever it was, I was going to have to handle it later on in the day. I collected all the trash and went to throw it away. And "later on" came a lot quicker than I had thought and hoped it would, because as I sauntered back to pick up my backpack, I found my principal giving me the same glare she gave me the day "I" flooded the football field. The glare that demanded an explanation, a damn good one.

I said nothing, and she said nothing. All she did was walk toward her office and flick her finger, suggesting that I trail along. I was taken slightly aback when I saw that we weren't going directly to her office. We were making our way to the gym; at least I thought we were. It turned out we were making our way to the side of the gym, the side that was perfectly displayed to everybody who passed the school or was on the football or soccer field. We stopped, and she pointed up. I looked at her then at the mural she so harshly had me look at.

"Did you not learn your lesson last time?" she asked.

I stayed quiet. The only words that came to my mind were "I guess not," and I knew that those were words that she would not appreciate the sound of.

"I cannot comprehend why I have no problems with you at all the entire year except for the beginning. You keep phenomenal grades, give great behavior in class, you are extremely helpful in every club you participate in, but you just have to cause havoc at the beginning of the school year." She paused. "And for some unknown reason, it always has to be this intense."

"I-I don't really know what you want me to say," I said questioningly as I studied her, thinking that perhaps I'd get an idea of what she wanted from me.

"So you're admitting to this? Again, you're not denying any of it?"

"That's right. I can't really see why I would. If I did, I couldn't prove anything, and all signs point to me being at fault, right? So give it to me straight."

She stood back in confusion and attempted to study me. Nothing about our encounters made sense, so I suppose she wanted to make them make sense, at least to make them make sense to her.

"Before I 'give it to you straight,' can you tell me why you did it?"

"I don't know." I looked down and confessed to a crime I didn't commit. "I want to be remembered for something."

"Even something bad?"

"Being forgotten is possibly my biggest fear, so even if I'm remembered for something like this, I'll take it."

She started walking back. I'm guessing I made everything make sense right then, and she probably found it somewhat sad; either that or she didn't believe me, thought my answer was crap, and didn't want to try to get the truth out of me anymore.

Thankfully, it didn't seem like she was having a bad day or on her period because my punishment wasn't as harsh. Well, more so, it wasn't going to last me all year like my last one did.

I went to class and told Lydia a summary of what had happened. She wanted me to spill everything, but I really didn't feel like telling the story twice, so I had her wait till the end of school so I could tell her and Tyler the whole story at the same time. They were both mainly interested in what amount of trouble I was in. I had guessed that was going to be the "best part" of the story.

I mentioned that I had lunch detention for the rest of the semester, that I had to help clean the mural and repaint it, that I had to miss the homecoming dance, and that I was suspended for a week. What I didn't mention was that I wasn't suspended for just any week. I was suspended for spirit week. I was missing out on every fun part of homecoming week and weekend. I obviously had to let Lydia know sooner rather than later, so I told her that weekend. She was devastated. She wanted to miss that week with me, but since I couldn't make up any of the work assigned that week, I knew I had to at least learn and master the material. I had to make her go.

Since Tyler had work and Lydia was at school, I had the week to spend a decent amount of time with Tyler's dad. Raymond didn't have to go to work until one o'clock, which was around the time that Lydia got home from school, so the week wasn't so gloomy. I knew that Tyler was more than glad to have his dad home, but I also knew that he couldn't even begin to imagine how happy I was to finally feel like I had a dad.

Ray and I spoke a lot about little things and had those conversations about nothing. But he also instilled it in me that even though Tyler and I weren't married yet, I was definitely family. He said I had been family for a long time, before Tyler had even proposed. I could never emphasize enough how amazing of a feeling I got from him telling me and truly making me believe all that. Because I remembered how it felt to not belong anywhere or to anyone and to feel like you had no family, like everybody around you had a family that you weren't a part of. That feeling was practically engraved into my soul. I knew I never wanted to feel that emptiness again, so I was beyond grateful that Raymond kind of told me that I would never have to.

Speaking of emotions, I was positive that Cara felt very proud of herself when she noticed that I wasn't in school for that entire week. Pride isn't always an emotion to feel proud of. It can come from bad places. And I'm sure the pride she felt then was coming from one of those bad places—vengeance.

When the week was done with and it was Friday, Tyler got home early, and Lydia flew over to our house the second school let out. When she got there, it almost felt like a reunion, which was completely idiotic being that it was only five days and we all saw and, or spoke, to each other every single one of those five days. But we were attached at the hip; it just felt particularly refreshing to know things were back to normal.

We turned on a movie not long after we had lunch—maybe second lunch—and actually sat down to watch it instead of just letting it play in the background. I wasn't exactly fixated on coming up with an idea to get back at Cara. I just came to the decision that because she took my homecoming away, I was going to make hers not so great. And I just figured that between the two days I had left, something would come to me. Lydia was a little more focused on fabricating a counterattack than I was. So leave it to her to have jumped up during *The Longest Yard* and holler, "I got it!"

Chapter 19

"*W*HAT EXACTLY DO YOU GOT?" I had to ask.

"A counterattack, stupid!" Lydia grumbled.

She yelled at me and smacked me in the face with a pillow. I have not the slightest clue why everyone loves to hit me with pillows.

"Okay, okay! Stop being violent. Let us hear your plan."

"Homecoming night, we steal the Fans' limo."

"How do you know they're getting a limo?" Tyler asked.

"I heard Rachel say so during third period on Tuesday," Lydia said while not hitting Tyler with any pillow.

Tyler and I agreed to Lydia's counterattack plan, but we wanted to finish watching *The Longest Yard*, so she sat back down and didn't further discuss the plan till after it had finished. We inferred that the limo driver wouldn't pay much attention to the kids in the back, so taking it, we guessed, would be a piece of cake.

We just had to wait to see when the Fans got there, wait some more to make sure nothing seemed too fishy, then we'd go and climb into the limo dressed up like we had been at the dance—once again to not seem suspicious—and finally, we'd drive away in an essentially free limo. We were at least making sure that Cara got to homecoming. I was sure finding a ride home wouldn't be excessively difficult. But it hit us—what fun would a stolen limo be if we didn't go out and make something out of the night, so we had some more plans to make.

On the night of homecoming, Lydia and I wore our prom dresses from junior year, and Tyler wore his suit, to look like all we were doing was attending a dance. Raymond took us to the dance; that way, we didn't have a car to pick up afterward. Barely twenty minutes had passed by when we saw Cara and her applaud squad get there. We chose to stand by for at least an hour before getting into the limo so it could appear that we ourselves spent our night having a good time at homecoming.

Time passed, and our plan started to take place. I have to admit, I was a bit nervous that the driver would notice that we weren't the right kids. Luckily enough, he didn't notice anything at all. When we got in, he just asked us where we wanted to go next. On the spot, I thought it'd be nice to go to a local ice-cream shop I loved. It was nighttime, so I'm sure somebody thought it strange, but anytime is a good time for grabbing some ice cream. The driver got us there fairly quickly, considering the traffic. I asked him if he wanted anything before the three of us went in; he seemed flattered but said no thanks. We spent about an hour inside, but none of us were quite ready to go home right away. Lydia had a wonderful idea of where we were going straight to after we had our ice cream: a tattoo parlor!

I asked her how she found out about this tattoo parlor, and she said a friend of her dad's got his tattoos there and heard that the artist who worked there was just about the best around. We gave each other a certain look, knowing who was really considered to be the best artist around—Larry. She thought that if we found Larry there, then we'd get tattoos that night, but if not, then we'd look at his work, think about it, and possibly go back.

Tyler asked about who this Larry guy was. Neither Lydia nor I could really even begin to explain how masterful Larry was, so we told Tyler to just define the word *best* in his mind, gave him a minute, and told him that Larry was the absolute best tattoo artist the world had ever seen. He was possibly the best tattoo artist the world would ever see. God really gave him a gift. It was breathtaking. Tyler sat back sort of amazed. Think about it, Lydia and I had eighty-two lifetimes under our belts; if we were calling this guy the absolute best, then he had to be miraculous at what he did.

Lydia was so anxious to find out if Larry was the guy Richard's friend was such a big fan of that as soon as we pulled up to the parlor, she was instantly out of the limo. Tyler and I followed, not as eager. I promised the chauffeur we wouldn't be too long, if long at all, and that we would be headed home straight afterward. He gave a slight smile and nodded; he assured me that, that was what he was there for. Tyler told him that he could go in if he had wanted, nodding again he said he just might if it took so long.

Knocking on the door Lydia peeked and walked in. She said hello a few times to see who might be there; since the lights were on and the door wasn't locked, she felt it was safe to assume at least one person was there. When Tyler and I walked in, a familiar face popped up from behind the counter. Lydia and I smiled our "very excited" smiles and turned to Tyler to tell him that was indeed Larry—the guy we were hoping for.

Larry said he didn't answer Lydia right away because the robberies in our town were still taking place. And even though they had only seemed to be hitting houses, he was right to think that one can never be too safe. The three of us were all dressed up; I suppose that was what settled him to believe we were no robbers.

"So you guys are looking to get tattoos? Piercings?"

"Tattoos!" Lydia said quickly.

"Cool. All of you guys are getting tatted?"

"I'm not," Tyler contradicted.

"Okay," Larry beckoned. "Just the ladies then."

"I'm first!" Lydia hollered.

Larry laughed a little at how forward Lydia was about how badly she wanted her tattoo. He asked her if she knew exactly what she wanted, and she replied with, "Of course." He told her that was a good thing and that she seemed like she was going to be fun to work with being that she was so enthusiastic. Those words just put her over the moon. She appreciated compliments more than one might imagine. I always thought it was very sweet.

I sat with Tyler in the open area as Larry went with Lydia into the corner area where he tattooed so he could draw her what she had in mind. I would say, so he could "try" to draw her what she had in mind, but it was like Larry crawled into your mind. He seemed to get everything right every time!

She wanted a small tattoo of a tiny sailboat out in the water. Some of the water was dark, like it was night, so the sun wasn't up to guide the boat or where it was going, but there was also lighter water. It was water that had been lit from a nearby, you guessed it, lighthouse. I went after she did and got my usual first tattoo: a lighthouse on my right hip to go along with my best friend's sailboat on her left hip. Her sailboat is supposed to be lost at sea, and my lighthouse is what's supposed to be the reason it finds its way. When she told me I was the reason she ever felt found, I cried like a little girl or, better, like a baby. It just meant a lot to me.

Both of the tattoos only took about an hour and a half, maybe a bit less. And Larry said he really liked us, so we didn't have to pay! I've always loved that guy. Before we got back into the limo, we asked Tyler if he was 100 percent sure he didn't want a tattoo. He said yes. He didn't know what he'd get, where he'd put it, or if it would be colored or a simple black and gray. Up until then, he hadn't thought about it. He had a real appreciation for tattoos but, for whatever reason, didn't think about getting any himself until we brought it to his mind.

I was sorry that I hadn't asked if he wanted one, wanted one that night, or if he knew what he'd get. He had always liked them in every other lifetime, so I just went off that.

We wanted to let the chauffeur go home, so Lydia just let her parents know she was staying at mine and Tyler's house that night. Surprisingly, Ray was still up when we got home. Lydia and I were proud to tell him and show him our fresh ink. He asked Tyler if he got anything, and when Tyler said no, he said Tyler was going to be addicted when he got older. Lydia and I knew that, that typically happened even in the lives when he didn't choose to wait that long.

I turned the TV on as we all started getting ready to go to sleep. During the moments I was grabbing Lydia pajamas, I heard that another robbery took place that night. I found it shameful and sad how people could do those sort of things. Of course, I didn't know if they had been led into those actions or if life had a way of "forcing" them into those actions. Either way, I wished they would've realized there were better ways.

We all fell asleep rather quickly. It made sense. We had a crazy enough night.

I considered not going to school the next day, but I had missed a lot of school, a lot of lessons, a lot of material. I was probably expected back by all my teachers; perhaps the teachers that had only had me previous years expected me to return. I did have spectacular attendance—when I could. I more than likely should have felt joyous to be able to return, but I just felt tired. I was in my own head. I was going back to thinking that I didn't have to care much, so I made Tyler and Lydia get me up no matter what it took. I pretended to be shocked when they automatically had the idea to hit me with pillows.

When I got to first period, Cara wasn't there. I couldn't think of why she wasn't in class. I also couldn't fathom why I even cared. Typically, I was relieved when she wasn't around. It meant she was off my back for a while. Suddenly, about forty minutes into class, I recalled I was signed up to donate blood that day for our annual blood drive. I always donated. I couldn't just pass on what I already volunteered for, so I told my teacher I had to go. She made me collect all my work before I left, though. No one was ever great at getting us in on time for our donation, so the fact that I was signing in an hour late was horrible. After I signed in, I had to check in with the office as well, so they wouldn't get me in trouble for being absent or late.

I ended up missing second period and third period, which was arguably my worst class to miss! I saw Cara having her iron levels tested as I was leaving. Again, I wondered where she had been, because she never dared to miss class.

Lydia was still waiting to donate blood by the time I finished, so I had to go to fourth period without her. I was lucky I was able to attend that class session because that's when we started to review the case of *Roe vs. Wade*. We only highlighted that day, but in AP government, pretty much every day was crucial in my opinion. The bell rang, and Lydia told me she was almost done. She felt a little dizzy, so she was sitting around for a while until she felt good about walking. I offered to go and get her, but she thought it was best that I went and reviewed some of the concepts with my calculus teacher. I agreed and went to my math class.

I stayed for thirty minutes or so. Since I wasn't allowed to make up work from the previous week, I had no work to pick up. I went to go and get Lydia, who was at our bench at that point. I had to text Tyler that I was going to be taking her home since she still felt faint and that he didn't have to go get me. When I lifted my head from my phone, I caught a glance of Cara and her of me. She gave me a dirty look, knowing that I was responsible for taking her limo.

I gave her a cheeky smile and arrogantly waved at her as I passed by without turning back. I don't know why, but at that moment, I noticed that our rivalry felt really good to me I'd even go as far as to say *fulfilling*! When she got me, I got this feeling of "Oh, it's on now." And when I got her, I felt adrenaline. I felt like I was winning in this game that didn't even really exist. I didn't know why, but I knew I was somehow winning in life. I was beating everyone.

Chapter 20

IT WAS THE NIGHT OF the Halloween carnival and probably an ideal night to embarrass the heck out of me. More games and rides were included that year, so a lot more kids went that year than other years. I don't know why or how, but I didn't even care if, that night, Cara had something planned. I guess that was one of the reasons why I even went; I was on cloud nine at that point. Like I said, I just felt like I was winning at life; no one could beat me, so I had nothing to fear.

To my fortune, nothing happened that night as far as Cara's pranks went. I actually didn't even see her there, for the carnival or to assist. That seemed abnormal. I did see Kathleen, Rachel, and Carter there though, so I figured she was probably somewhere with Cynthia. The five of them were always together, so if you saw only three of them somewhere, it was only natural to assume the other two were together someplace else. I'd later find out that assuming really is always a stupid thing to do, and I shouldn't have done it then just like I never did any other time.

For the rest of the semester, my life remained quiet and unshaken. Cara left me alone. We barely saw each other, and every time I did see her, she didn't bother to look at me with eyes full of resentment. It was senior year though. What did I care if this frivolous battle between the two of us continued or ended? If she got me, she got me. I'd find a way to get her back. If she didn't, she didn't, and that would be the end of something that really went on for too long a time.

I definitely had other things to consume my mind: hanging out with my two best friends, doing well in school, and planning my freakin' wedding for goodness sake! All that was a lot better to think about than thinking about getting thrown in the school's dumpster or something like that.

By the time winter break ended and we were all back in school, all the seniors could only talk about the things that all high school kids look forward to until they actually happen. Getting gowns, decorating caps, our last spring break, senior ditch day, and the senior prank were all things that were sought-after. I couldn't tell you how excited everyone was for everything on that list. But most of all, we were excited for the senior trip. Sadly, the school was keeping the destination a secret until February, two months before we left. I paid my money the day we got back to school. I was way too psyched to wait, but of course, I couldn't pay our class president (Cara), so I gave my money to Carol to pay for me. She was a dependable person, so I felt confident counting on her.

No one knew when senior ditch day was, but Cara assured us that it was soon. She said that she would be sure to tell us the day before or the Friday before, so we could make sure that we had everything straight. It turned out that student council—the Fans—were going to drop notes into all the seniors' lockers that had the date of senior ditch day. I couldn't be positive if I would get one or if Lydia would either, so I was glad that Harold ended up telling us. He overheard the Fans saying so while he was working. He told us where we were meeting at as well.

As I thought, Lydia and I both didn't get notes like we were supposed to one Friday at the beginning of February. That Monday, at least 95 percent of the senior class was gone. Some kids had assignments or tests that were just too major to miss. Harold apparently got the date wrong. We weren't mad though. Cara probably figured out that we were friends with Harold and wanted to make us think that we were one step ahead of her. And as much as it pains me to admit, her plan worked.

So we got excluded from senior ditch day. It sucked, but Cara had done worse to me; that was for sure. If that was all, I decided that our war was over. I didn't have to come up with some sort of elaborate plan to get back at her. Instead, all of us seniors who had to miss out on senior ditch day were going to have a ditch day of our own. I took note of all the seniors that were at school when they "shouldn't" have been, and I gathered them up to have a meeting with Lydia and me. We found a date that was good for everyone, which wasn't too hard because there weren't too many of us, and awaited February 16.

Our ditch day started at nine o'clock, late enough to let some kids sleep in if they wanted. We met at an amusement park just outside town. And because it was a school day, there wasn't really any lines at all. We all stayed together for only a little while, then we grouped up and separated. Even after school, there didn't seem to be much of a line at any game or ride. The entire group stayed there until past four thirty! We were all having such a good time that we insisted on keeping our ditch day going. We crowded a restaurant even more out of town for dinner then went to a not-so-popular lake that was closer to town but not so nearby. The lake was somewhat hidden, and not a bunch of people knew about it; only two kids in our group had known about it. That was the only reason it wasn't popular, because honestly, that lake was one of the coolest places I had been to in a really long time. All of us promised to keep it a secret so that it would only be our secret, kind of like a lake God made especially for outcasts. To me, that was the best part.

The next school day, it felt like I had a ton more friends. I don't know if the other kids felt that way because a lot of them probably already were friends, but if they did feel that way, that makes me feel pretty enthused.

Caps and gowns came in, and for the entire day, the senior class was basically all matching. I was nervous about getting mine dirty, but I just had to get a feel for what it was like having it on. Everyone was talking about how they wanted to decorate their cap or bragging about their original idea, but there were a few seniors who wanted to keep their ideas a secret so that nobody else could even think about stealing it from them. For example, there was a set of twins who were doing matching caps. They had some inspiration from their favorite movie. When they both would not dare tell me, I was even more eager for graduation just so I could see how their caps came out.

The senior prank was pretty great. Out of all my lifetimes, I think I like this one the most. All week, kids from the senior class had been taking staff members thoughtful gifts such as coffee, candy, and flowers. So at the end of the week, it didn't seem so suspicious when we went around handing out brownies to janitors, teachers, security guards, counselors, every member of the school's staff. I hate to admit that we even got some of our cool staff members, but that's the way the game goes. I wasn't one of the seniors handing out the brownies, sadly. I wanted to be, but I didn't have a completely clean record with the principal, so I was just one of the kids who made our plan not so suspicious. I gave out the flowers.

Either you're wondering how the heck this was a prank or you're thinking we got our faculty members high. No, we didn't do that. We did something even better. Every single one of the brownies we handed out had laxatives in them! It was the funniest thing ever. I'm sure that day any part of the staff that took a brownie, which almost all of them did, hated the seniors with a passion. I'm sure they loathed us right after they finished, well, you know. I would think that our principal was livid enough to want to suspend all of us, but she couldn't suspend all of us. Well, maybe she could have, but she didn't. Not one of us got into trouble. Maybe she just came to terms with the fact that it was a joke and that, in reality, we just had to do it. We didn't have a choice. It's what seniors do.

The lowerclassmen were wondering what on earth was going on that day, so we felt very entitled to the right to brag about it. They, especially freshman, looked at us as if we were the ultimate prank-sters, best in the world. Who knows, maybe we were. Some of them told me it really sucked that they couldn't have thought of that first. And now, they had to top such a brilliant idea like ours. Okay, maybe they didn't say *brilliant*, but they did love our prank. It was definitely a senior prank to beat; that's the truth.

Our last high school spring break was really the last thing we were all pumped for together, because obviously, not every senior could go on the senior trip, but we did all get time away from school. I found out in my first-period English class that the school arranged for us to go to Finland for an entire week. That was the best news!

I hadn't been to Finland for a long while, and I personally loved it there. It was beautiful the last time I saw it, so you can imagine that I missed it and that I was basically electrified to visit.

April came, and the senior trip was only a week away. The trip started a week before spring break did, so I was going to get three weeks off school instead of only two. Lydia and I collected all the work we were going to be missing and stayed in for lunch for certain lessons so the work would undoubtedly be a breeze. Also, in preparation for the trip, Lydia and I went to a bunch of stores just searching around for anything we might "need" in the plane, in the hotel, during the trip. Tyler was clever enough to look up cool things to do and places to go while we were there. He admitted that he was a bit jealous but that he was glad that we were going to have sister time and an overall good time. I promised him that I'd take him to Finland at least for a short while so he could experience the food, the land, the scenery, and everything else. He loved the sound of that.

The week felt incredibly lengthy, but Thursday finally arrived. I had Lydia stay with me and Tyler that night so we could pack together and so we could travel to the airport in just one car. We had too many things, so Lydia and I didn't pack everything we thought we needed. Only making room for the essentials, we managed to fill up four luggage bags.

Friday morning, both Lydia and I woke up at four o'clock, maybe even a bit earlier, without any struggle. We were both just so excited for our trip. I don't think either of us even wanted to sleep on the plane, so it wasn't like we got up easily, because we knew we'd be napping soon. We got dressed, ate, and loaded up the car. Ten minutes after letting the car warm up, we woke up Tyler and Raymond. Ray had to come so Tyler wouldn't have to drive all the way back by himself. Thankfully, they got up quickly, because they knew that as soon as they took us, they'd get to go back home and sleep.

So we were off to the airport, Lydia and me as excited as ever. On the way there, shockingly, no one slept. Once we got there, Tyler got down with us. Ray didn't want to get down; he said the airport was too busy of a place to be if you didn't have to be there. I will give him that much. When we walked in, it was crazy. But nonetheless, we got to the gates without any issues. Lydia hugged Tyler goodbye and promised she'd send him lots of photos on the trip so it'd be just like he was there with us. And he promised her he'd do the same so it'd be just like she was home. It was the best of both worlds, I guess. I hugged Tyler goodbye too, but longer. I didn't really want to let him go and wished that he could come with us to Finland. He said he wished he could too but that a week wasn't too long and that he'd call me every night to tell me good night. We told each other that we would miss each other and that we loved each other. Finally, I kissed him and let him go. Lydia was already waiting for me to get through security, so I hurried into the line, looked back, and waved at Tyler before he started to leave to the car.

I got through security after a few minutes, and when I put my shoes back on and whatnot, Lydia and I went straight to get coffee. Our enthusiasm seemed to be wearing down, but only slightly. Still, the coffee just felt necessary. About halfway through my coffee, I needed the restroom, so I handed Lydia all my things and went. Right when I got back, they announced our flight was boarding. I asked Lydia if she needed to go; she said no. But I reminded her that it was going to be quite a long flight and airplane bathrooms aren't exactly pleasant. That convinced her to go just to be sure, so she gave me all her things, and I waited. As I waited, I was very surprised to see Cara coming up to me.

"Hey, Melenium," she said with a smirk on her face.

"Hi," I said back as I turned away, knowing that I didn't exactly want to talk to someone I found so wicked, and not in a good way.

"So our little game, it's pretty much over?"

"Yeah. I'd say so," I replied, making eye contact now.

"You think you won?"

"Actually, yes. I do think I won."

Cara laughed a small laugh.

"I don't," she said. "I think I won."

"Well, I guess we'll have to wait and see."

"I guess so. You will just have to wait and see."

Still with that smirk on her face, Cara walked away and onto the plane.

Lydia walked out of the bathroom, and I told her about the small conversation I had just had with Cara moments ago. She told me to try to forget it, we had a trip to enjoy, and we couldn't let her ruin it, not even only a little. I agreed, and we went to get in line to board the plane.

"Legend, Lydia Legend," Lydia said so she could get on the plane.

The lady nodded with a smile and told Lydia to make her way onto the plane.

"Melenium Champion," I said.

"I'm sorry, your name isn't on the list for this flight."

"That's not possible. It has to be."

"No, I'm afraid I can't let you on without a reserved seat."

She handed me the list, and my name, indeed, was not on it. As I handed the clipboard back, a man came up behind me and tapped my shoulder.

"A young lady asked me if I could give this to you. She had to board her flight, but she said that it was important."

I opened the envelope I was just given, and I saw that inside it was an old check and a note. The note read, "You didn't think that I was so rotten that I'd keep your money, did you?" Sure enough, the check was the check I had signed weeks ago and had given to Carol to turn in for me. It was torn up in six pieces.

My phone rang right then. It was Lydia asking me why I was taking so long. I texted her back, telling her that I couldn't go, because on top of the fact that I didn't have a reserved seat, the plane was full. And just after I pressed Send, I saw the last two kids get on the plane ready to leave, so I couldn't purchase a ticket. Lydia asked me if I wanted her to get off the plane just before they left, and I, of course, told her no. Carol and Julian would be with her, so I told her to try to just have fun as much as she could.

I sat down at the gate for a while in disbelief. When I finally could do it, I called Ray to come and pick me up. I knew that if I called Tyler, he would stay asking too many questions that I did not feel like answering. Feeling bad about having to make him make his way up to the airport a second time, I decided I was going to buy us all dinner that night. It wasn't like I didn't have the money. It was all there sitting pretty in my account.

I waited in a lounging area that the airport had while Raymond and Tyler made their journey up there, again. I saw Tyler walk in through the doors. I thought to myself, *Why didn't he just call?* He noticed me before I went to him, and he hugged me. Oh, that was why; he realized I really wanted and needed a hug. Like I expected, he started asking questions. Before we got to the car, I put my finger over his lips, and he stayed quiet. I shook my head, turned away, and then kept walking. I couldn't answer any questions yet. I was feeling too many emotions, and they were all awful.

I climbed to the back seat of the car, put my seat belt on, and pouted, looking out the window and waiting for us to start our way home. I noticed Raymond look at Tyler to silently ask him what was wrong. Tyler shrugged and mouthed, "I don't know."

I would've spoken, at least enough to answer their questions, but I really couldn't. I had to hold my facial expression in place. It was the face you make when you know that if you move or speak a single word, you'll start bawling out tears. And I didn't want to start crying. I know that bottling your emotions up is a bad thing, but I don't think anyone likes talking about how terrible they feel, especially not right away. Hyperventilating, runny nose, cheeks burning from all the salty tears were simply not something I enjoyed, so the entire way home I was silent.

When we got home, I rushed out and went to bed. I let myself cry there, not loudly like I honestly would've preferred, but a lot. I wet my pillow so much that you might've guessed that a tired dog slept and drooled all over it. That wasn't the most comfortable way to try to sleep, so I stole Tyler's pillow. In no time, I was passed out.

I woke up five hours later with my bags unpacked, my pillow dry with a new pillowcase, and food ready for me on the side table. Man, God blessed me with the best fiancé ever! I went downstairs and saw Ray and Tyler playing Madden on the Xbox. I found it sweet that they were trying to stay quiet to let me sleep, because they were typically extremely loud when they played against each other. I went and sat down to watch, and they paused the game to ask me if I felt better. I confessed that I didn't feel much better, far from happy, but the nap helped. I had calmed down, and I was ready to talk.

Ray said that he would save the game, we could have an early dinner, and we'd all talk then, but I said no to that. I wanted to watch them finish their game, to see who won. And I wanted to treat the both of them to dinner at one of our favorite restaurants. The final score was 24–32. Tyler lost. He kept repeating himself, saying that Ray got lucky and that they had to play another game. I found it pretty hilarious and was relieved that the focus wasn't on me for the time being.

When we got to the restaurant, I told Tyler and Raymond the whole story of what happened that morning. They were both pretty blown away with how terrible it all sounded. It almost seemed like I was making it up, because honestly, what kind of person even does that? I started to realize that this whole thing probably wasn't just about who topped our class anymore. It had to be more than that; it just had to. Raymond asked me if I still wanted to go and, since I had my money in the bank, why I didn't buy a ticket so I could be with Lydia. I explained to him that since it was a school trip, the tickets were at a discount—a very good discount—and I definitely couldn't afford a full-price ticket. It was a real shame, but after covering the main story, I didn't want to get into the details. I barely wanted to talk about it at all. So we switched topics for the rest of the night.

I had already napped for a decent while, but I was still ready to go to sleep at eleven o'clock. I wanted to stay up until I heard from Lydia, but I didn't want to spend the night constantly checking my phone. Tyler was real tired as well and was in bed thirty minutes before me. I was on the brink of slumber when I heard my phone go off. I picked up my phone and saw that Lydia sent me her first picture of the week. It was her in her hotel room. I texted her back, telling her the room looked gorgeous and I was so jealous. She responded, saying that she had a way to make me less jealous. I asked her how, but I fell asleep seconds after I hit Send.

I got up in the morning and checked my phone. Lydia sent me a message telling me that Cara was her roommate for the next seven days. Following that message was a photo of her making a pouty face.

She was right. I did feel less jealous. But I did feel bad because even though most of their time in Finland wasn't going to be in the hotel, I was sure Cara wasn't going to give her a very easy time.

As the weekend went by, I was okay, but I was still upset. When I went back to school for my last week before spring break, I was still okay, but I noticed something. I was actually very angry! I was infuriated, truly furious that Cara had the audacity to take an experience away from me. In our earlier years, it seemed as if she was just trying to coerce me to stop trying completely in academics so she could pull ahead in our graduating class, but now it all seemed like it was that she was out to get me. It seemed as though she just wanted to be mean and bully me, to make me sad and heartbroken in certain situations of my life.

I obviously have to admit that there are things that I did to her that I really should not have, done things I'm not greatly proud of, but I looked at it only as if she deserved it all. I omitted the golden rule. I made it "Treat people how they treat you," not "Treat people how you want to be treated." That's why at the end of that Monday, I told myself that I did indeed get mine, but I was going to make sure that Cara got hers.

Chapter 21

*A*S THE WEEK WENT ON, my phone was going off constantly. Lydia wasn't only sending me some photos; she was sending me every photo she took. And sometimes she would send one just to say hi. I thought it was sweet, and it made me smile. But even though I had calmed down, I was still livid. Cara Montoya had a huge target on her back, and I was determined to hit it.

Having all the time I had, I, for the first time, came up with a diabolical plan or "counterattack" of my own. I stayed thinking about it all day so I could fix the kinks and work out the details. The second I had it all figured out, I sent Lydia a photo captioned "I got it!" She replied with a compilation of question marks, not too positive of what I was talking about. I knew that if she was out, she wouldn't really be able to talk, and if she was in her room, she wouldn't be able to talk at all because Cara would be around. So I spent fifteen minutes typing out a text message telling her everything about this facinorous arrangement I had devised.

I couldn't wait to hear what Lydia thought and what she possibly had to add on. But I had to. It was over an hour before she got back to me, and when she did get back to me, I was quite taken aback. She texted, "I'm not too sure about that :/" The emoticon showed that she didn't have much approval for what I had thought of. Her answer was short, and I kind of found it unsettling. I didn't know what her response was even supposed to mean. This whole time, I hadn't seen her so resentful; she didn't even want to suggest anything different. I went to Tyler to see what his reaction would be. He really had no comment and didn't say anything on why he thought Lydia replied with such a standoff approach.

The two of them being so resilient toward what I thought was an ingenious plan led me to act aloof. Typically, getting back at Cara for how poorly she treated me left the three of us elated, but now for some reason, the two of them were left uncertain, as if something happened and altered how they perceived our actions. It was as though the last four years were repugnant and unnecessary. But how could that be? Nothing at all had changed.

The next day, my phone stayed completely silent, and I wondered why Lydia wasn't sending me pictures. I tried not to focus on it and played outside with Neptune and Gadget while Tyler was at work. At eight forty-five, my phone rang with a message from Lydia. It was her lying in bed, saying that she forgot to charge her phone overnight, so it was out of battery all day. That relieved me of some stress I didn't want to believe I had. Later she said she had Carol take a bunch of pictures and she was going to send them to her. And then she'd send them to me.

Friday morning, I made the decision to not go to school. It was the day before spring break; how important could it honestly have been? Lydia texted me in the afternoon right before she got on the plane to let me know she was coming home. I was glad that she was going to be back soon and we could spend spring break with each other. I told her to call me when she landed even though I knew it would either be very late that night or very early the next morning.

That day, I had a lot of coffee and a bottle of Pepsi; with all that sugar, I don't know how or why I went to bed so early. So the next morning, I had a missed call and three text messages from Lydia. I got out of bed to make breakfast and started to call her back, but I hung up once I heard her ringtone coming from the living room. I ran and hugged her tight. I always hated being without her. Tyler came in, and I was surprised he was awake, but less surprised when he confessed that it was only because he had to be at work soon. He had made the two of us breakfast knowing that we had to talk all about our time apart. He kissed me before he left and told Lydia that when he got off work, she would have to tell him all about her trip as well. She laughed and said she would gladly do so.

We sat down at the table, and I told Lydia I wanted to hear about her week first. Barely eating at all, Lydia told me all about Finland and about the things that were new and things that were still the same. For at least twenty-five minutes, she ranted on and on about the northern lights. But of course, I did not interrupt once. I gave her my undivided attention. I would say that it was easy because she was chatting about it so enthusiastically that I was wavered to believe that even the twelve-hour plane ride was fascinating. When she finished, we stayed talking because I obviously had some questions lined up for her, and she was very excited to answer them. We went back to the living room, and she showed me all the videos she took that she hadn't sent to me. The trip seemed pretty exhilarating and even more then; I wished I had been able to join her.

That led me to tell her about my week. There wasn't too much to tell, definitely not as much as she had, but I stretched some stories out, and more than once did I go off topic for longer than I should have. But like me, Lydia didn't interrupt a single time and gave me her undivided attention. I really got into my storytelling when I came to telling her about my plan to get back at Cara for excluding me from the senior trip. I noticed Lydia's smile dropped once I started talking about it, but I inferred that she was just trying to focus on all the beautifully devious details, so I kept on. I finished, and I was once again waiting anxiously for her response. I thought that perhaps hearing it over again would brighten her up to the notion. It didn't.

"I still don't really know about that," she said, making that expression of disapproval.

"What do you mean, Liv? You're usually so pumped to think something up or carry the plan out."

"I know but—"

"Do you want to think of something? Is that the problem, 'cause if that's what it is, I have no problem handing the wheel off to you. I mean, you always have great ideas."

"That's not it, Mel…"

"Then, what is it?" I looked at her with concern and curiosity.

"I-I just think that," she took a breath, "I just think we shouldn't do anything."

I stood up.

"What?"

"I don't think we should do anything."

"Are you being serious right now?" My voice had risen. "Liv, do you remember what she did to me a week ago? And two months ago, a year ago, and the year before that?"

"Mel, I know. She's been horrible, but that doesn't mean we have to be horrible back!"

"Listen, I'm just not okay with her getting the last laugh. I don't know how you can't understand that."

"I do understand. But, Mel, you gotta be the bigger person here."

"Screw being the bigger person! I've been the bigger person this whole time, every single lifetime. And every single time, the asshole who wasn't being the bigger person won."

Pain really got to me. I didn't know what I was saying. All I knew was that I was hurt and I wanted someone to hurt, not with me, but more than me. And instead of me.

"How, Melenium? How did they win?" she asked.

"Because at the end of it all, I was still hurt! I'm tired of being the one who always has to just get over everything."

"I know, and I know it sucks, but you have to listen to me. I mean, Tyler agrees with me."

I was pretty startled. Tyler never told me about Lydia saying all of what she was saying then. He told me everything, and now he was omitting things from our conversations? That made me even more hurt than I was before.

"So you're the one who made him turn down my plan."

"Yeah, I guess."

"Can you at least tell me what made you have this change of heart?"

"I can't," she said, looking down.

"Well, fine."

In that moment, I started having an anxiety attack, but I didn't want her comfort or her presence around me. I only wanted to be alone. So I ran straight to my room and right to my bed. I curled up and started breathing heavily. I felt my eyes starting to water, and then the first tear fell from my left eye. I threw the blanket over myself and started to whisper to myself and to God to see if I could regain my composure. Lydia was knocking on my locked door, begging me to let her in, but she was the reason I was crying. It was her fault. Why would I let her in?

In the midst of all the havoc, I somehow fell back asleep. I don't know for how long, but when I woke up, I felt a hand rubbing my back. It was Tyler's. And I heard his voice; he was talking to Lydia. She stayed waiting outside my bedroom door. That broke my heart a little bit. Why did I always shut her out? Neither of them noticed I had woken up, so I closed my eyes and listened to what they were saying because I knew it had to be about me. Tyler asked Lydia if she told me what she had told him. She said no and that she didn't know if she should. They didn't talk much longer, but Tyler told her that he would decide and, if so, he would tell me. So he asked her to come back in the morning. Lydia said she wanted to be there when I woke up to make sure I wasn't made at her. I decided I wasn't. But Tyler told her he really wanted to tell me alone so I didn't feel bombarded.

Lydia left, and only minutes later, I got up. I asked Tyler what it was that he and Lydia didn't want to tell me. He refused to tell me right then. He said he wanted to wait till I had really calmed down; it didn't seem like I had. I inclined that he tell me. I honestly felt offended that he thought I was too unstable to hear news that he and Lydia were obviously able to handle and handle well. The fact that that made me upset, he said, was the reason he knew I wasn't ready to be told.

I didn't start having a second anxiety attack, but again I ran out and wanted to be alone and unbothered. As I was on my walk, I saw Rachel and Cynthia. They were talking about planning a graduation party for the both of them and the rest of the Fans. Rachel thought that it was best if they only made final decisions when the five of them were with one another. Cynthia concurred, so she suggested that they all meet up at her house that night. Rachel told her that wouldn't work because Cara was busy that night and would be at a fancy restaurant having dinner. I stopped listening then and chose to execute my plan alone. Lydia and Tyler might not've agreed with it, but they didn't feel, know, or comprehend my pain or how badly Cara had been hurting me those past four years. They didn't get my reasoning, but I did. My plan was flawless, and I was not wrong in thinking it up or in carrying it out. I wanted it to stop more than either of them understood, and the way I saw it, that plan was the only way to make it stop.

I made a few stops to get what I needed and went to the restaurant Cara was going to be at right away. I had bought a pack of water balloons, and maybe that doesn't sound so ruthless, I know I didn't think so, but it was still a glorious plan in my opinion. I stayed on the side of the restaurant with the hose. I filled up balloons with dirt and water and shook them so the balloons would be mud balloons. When this all really began, I was getting splashed frequently with cold, muddy water. I was going to have it all end this way, except now the tables would be turned. Cara would be on the receiving end.

After I finished, I just waited patiently, but at the same time impatiently. I wanted Cara to experience her karma as soon as possible. And it was like I say, karma's a bitch, but only if you are. And for the past four years, she was.

I saw her car pull into the parking lot. It was go time. She stayed inside her car for a while. She was alone, so I didn't know why. I couldn't think of her doing anything else except, perhaps, fixing her makeup. If only she knew how pointless that was going to be. She stepped out of her car and walked a few steps; that's when I stepped out and started pelting her with my mud balloons! I hit her shoes, her dress, her legs, her hair, her face—side profile and all and maybe even everything else. I knew that I threw the balloons hard. I could hear it in the way they popped. It was hideously satisfying.

Cara started sobbing lightly. That was when I stepped out a tad more. She looked up at me drenched in muddy water; I couldn't tell if she was actually crying or just upset with what just happened. Then I looked at her and said, "Game over. I won." We both shifted stares when we heard a voice.

"Cara, hurry. Your dad has been waiting…six…years."

The sound of heels sped up, and I heard Cara's mom ask her what happened to her and if she was okay. Cara started sobbing louder, and her breaths got faster and less consistent. Man, did I know how that felt. Cara's mom must not have seen me, because she said nothing, but I still started to run anyway. I don't know why, for how long, or how far. I guessed that maybe I wanted to focus more on my breathing and my trail than focus on the fact that I had just completely ruined a daughter's date with her dad, whom she hadn't seen in over six years.

I stayed walking, and by the time I realized where I was, it was real late. I had seven missed calls from Lydia and nine from Tyler and four text messages from both of them. Where I was, was nearby Larry's shop, so I headed over there. I was so lucky that he was there. He asked why on earth I was out. I didn't want to explain, so I just told him it was a long story; thankfully, he took my answer and asked no questions. I made up my mind and called Tyler, knowing I couldn't stay there all night. I had to let Larry go home.

Tyler picked up almost instantly, wanting to know where I was. I told him I was at the tattoo parlor we went to for homecoming. He said he didn't quite remember where that was but that he would find me. A literal minute later, he texted me, saying for me not to move. He knew me too well. I probably would've walked to some place he was more familiar with to make it easier on him. Tyler didn't take too long. I didn't think maybe fifty minutes after we got off the phone. He went in and thanked Larry for "keeping an eye on me." Larry laughed and said it was no problem; he guaranteed him we were already pals.

When I climbed into Tyler's Jeep, I tried changing the subject that hadn't got started. I was willing to talk about basically anything that wasn't related to what I had just done. But as you might've wisely predicted, Tyler wasn't going to let me off the hook that easily; actually, he wasn't going to let me off at all. He hit me hard with the questions, asking me where I had been and what I had been up to. I angrily crossed my arms and refused to answer him. He tried to demand that I answer him, but I kept my mouth shut. Holding in my tears, I was hoping that he'd do the same. For the car ride, he did, but then we got home, and he began with the questions again. I jumped out of the car and slammed the door closed. Then I stomped my way inside the house and to our room. Still, I was hoping that he would let up on me and realize that I wasn't in the mood to be asked questions. I was only in the mood to be left alone. He should've realized that I was going to tell him the whole story when I felt like it, when I was ready.

He lost his patience with me that night and barged into the room fuming.

"Melenium, you have to tell me now!"

"No, I don't! I don't have to do anything!" I answered back.

"Yes, you do. I wanna know, and I wanna know now." He stared at me with a good amount of fury in his eyes. "Melenium!"

"All right!" I shouted. "You wanna know what I did? I just pelted a girl with balloons full of mud. She hadn't seen her dad in over six years, and I ruined their first time seeing each other in that long of a time!"

"You what? How could you do that?"

"I didn't know, okay? I didn't know." I paused. "But you did. Why didn't you stop me? Why didn't you and Lydia tell me what was going on with her?"

"We didn't want to upset you. Being that most of that time, you were screwing with her."

"I was screwing with her? Don't you mean we were screwing with her?"

"I guess, but it was mainly you. I mean, you started it."

"You've got to be freakin' kidding me right now. You're the one who started it. I planned on playing the innocent, good girl till everything ended, but you told me I had to do something."

"I didn't tell you to take it this far."

"And are you just totally forgetting everything she did to me? If you want, you can say she's the one who really started it. It's a justifiable statement."

"I didn't forget about what she's done, but that's no excuse."

"You're right! It's not an excuse. It's a reason."

"You know? I'm getting the impression that you wanted to do all this. You wanted to hurt her. This was your opening, and you took it."

"Now that's ridiculous! You honestly believe I wanted all of this to happen? So you know how crappy I feel right now? God! You're out of your mind!"

"I'm out of my mind? You're the one who claims to have lived eighty-two damn lives and remembers them all."

"So now you don't believe me?"

"I don't know! I don't think I should. I mean, the very thought of that is mad! Disturbed! Demented even!"

"You don't mean that." I wept.

"I just might, Melenium. I mean I don't remember anything. Why is that, huh? Why can't I remember anything but you and your sister can remember eighty-two lifetimes?"

I didn't want to answer.

"See, you can't tell me. For all I know, you and Lydia are both complete nutjobs who just wanted to pull one over on me or anybody dumb enough to believe you. You guys are, more than likely, just completely delusional!"

That right there made me crack. He was not going to say that about my little sister.

"Okay!" I hollered. "Okay, Tyler, you wanna know why I remember, why she remembers?"

"I'm waiting," he expressed arrogantly.

"It's because I committed suicide!"

He stood up right and lost all arrogance in his face.

"That's right. I committed, I killed myself, I took my life! Any way you wanna phrase it, I did it. Wanna know how? I got a gun, put the barrel to my head, pulled the trigger, and shot a bullet straight through my skull on the side of a freeway! Nobody would've noticed I was gone, but the school reported all of my absences. When they found my body, Lydia saw it on the news and had to identify me. Only years later, she did the exact same thing, in the exact same place! We didn't have anyone to give a damn about us, so we had to do it somewhere at least kind of obvious. My little sister cut her life short, and it was all my fault! Our first lives, I took them away. God said we had to remember so we'd never give up on ourselves and do it again." I rubbed my tears away. "And wanna hear the best part? The day I did it was the day before I was supposed to meet you."

Tyler took a step toward me, probably to console me, but I stopped him and told him not to touch me. He stared at me speechless. He didn't know what he could do or what he could say. But I didn't need him to do or say anything; what could he have? I was breathing heavily, and yet I felt I couldn't breathe at all. I didn't want to be near him, so I quickly walked away. He stayed stunned and frozen and still.

Chapter 22

$\mathcal{F}$OR THE SECOND TIME THAT night, there I was, running away. I sat down on the sidewalk once I couldn't torture my lungs any longer. Panting harshly, I threw my head back. I still felt like I was being asphyxiated by the night, but my legs begged me for rest, so I stayed motionless. I rested my arms and head on my knees, listening only to crickets, my breaths, and the very occasional passing car. I ignored my aching heart and painful thoughts. At least, I tried to. It was close to four o'clock in the morning when I knocked on my sister's window. Slowly and carefully, she assisted me into her room. She worriedly asked me what I was doing there at that time in the night and pondered if things were okay at all, since I had been away for so long. I could only tell her that I would explain later; reliving the ending of my first life made me want to make sure Lydia was all right in every way more than ever before. That meant that I needed her to be fully rested.

I didn't sleep that night; I didn't really care to, but I was feeling exhausted not only from the lack of sleep but also from the running and the crying. Close to nine o'clock, I started to really feel how tired I was and began to fall asleep. But just before I did, I heard Lydia wake up. I sat up so I wouldn't give her the impression that she woke me up. She peaked in the room and walked in slowly. She asked me how I was feeling. I shook my head, looked her in the eye, and confessed that I wasn't feeling great.

Questions weren't exactly something I needed right then, but I knew I couldn't make this another time I chose to shut her out, so I let her ask away. She asked only a few, just to get the answers on how to go about making me feel better. We talked about mine and Tyler's fight, everything he said and everything I said back. I told her that I told him the whole story, even why she remembered it all. I hoped she wasn't mad, and she said she wasn't. When she finished asking me about the fight, I took a deep breath and admitted I had to tell her more. I had to tell her about Cara.

She stayed quiet as the story spilled from my mouth, and when I finished, she took a deep breath and admitted that she had a strong urge to lecture me, but she sort of knew that she didn't have to. She knew that I knew what I did was wrong, stupid, childish, and spiteful. I didn't have to hear what I already knew. I proved that the second I gained the guts to rat myself out and told her what I had done.

I laid my head on her shoulder and cried a little. She laid her head on mine and told me that it was okay and I was fine. After a few minutes, she patted me on my knee, got up, and told me to go with her to eat. But I didn't want to eat. I wanted to simply lie down and be sad. It wasn't her fault, but I really wanted to be alone.

I'm positive that anyone and everyone who reads this knows what it's like to want nothing more than to be alone. And I'm also positive that a vast majority, if not all, of who read this know that it is terrible when somebody you love tells you they just want to be left alone, because you really do not wish to leave them alone. You want to be there for them.

That was the situation then. I craved no company but my own. And Lydia wanted to grant me hers. But she understood that for, however long, the best thing she could do was give me space. I would get better on my own time, and when I got better, enough, I'd ask for the company she was saving for me.

I spent a week in the guest room feeling all sorts of emotions, including emotions that I thought I'd never have to feel again. I would hear Lydia talking to Tyler and strictly told him not to come over and see me. She said she wasn't mad at him, but I think she was, at least to an extent. She probably didn't want to be, but when someone hurts someone else that you love, you'll always store up some resentment toward them.

The first day I spent disgustingly sad, the kind of sad where snot is dripping onto your lips and you barely even notice because you barely even care. I couldn't stay quiet because I was crying too hard; I couldn't catch my breath. I didn't even leave the bed. That told Lydia she was going to have to take care of me a little. She would go in the room and make sure I ate at least twice a day. She made sure I took showers. And she made sure I changed my clothes daily. I couldn't stay in snot-covered clothes for longer than a day.

Days 2, 3, and 4 were the exact opposite; I didn't make a sound. Late afternoon, Lydia would come to check and see if I was sleeping and if she doubted it she had to see that I was still there. I let my emotions melt. I guess they all mixed together because I didn't know what to feel. Mostly during the course of those three days, I felt empty.

The fifth and sixth days were a mixture of the two. I stayed quiet, but I cried almost nonstop. I felt something that I was certain I'd never feel again, and I definitely was convinced that if I did, I wouldn't feel it so strongly and with such depth: the desire to die. I lay there and stared at a blank white wall, and the words "I want to die," "I wish I were dead," and "Maybe I should kill myself" ran over and over again, repeating in my head. When the day switched to night, I concentrated on the wall that now wasn't white; it turned black, and I started to picture the word *death* written across it. My mind was screaming, yelling for help as I stayed silent. I realized that I didn't want to be dead; no, it was much more morbid than that. I wanted to be dying. Despite me wanting to not have to hurt anymore, I craved pain, but only the ultimate pain: suffering. The kind of pain that made me want to give up, but I couldn't; that wasn't a luxury I was given. I wanted that. That was another night that I went without sleep. In the morning, after the wall turned back to white and Lydia brought me food, I wrote a suicide note. It was mainly to Tyler. It didn't explain much, but it did say that if he'd have me, I'd never be gone and that went for anybody else who'd have me. I asked God to take me away. I told Him I didn't belong in this world, I wasn't made for it, and I wasn't meant to be here. I asked Him to take me and never put me back. I didn't want to have to do it myself. But He didn't. The letter was short, but despite that, I read it to myself for hours.

Lydia came in with dinner. I asked her to eat with me. I didn't say anything, and she didn't say much, but having her there gave me a sense of security. When I was done eating, she placed my plate on top of hers and stood up. I stood up and took the plates from her. I laid them on the desk, and I hugged her tight and for a long time. In the middle of it, I noticed how I was breathing. I noticed how she was breathing. I noticed my heartbeat. I noticed her heartbeat. When I let go, she asked me if I was okay. I took a few seconds to think about it and thought that the appropriate answer would be yes, so I said yes. She smiled and said "good." I turned around, went to the bed, and told her good night.

I fell asleep, but being the insomniac that I am, I woke back up at two o'clock in the morning. I stared at the ceiling for a while, but I got uncomfortable and turned over to stare out of the window. I noticed the moon wasn't like my wall. Despite the darkness, the black holes, and the meteorites, the falling stars, and the lifeless planets, it stayed white. It shone very bright and lit up the night.

I left a note for Lydia to find and sneaked out the window. I couldn't put this off any longer. I couldn't live anymore, not knowing I did another soul so wrong. No, I didn't go and kill myself again, if that's what you thought. I went to go find Cara to give her the biggest apology anybody had ever heard.

I was absolutely clueless when it came to knowing where Cara lived, but I knew where Kathleen lived, so I walked all the way over to her house. I knocked on her door when I got there; that was probably pretty rude. I didn't think to be mindful of her family, and I had forgotten that I was out at a ridiculous hour. Kathleen's dad came to the door and asked me what I was doing there. I told him that I had to be somewhere very important but I couldn't go without seeing Kathleen first. He invited me in and told me to wait while he got Kathleen out of bed. She walked in, very surprised to see me. Like her dad, she asked me what I was doing there. I gave her a synopsis of what had happened the week before, and I told her that I felt like the worst person in the world for it and that I needed to know where Cara lived so that I could apologize for all of it. She gave me her address. I was going to be on my way, but she stopped me. I guess she wanted me to feel less guilt because she told me that Cara actually saw her dad in October. That was why she wasn't at the carnival that night. Her dad didn't go home straight away, because he wanted to help his friend who was suffering badly from PTSD. Lastly, she told me not to go there right away; it was too early.

I thanked her and went back out to find Cara's house. I was able to find it without struggle, but I waited till nine o'clock to knock on Cara's door. I was nervous and felt my heart pounding. When Cara opened the door, I just lost my ability to talk; I had a lot to say but didn't know where to start. She was going to shut the door in my face, but before she could, I yelled "Wait!"

"What?"

"I-I really need to talk to you. Can I please talk to you?"

She thought about it, probably considering just closing the door again, but then she let me in. I stayed nervous convinced that she hated me more than ever and wouldn't actually listen to a single word that I had to say. We sat down in her living room, and suddenly I felt my face getting hot, tears were tempted to come out, but I knew I wasn't there to break down, not right away at least.

"I'm sorry."

She looked at me for a moment then asked me why.

"Because I did something really awful to you. And…and not even just last week, but also over these past four years. I wasn't very nice. I was the opposite of nice. I was just plain mean. I have never wanted to be the reason anybody had a bad day, and I gave you a ton of bad days."

"Maybe, I mean, yeah, but…but I think I should be the one saying sorry. I got really bitter over you being better than me, and instead of trying harder I just made you a target. On top of that, I made my friends do the same."

"I did that too."

"I can't blame you. I caused all of this. What happened Friday, I basically asked for it."

"No, don't say that. I wouldn't blame you. I wouldn't blame anyone. We just…we took a stupid thing like grades and made it an important thing. It got out of hand, and next thing we knew, we were taking it too far."

Cara and I cried over some things, laughed about other things, and told each other to completely forget about everything else. We stayed talking, and she even had me over for dinner! I didn't leave until eight thirty that night. I couldn't imagine how much I let an evil vengeance overwhelm me. It made me forget about forgiveness and mercy and turned me ruthless. I hate that.

I gave Lydia a call to let her know I was all right. She offered to pick me up somewhere, but I wanted to walk. It gave me more time to gain composure, because then I was on my way to go talk to Tyler. That nervousness truly ate away at me; the closer I got to home, the more I felt like I was suffocating.

I drew some relief when the driveway was within sight and I could see that Tyler's Jeep wasn't there. When I approached the door, I wasn't certain whether or not I should've knocked, so I did what Lydia always did, knocked lightly and peeked inside. Ray came to the door and asked me why the heck I was knocking to come inside my own home. I let out a small laugh. It felt good to see him. He asked where I had been; I told him Tyler and I had a fight and so I had been staying with Lydia. He said he'd beat Tyler up for me if I wanted him to. I laughed again and told him maybe another time, but right then all was forgiven. I asked him where Tyler was at and if he knew when he'd be home. Ray told me he just went out somewhere and only knew that he'd be home before ten o'clock.

I went to my room and waited. I had less than an hour before he got home. Why did that scare me? And why did that also give me a feeling of euphoria? If Tyler didn't tell his dad anything, I guessed that, that meant we weren't broken up. That's more than likely where the euphoria came from. All of a sudden, I heard Tyler's voice yell to his dad that he was home, and his footsteps came closer and closer. I stood up and stared at him when he opened the door. He took me into his arms, and I embraced him like all my lives depended on it. I smiled and cried, burying my face into his chest. He kissed my head then whispered something to me.

"I remember."

I let go of him only slightly and asked him to repeat what he had just said. He let go of my hips and revealed to me his wrist. Tattooed across it was the word *alive*.

"I remember."

I hugged him even tighter. I couldn't believe it. He actually remembered it all. All I knew was that what had happened that past week, everything with Cara, our fight—all of it was forgotten. It didn't matter. All that mattered was us.

Chapter 23

*L*YDIA, TYLER, AND I SPENT the rest of spring break doing whatever it was we could do to have fun and enjoy one another's company. Two weeks after getting back to school, finals began. Cara and I wished each other good luck and even studied together for our calculus final. Crazy, right? I studied!

After tests were graded and final grades were sent in, Cara and I wanted to know which of the two of us ended up winning valedictorian. We went to the counselor's together to find out, but they wouldn't tell us. They wanted to make it a surprise on the day of graduation. I loved surprises, so I guessed it was fine.

On graduation day, I sat eagerly waiting to find out the result of my efforts through all my school years. Our principal was up at the podium and announced to everyone that the race was tight and had gone back and forth all four years of high school. Of course, she added in that both Cara and I should be very proud and blah, blah, blah. But at the end of it, she announced my name as valedictorian. I was overjoyed, more than I ever expected to be. I ran up to the podium and was ready to make my speech.

"Wow. Umm, I don't think I was ready to actually receive this title, but I'm beyond grateful that I now have. It wasn't easy getting here I can tell you that much. I learned a lot about myself these past four years. I learned a lot about the person I am and the person I wanna be. But I'm rambling a bit, I said more than enough last year." I held up my hand and showed it off to the crowd. "I said yes." They all cheered. "I think the real person who should be up here is Cara Montoya. Cara, come on up."

A huge smile grew on Cara's face, and she ran up onstage and hugged me tight.

"I can't believe you just did that." Cara laughed. "I don't even really know what to say. I guess I mainly wanna say thank you to everyone. Thanks, Mom and Dad, you guys always supported me and told me I could do anything especially when I thought certain tasks were too hard. You taught me that 'too hard' only existed in the worlds of people who gave up too easily. And thanks to my best friends Cynthia, Carter, Rachel, and Kathleen. You guys loved me through a lot of shi-stuff, and I know you didn't have to, but all four of you did anyway. I wasn't always the most lovable person, but you guys still loved me. And I really want and need to thank Melenium. Mel, you pushed me to try harder in everything I did, and that definitely made me a better person. You taught me how to be a better person and taught me that I'm always going to want to be one.

"I'll admit to everyone here that these have been the worst four years of my life! But no doubt about it, they've also been the best.

"I'm honored to be in this graduating class because I don't think any group of people could've showed me a greater time. Congrats to all of us.

"We did it!"

Cara ran up to me again and said thank you. I told her she really deserved the spotlight.

"So #TeamCaraMel?" she asked.

"Freak yes!" I told her. "That is probably the best ship name anyone has ever heard."

After graduation was over and we went to a few parties, Tyler, Lydia, and I decided to drive to mine and Tyler's house to pack a few things then head out of town to have our wedding!

I already knew the things we needed, so I told Tyler and Lydia to stay in the car, keep the engine running, and let me grab everything. It'd be quicker. They agreed and stayed in the car while I hopped out.

I opened the door with my key, and as fast as it opened was as fast as I felt a bullet shoot through my torso. I fell on the floor and saw that the house was being robbed. I looked at the man who shot me. It was Harold! He started panicking, whispering "Oh my god.

Oh my god" to himself. One of his friends grabbed him by the shirt, telling him they had to leave. He asked, "But what about—" His friend cut him off, saying I didn't matter; they had to go. Harold turned around and started running.

I'm sure that Tyler saw them running to their car and noticed them driving away so hurriedly.

Tyler and Lydia ran in and started freaking out when they saw all the blood I had already lost. Tyler screamed for Lydia to call for an ambulance. I gathered enough strength to tell them that it was Harold who shot me. Lydia ran to grab her phone from Tyler's Jeep. I knew I wasn't going to make it, so I just held Tyler's hand and told him to not let go.

He was crying and telling me that I'd be okay. I kept telling him I wouldn't be, but he couldn't accept that.

"Tyler. Tyler, listen to me, next time, okay?"

"No. I can't lose you."

"You're not losing me."

He cried more. I touched his cheek and had him look me in the eyes.

"I promise not to fight when You call me home."

He looked at me with tears still streaming down his face. He nodded and squeezed my hand a little tighter.

"And for right now I will freely roam."

"I am not too sure of what I know.

"But I promise to believe in my time to go.

"I will not take what is not completely mine.

"And I will not argue when You say it is time."

He brought my hand to his lips and kissed me goodbye.

And I spent my last breath telling him, "I love you."

Epilogue

I'M TWENTY-THREE NOW. I HAVE no shame in telling you all that I bought myself a wedding dress when I was nineteen. I have been saving up for the wedding since I was five.

Tyler found me yesterday. I was walking along Time Square, and he went up to me and asked me to marry him before he even said hello. He told me that he purchased a ring the second he was able to afford one he found better than good enough so that he could propose instantly.

He already found Lydia. I'm meeting up with her tonight. She already has her dress picked out for the wedding.

Tyler and I are getting married for the first time tomorrow! It won't be anything extravagant, but later on, we'll have a wedding, that is. But for right now, I'm happy with something small and real cute.

Suicide Letter

*T*YLER, I'M SORRY FOR EVERYTHING. I really wish it hadn't ended the way it did. Just know that I love you and that will never change.

I'll be singing to you with every breeze of wind you hear.

I'll be hugging you with every ray of sunshine you feel touch your skin.

I'll be kissing you with every drop of rain that falls on you.

Lydia, I'm sorry I left again. I love you, and I need you to stay strong without me. Don't do what I did. You're better than that. You can stand up to your problems.

I'll always be with you.

To all my other friends, I'll miss you. If you're hurting, don't resolve to suicide. I know I did it, but that was me, a mistake I made. It doesn't make anything painful go away; it only throws you into a deeper and darker hole that is truly lifeless.

The world is alive. Be alive with it!

—Lennie

About the Author

KIMBERLY CRUZ IS A TWENTY-ONE-YEAR-OLD writer from New Mexico. She has always had a love for writing. At the young age of ten, Kimberly decided that a normal life just wouldn't cut it for her and she had to follow a passion that burned inside her. There were a few things that seemed to have lit her path, but all of them proved to only be temporary. Throughout her years of exploring, however, writing was always right there. When high school came along, she finally noticed that the passion burning inside her was indeed writing! It had been right in front of her all along.

From short stories to poems and full-length books, Kimberly was creating art through words anytime she could, even in school when she should've been doing other tasks, like paying attention to her teachers teach. One day, a friend asked that she write her a little something. That really seemed to fuel her fire. Said friend read it, loved it, and started to share it; before she knew it, more friends wanted her to write them "a little something."

Life seemed to be running at her fast, so she had to run at it faster; at seventeen, she was determined to make a whole new world by moving her ideas from her mind on to paper. After finishing one piece, she decided she'd like to continue to make worlds of her own through her own words as long as life would let her.

CPSIA information can be obtained
at www.ICGtesting.com
Printed in the USA
LVHW050708030519
616300LV00001B/10/P

9 781645 441137